THE SAGA OF HARLAN WAUGH

TERRY GROSZ

WOLFPACK PUBLISHING
— EST 2013 —

The Saga of Harlan Waugh
Terry Grosz

Paperback Edition
© Copyright 2016 Terry Grosz

Wolfpack Publishing
6032 Wheat Penny Avenue
Las Vegas, NV 89148

ISBN: 978-1-62918-438-8

CONTENTS

DEDICATION

As I sit quietly in my study musing over days long gone while listening to the music of Yanni, my eyes scan the walls decorated with mementoes representing a thirty-two-year career in the service of the people of this country. This service was not of a military nature but involved protecting the national wildlife heritage of the people of the United States.

Interspersed throughout those career memories are family pictures from happier times: outings with our grandchildren, fishing trips to Alaska with my bride, elk and deer hunting and processing the carcasses in the garage with our two sons, float trips on the Powder River, and pictures of our parents before they all crossed over the Great Divide.

Of note is a picture on top of my computer shelf of a distinguished Littleton police officer who watches over my every move. It shows a bear of a man whose arms were the size of most men's legs and who contained in that carcass a good, gentle heart as big as Mother Nature's outdoor world. It shows a man who, while elk hunting near Walden, Colorado, saw the first wild gray wolf that was black in color three years before it was officially recognized as having been "discovered." It shows a man who was so strong that he could lift a dead, full-grown elk into the back of a pickup by himself, yet swing his daughter up onto his massive shoulders with an innate gentleness not of this world!

It shows a man who, like his dad, married the love of his life. He was so proud that his second child was on the way that he was fairly bursting at the seams to tell anyone who would stand still and listen. It shows a police officer who was acknowledged by his peers as one of the very best, and that law enforcement community still mourns the loss of this man who was a friend for all seasons.

It shows a man who was such an excellent cook that even God would have liked to come down to partake of his meals. It shows a man who was so steadfast in his faith in a supreme being and a life hereafter that his vision of life's path was unshakable. It shows a man who saw the world through glasses of many colors and shades and lived accordingly.

The picture shows my younger son, Christopher, who passed away of natural causes on October 13, 2005, at the age of 35.

I know of no greater loss a parent can suffer than the loss of a child.

It is to this bear of a man—a good Christian, an excellent cook, an outdoorsman par excellence, a fisherman beyond compare, a valued member of the law enforcement brotherhood, the type of man most of us aspire to be although we don't succeed, a holder of the Medal of Valor, a crack rifle and pistol shot, a beloved son and warrior—that I dedicate this book.

Rest in peace, my son, until we are together once more to range over the land; enjoying its breezes, appreciating its wonders, and laughing like we did when we were together...

ACKNOWLEDGMENTS

The character Harlan Waugh does in fact exist in reality. The real Harlan Waugh was a police officer for the City of Littleton, Colorado. As in the story, he is as bald as a river rock, is a crack shot with a rifle (a former U.S. Marine Corps sniper and was a S.W.A.T. member), is frank but level-headed, has a love of life that knows no bounds, has the highest ethics and a warm personality that can turn deadly serious in times of need or danger, is a loving father, and is one whom very little in life scares or concerns. He truly is a man for all seasons who became a close family friend through our police-officer son, Christopher.

As in the story, if Harlan takes a liking to your miserable hide, he is a friend for life. But break the laws of the land or the principles of humanity and, if justified, he will hunt you down as ruthlessly as the Harlan in the book did one Bosco de Gamma...

I acknowledge not only the use of this towering, courageous man's good name but the very essence and spirit with which he lives and faces all aspects of life to cloak my main character in the book.

Thank you, Harlan, for the grist of the story, and even more for the love and brotherhood you share with my family and shared with Christopher before his untimely crossing over the Great Divide...

"Wagh!"

THE SAGA OF HARLAN WAUGH

THE AFTERMATH

Dᴜʀɪɴɢ ᴛʜᴇ ʟᴀsᴛ ᴍɪʟᴇ ᴏғ ᴛʀᴀᴠᴇʟ, ᴛʜᴇ sɪᴄᴋʟʏ-sᴡᴇᴇᴛ smell of death permeated the crisp, late August afternoon air. Harlan was more than familiar with that smell, and he grimaced and narrowed his eyes to a higher level of alertness. A month earlier on the Yellowstone River, while he had been preparing for the fall beaver trapping season with his younger brother and two fellow trappers, they had been ambushed by a band of deadly Blackfoot Indians. Before the four men could reach any kind of redoubt, three lay dead in the late summer sun, full of arrows. Harlan had escaped and made it to a rocky outcropping on high ground with his group's horses and mules. For the next four days, he held the Indians at bay with his remarkable sharpshooting ability and several highly accurate .54-caliber Hawken rifles.

Harlan had been raised by his father, a superb big-game hunter who, for years, had supplied meat and hides for the pioneer settlements nestled in the Appalachian Mountains of western Pennsylvania. He had been taught by his dad that when shooting he should hold tight, relax his breathing, and squeeze the trigger as if the rifle was the love of his life. Above all, he had been told not to waste powder or shot because they were hard to replace in the wilderness.

"One shot, one kill," his father constantly preached until the day he died at the hands of a band of Indians who were upset by his intrusion into what they considered sacred hunting grounds.

Harlan never forgot, putting those words of wisdom into practice during his previous five years roaming the western wilderness as a free trapper and mountain man. During those four terror-filled days and nights on the Yellowstone, Harlan did as his dad had preached. Every time an Indian raised his head to shoot or presented the smallest of targets, a one- ounce, .54-caliber lead slug would strike that individual and kill him instantly. Soon the band of Indians, dismayed by their continuing losses, abandoned the straight-shooting mountain man for quieter pastures. After waiting another day on his rocky outcropping to be sure the hostile Indians had vanished. Harlan led the hobbled, thirsty, and starving pack-animals out to pasture along the Yellowstone River.

Then he commenced the grim task of burying his brother and friends, made all the more difficult by the sight of their bloated, fly-covered bodies, heavy with the sickly-sweet smell of eternity.

The magpies and ravens had not made his task any easier as the hungry birds had picked clean the dead men's faces, down to their glistening white skulls.

After burying the men along the Yellowstone and covering the site with large rocks so the wolves could not dig up and eat the rest of their bodies, Harlan headed south with the livestock, the men's effects, and the previous season's trappings. Dangling from the five mules at the end of the pack string were the freshly salted scalps of eleven Blackfoot warriors as a grim warning to all others with evil intentions. According to their own traditions, these warriors would forever be forbidden to travel the Happy Hunting Grounds because they lacked their hair and the skin that held it in place.

Keeping to the densely brushed creeks and river bottoms. Harlan moved due south until he felt he was out of the territory of the dreaded warriors from the Black-foot Nation.

After all, one man, no matter how good a rifle shot he is, will find more than his match out west if he ain't care-ful. Especially when leading a valuable pack string of horses and mules loaded with furs and other white man's necessities of life, he grimly thought.

Entering a small valley south of the Willow Lake area, just north of what is today Pinedale, Wyoming, he chanced once more upon that telltale smell of death that reminded him of the events on the Yellowstone.

Slowing his horse to a cautious walk, Harlan continued following a small stream toward Willow Lake, where he planned to set up camp. When he came to another large opening surrounded by tall cottonwoods and good grass, the nightmare associated with the smell of death began to reveal itself. In the stream lay numerous bloated bodies of Indian women and children filled with arrows. Nearly all of the bodies had been scalped and mutilated. His horse sidestepped the body of an Indian woman still holding her dead baby as Harlan examined the markings of her dress from the saddle.

Crow, he silently figured. Probably a hunting party far south of their territorial range and into that of the Lakota. Once discovered by the Lakota trespassing on their tribal hunting grounds, well...

Continuing, he found more bodies of women and children who had run for the protection offered by the brushy creek bed only to find that it was their place to die. He could smell the oily pine-wood smoke of camp-fires and meat rotting on drying racks, abandoned but still heavy and pungent in the air. Emerging from the dense brush by the creek but partially hidden at the forest's edge at the meadow's opening, he got his first look into the valley of death.

Clustered along a small rise in the valley were the burned remnants of thirty-two Indian tepees. Scattered throughout were the bodies of numerous men, women, and children along with several dead horses and the corpses of most of the camp's dogs. The silence of the scene was broken only by the melodious croaking of the ravens and calls of the crows and magpies, scared away from their feeding frenzy by Harlan's sudden appearance.

It appeared from the bloat of the bodies that the fight had occurred several days earlier, he thought as his eyes carefully swept the area for any signs of lingering danger. Looking closely at several bodies of men filled with numerous arrows and horribly mutilated, as was the custom of the time for many tribes of plains Indians, he noted that the arrows were from the Lakota and their allies the Northern Cheyenne. Knowing those Indians could be just as mean as the dreaded Blackfoot, he moved his pack string deeper into the comforting brush surrounding the creek. Determined to be rid of the oily, clinging smell of death and the sight of battle, Harlan continued along the creek toward Willow Lake.

Zip—thunk went an arrow into his saddlebag! Harlan's horse, spooked by the surprise impact to his side, bolted forward. Pulling the horse quickly to a stop, he whirled in his saddle to face his unknown assailant, quickly pulling back the hammer on his Hawken in one smooth, practiced motion for the battle that was sure to follow.

Standing with a distinct wobble, not twenty feet away, was an Indian boy who looked about twelve or thirteen years old. An arrow was stuck deeply into a festering wound in his thigh. Off to his side stood another Indian boy of about nine or ten whose entire body was trembling violently, like aspen leaves in an early fall storm. It was obvious that the younger boy had seen more than his mind could reasonably tolerate and was in deep shock.

The older boy was trying to notch another arrow and do a better job than he had the first time. Realizing that these two boys were probably all that was left of their band, Harlan quickly raised his hand in the sign of peace, putting on his best smile. Because much of daily existence in the West was painted in blood if one were not alert to the dangers at hand, his free hand went to the horse pistol in his belt.

Trying to draw another arrow in the bow was too much exertion for the boy's weakened body, and he suddenly toppled over the stream bank, landing smack-dab on the nock end of the arrow shaft protruding from his thigh. With a screech, he dropped his bow and arrow, passing out as the shaft was forced clean through the thigh.

Dismounting and scrambling over to the boy, Harlan grabbed his bow and tossed it next to his pack string so it couldn't be used against him. Seeing that the boy was out cold from the pain of the arrow passing through his thigh, Harlan scooped him up in his arms and walked back up the creek bank. The boy's garb showed that he was a Crow Indian.

He more than likely ran to the creek for protection but didn't escape before he had bought an arrow in the leg, he grimly thought.

Splitting the young Indian's buckskin pant leg with his knife, Harlan discovered a blue-black, festering wound caused by infection from the arrow. He took the opportunity to pull the rest of the arrow shaft through the thigh while the boy was out cold. With the razor-sharp tip of his gutting knife, Harlan trimmed the putrid flesh around the entry wound down to that which bled freely and looked healthy. Pulling a small flap of dirty buckskin from the entry hole as well, he washed the wound with water from his canteen.

Then Harlan wiped the wound dry and poured a small amount of gunpowder from his powder horn into the arrow's entry hole. With a spark from his flint and steel, he set the gunpowder aflame. The leg involuntarily jerked as the powder flamed high, then quickly died out. Along with that, came the smell of burned powder and flesh. Kneading the back of the small thigh with his hands, Harlan managed to get the wound to bleed freely from the exit hole, further cleansing the wound.

Stepping over to his lead mule, Harlan unpacked a piece of clean gun-patching material and tightly bound the boy's thigh, covering the wound. Then it dawned on him that in the rush of the moment with the first Indian boy, he had forgotten the younger child. Quickly turning, he saw that the boy had not moved an inch and was still trembling violently. Harlan walked slowly toward him so as not to scare him any further, holding out his hand in a friendly gesture.

When he reached the young boy, whose dark eyes never left the trapper's face, he gently picked him up. Holding the shaking boy, he carried him back to the pack string and sat him down by the wounded boy, who was now coming out of his spirit world. Realizing how much terror the little one must have undergone, Harlan reached up to his saddle bag, with the arrow still firmly sticking out of it. Fortunately, the arrow had not penetrated all the way through into Harlan's horse.

It had been stopped short by the large amount of hard buffalo jerky in the saddle bag. Opening the flap, Harlan took out a piece of jerky and, kneeling back down, handed it to the shaking boy. In a flash, the child grabbed the jerky and savagely tore at the tough strands of dried meat as if he hadn't eaten for a month.

A low groan brought Harlan's attention back to the boy lying on the ground. He was looking up at Harlan with the fierceness of his kind, born from a thousand years on the unforgiving prairies and mountains of the West. Harlan again made the sign of peace, and this time the boy seemed to comprehend its meaning. Tears welled up in the youth's eyes, and he let all the terror and misery flood from his heart over his losses from the recent attack. He was crying over the loss of his parents, a way of life, and almost his own life. Now he was faced with an uncertain future as he looked up at this massive white man dressed like a cross between the feared grizzly bear and a buffalo!

In the next instant, the younger boy flew into the older one's arms, and Harlan realized they were probably brothers. Then the tears of loss really flowed between the boys. In a few moments, the older boy regained his composure and watched Harlan to see what he was going to do with the two of them.

The younger boy did the same, still trembling violently. Realizing that staying there in the valley of death was not wise, Harlan picked up the younger boy and gently placed him in the saddle on his dead brother's horse. The horse was very gentle and accepted his load without much interest as he looked back toward the new weight.

The boy continued trembling but seemed to accept his new lot in life, especially since the contact with the horse was familiar and comforting. Realizing that the wounded and weakened boy was another matter, Harlan took an ax from one of the pack saddles on a mule. At first, the wounded boy looked like he thought he was in danger again, and the smaller boy stopped eating his chunk of jerky to observe Harlan's actions.

Quickly selecting a small, nearby lodge-pole pine tree, Harlan cut it down, then limbed and trimmed it to the size he wanted. Another pine of like size soon joined the first. Cutting another gentle horse from the string, Harlan deftly constructed a travois and tied the front end of the contraption to that horse's saddle horn. Removing a buffalo robe from another mule's pack frame, he soon had a completed travois ready for travel.

Picking up the wounded boy, he gently placed him face-up on the travois. Then Harlan went to his saddlebag and brought forth another slab of buffalo jerky. He handed it to the lad on the travois, and there was a short stand-off before he took it. Soon, though, he was eating the jerky as hungrily as his ravenous brother.

Rearranging the pack-string so the boys would be close together for the comfort nearness offered, Harlan remounted his horse. With a careful look around to make sure his tree-chopping sounds had not attracted hostile attention, he continued downstream toward Willow Lake without a backward look at the scene of death. The wounded boy's bow was packed onto one of the mules bags in case its rightful owner would want to use it once again someday.

2

WILLOW LAKE

WILLOW LAKE WAS LARGE AND BEAUTIFUL BY ANYONE'S standards. It had good water and lots of firewood; lush, knee-high meadow grasses growing clear to the lakeside, and was fed by many surrounding beaver-laden streams.

A natural haven for any mountain man, Harlan thought with a grin of anticipation as he looked over the familiar area from his saddle.

Harlan and his trapper friends who died on the Yellowstone River had stayed at Willow Lake two years earlier en route to the Yellowstone. During that stay they had constructed a stout horse-and-mule enclosure and several lean-tos. Initially, some of the group had favored staying to trap in that area. However, the tall tales they had heard from other trappers in St. Louis and the lore of the Yellowstone had gotten the best of the men. As it turned out, with one exception, it got the best of them not only in thought but, in deed as well...

Surveying their old campsite, Harlan noted that the previous winters had been harsh on the lean-tos. They were flat on the ground, and their supporting poles had been scattered. The corral was another matter. It had been built hell-for-stout to keep Indians from stealing the valuable livestock and, with a little work on Harlan's part, would soon return to its former strength.

Slipping easily off his horse, Harlan untied the following animal and led him, still pulling the travois, into the shade of the timber. There he checked on his wounded traveler before tying the reins to a lodge-pole pine. Returning to his pack string, he lifted the still trembling younger boy from his saddle and carried him over to the travois where the wounded boy lay.

He lifted the child up and placed him next to his brother. Both boys watched Harlan with wondering dark eyes but said nothing, either in their native tongue or in sign. Harlan figured they were still too scared to do anything but look and listen, which he understood and respected.

He had work to do, so he left the boys where they could watch him and headed for the old corral. After an hour of hard work, the corral was ready to accept its new livestock. Unpacking four horses but leaving the fifth still tied to the tree with the boys, he quickly hobbled them and turned them loose in the nearby meadow to graze.

He carefully arranged their packs and saddles in a

half-circle redoubt in front of the area where he planned to erect a sleeping lean-to. Bringing up the six mules, he unloaded their packs, hobbled them with double hobbles (because mules had a way of traveling great distances even when hobbled), and released them to graze with the horses. One horse was now left alone, separated from his companions and still tied to a tree with the travois. Hustling over to the now very nervous horse, Harlan untied it and led it to the corral.

Tying the horse to a stout corral pole, he carefully unloaded the wounded boy and gently laid him in the shade by the packs. Turning to retrieve the trembling child, Harlan was surprised to find him standing at his side. He guided him back to his brother and through sign language bade him to sit still, which the boy did. Harlan returned to the horse, removed the travois, unloaded the saddlebags, hobbled the animal, and turned him loose to feed and water with the other stock.

Man, I never saw a happier horse, he thought as the animal kicked and crow-hopped his way across the meadow in happiness over rejoining his buddies.

For the next four hours, Harlan sweated profusely as he constructed two lean-tos from the forest's materials at hand: one for him and the boys and the other to keep the summer- afternoon rains off the packs of gear and beaver plews. Before the fatal battle on the Yellowstone, Harlan's group had done quite well trapping beaver, and eight packs of cleaned and pressed beaver plews bore mute testimony to that fact. He brought in armloads of soft green fir boughs for bedding materials, and soon the sleeping lean-to was ready for habitation.

None too soon, he figured as the skies to the northwest darkened and then opened up with a typical afternoon thunderstorm. He hurriedly gathered the rifles and sleeping furs under the cover of the fir-bough roof. Running back outside, he gathered the wounded boy into his arms and, gesturing to the trembling one to follow him, ran for the shelter. Soon they were watching the thunderstorm sweeping over the area, dumping buckets of cold rain and then wandering off toward the southeast. Within moments, the sun reappeared, and steam began to rise from the ground, accompanied by the fresh smells raised by a recent rain.

"A good sign," Harlan mused, remembering his dad saying, Rain is a sign of new life.

As if on cue, another good sign appeared at the edge of the meadow some fifty yards away. A large, fat mule-deer buck looking for succulent feed at the meadow's edge soon joined the trapper and the Indian boys—but not in the manner it had anticipated...

Sitting by a small fire that evening, one designed not to attract attention, Harlan smiled. Both boys had been fed by the fat buck, as had he. The remaining meat hung high in a nearby tree, out of reach of any passing varmint. The lean-to he had constructed had kept out the summer rain, and both boys were sleeping quietly in thick, warm buffalo-hide furs. However, the older boy's wound seemed to be no better, and he was still running a temperature.

Tomorrow I will look in the lake's meadow for a poultice, Harlan thought with a furrow of worry crossing his brow. That should do the trick in the fever department.

Memories of his brother and two friends crowded into his thoughts. With the death of his brother, he alone remained of his entire family. All the rest had been killed by hostile Indians. A heavy sadness slowly fell over him as he sat by the fire, pondering his fate.

He now had two young boys in his care. What should he do with them? Many white frontier communities would not accept a white man with Indian children. Neither would many tribes of Indians inhabiting the West, especially those who hated the horse-stealing Crows and who would recognize the boys' tribal origin.

Even other fur trappers, most of whom had lost friends and family members to hostile Indians, could show a mean, Indian-hating streak, especially those at a rendezvous with a snoot-full of the fiery liquor normally sold at such events.

For now, he let those thoughts slide off into the heavy stillness of the night. He still had the results of his group's earlier trapping activities from the Yellowstone, which would leave him well-off though not wealthy. He had the trapping season before him in the Willow Lake area, which was in the territory of the friendly Snake Indians. He had more than enough goods and supplies because he had all that had been purchased to provide for a four-man party during a year's absence from civilization. He had a healthy mule and horse string and was in possession of five good Hawken rifles. He also had four horse pistols, much lead and powder, and more than enough beaver traps.

However, he was alone in a land that could kill or cripple a careless individual in an instant. He had no one to come to his aid or even know of his existence if he were to break a leg, take deadly sick, be attacked by varmints, or die. Soon, the cloud of loneliness began to crowd into his inner space once again, along with the heavy darkness of the night. For the longest time all he could hear was the soft tinkle of the bell from Martha, the lead mule, as she fed in the nearby meadow and the quiet crackling of dry pine wood in his small fire.

Then Harlan's stooped shoulders straightened, and his eyes burned fiercely. "By God! This is the life that I always wanted. This life is my choosing, and this is my land to explore and enjoy. And by God, that is what I will do. I will trap and live off this land until it claims me. I will travel its length and breadth to see what it has to offer and then do it once again just to make sure I ain't missed nothing.

If possible, I will raise those two boys as my own, and the three of us will become a family. Together we will see what this great land has to offer its newest orphans. Yes, that will be my lot in life. And when it is over, I will step across that Great Divide, meet my old family once again, and tell them of the wonders I have seen."

It was as if a great emotional load had been lifted from Harlan's shoulders once he had fortified his mind regarding his lot in life. Getting up, he used the toe of his moccasin to push fresh dirt into the small fire until it was no more. Making sure it was out so as not to invite any two-legged varmints to his campsite, he shuffled off to the lean-to with the characteristic trapper's walk born of years of living in the backcountry.

Once there, he made sure the boys were sleeping soundly. Then he took one of his Hawkens and stood it at the ready alongside a nearby tree by his sleeping furs. Taking another, he stood it next to the side wall of the lean-to in case the first rifle was not enough for whatever came his way in a bad or hungry mood. Removing his pistol and placing it by his head, he pulled the buffalo robe up around his chin and looked out at the star-filled night. Lying there for a few moments, he began to sense the cold of the night cooling the end of his nose. Soon he fell into a light sleep. Off in the distance a lone wolf's howl enticed several others from a nearby pack to join in the mournful song.

Yes, this is the life I have chosen, was Harlan's last thought as he dreamed of many things.

Overhead a million stars blinked their approval and welcome at the newest family on the frontier.

3

TROUBLE

DAWN THE FOLLOWING MORNING FOUND HARLAN standing by the fire, warming himself. His practiced eye roamed the meadow, counting the horses and mules. All were still there and getting fatter by the moment on the lush grasses. Grease spattering at his feet told him it was time to turn the generous chunks of venison steak cooking in a cast-iron frying pan loaded with bear grease.

He stuck the steaks with the point of his knife and flipped them over. Next to the frying pan sat an old spouted pot with a dark brew of coffee liberally laced with the grounds whirling away in a boil. Soon the fresh mountain air was filled with great smells.

Looking back over his shoulder, Harlan could see the younger boy standing in his bedding furs, looking hard at his still prone brother. Sensing that something was wrong, Harlan strode to the lean-to. The Indian boy with the wound was shaking violently and groaning. Kneeling, Harlan placed his hand on the boy. His body felt like it was on fire!

Realizing that he had to get the fever down quickly, he scooped the boy up and walked toward the lake. The boy's eyes were barely open, and he seemed to be deep in the clutches of the Great One. Removing the boy's dirty clothing, Harlan slowly immersed him up to his chin in the cold waters of the lake.

The boy's small body convulsed as the cold water closed in around his young frame, then lay still, as if he had passed out. Turning him on his side, Harlan examined the exit hole made by the arrow. It was a deep reddish-purple and swollen. Taking out his knife, Harlan thrust the tip carefully into the old wound channel. A greenish-yellow pus began trickling like a ribbon into the clear waters of the lake.

Taking the boy's thigh with both hands, Harlan "milked" the area around the exit hole until a flood of pus squirted from the wound. Soon that stream turned to a trickle, and then a stream of bright-red blood began to flow into the water. Harlan let the wound bleed for a while, cleansing it, then lifted the boy from the cold water and carried him back to the lean-to.

The smaller boy just stood there as if too scared to move for fear he too would be doused in the icy water. Harlan had to smile. Wiping the wounded lad dry with a rabbit skin, he laid him back down under a thick buffalo hide sleeping fur. Then he went to the meadow by the lake and harvested some western yarrow to make a poultice. He put the yarrow leaves, roots and all, in a tin cup and crushed them into a poultice with the butt end of his knife. He then applied the sticky poultice to the exit hole and bound it tightly into place with a clean gun-wadding rag. Feeling the boy's forehead, he grinned with satisfaction at the already sharp reduction in body temperature.

The icy lake waters did their job well, he mused with a grin. 'Course, water that cold would do most anything for what ails anyone.

Scooping up the younger boy, he carried him over to the fire and put him down on a log that he had pulled over for a seat. Soon the boy was wolfing down hot venison from the cast-iron frying pan.

All the while, Harlan's practiced eye continued roaming the edge of the forest and length of the meadow for any sign of trouble. Finding none, he sat down, and the two of them finished off the rest of the still cooking venison. Walking over to the hanging mule-deer carcass, Harlan sliced off another chunk from the hindquarter and returned to the fire. Soon more venison steak danced merrily in the hot cast-iron pan, filling the air with more great smells. Harlan poured himself a tin cup of the ugly-looking boiling coffee and gratefully swilled down a mouthful of the burning liquid, grounds and all.

Suddenly Harlan noticed that the mules and horses were frozen in the pasture, looking in unison into the edge of the trees bordering the meadow. Signing for the trembling boy to stay by the fire, he grabbed his, always-at-hand, Hawken and stealthily sneaked toward the livestock.

Keeping to the edge of the trees, he soon spotted the object of the animals' attention. In one word: trouble. A large grizzly bear was standing on its hind feet, intently watching the livestock some thirty yards away from where Harlan stood. Low on bear grease and knowing the bear would be loaded with fat this time of the year, which would produce some of the best cooking oil once rendered, he swung his Hawken up to rest along a nearby tree. Boom roared the great rifle in the cool morning stillness, and the grizzly bear was no more after being hit squarely in the ear.

Quickly reloading in case the bear had some friends or the sound of shooting drew the attention of any nearby Indians, Harlan stood stock-still, watching and listening. After discerning no sights or sounds of danger, he returned to his fire only to find the venison left in the frying pan resembling a lump of coal. Dumping the burned meat onto the ground, he greased the pan once again and put more meat into it.

This time I need to pay more attention to my cooking, he thought with a grin.

Over to the bear he went, and in no time he had it skinned out, with the fur side lying on the ground. On the meat side of the skin were the hams, front shoulders, and ribs cut out and ready for hauling. He had dragged the guts a short distance away for the varmints to enjoy, and two gray jays had already claimed the pile as their own. Grabbing a front shoulder with one hand and the Hawken in the other, he trotted back to the campsite. Hanging the shoulder on a pack frame to keep it clean and off the ground, Harlan went back to the fire, and he and the smaller boy hungrily laid waste to the venison frying in the pan once again.

Damn, there is nothing like a gutful of fresh venison and scalding-hot coffee for breakfast in a country as beautiful as this, thought Harlan with a grin as he surveyed his surroundings once again.

Turning to see the wounded youth lying propped up on his elbows, Harlan sliced some more steaks and tossed the rest of the venison into the frying pan. Rising to his feet, he shuffled over to check on the youngster.

Inching and squirming himself over until he could lean against a pack of beaver plews near the bedding, the youngster smiled weakly at Harlan and made the sign of peace.

Harlan quickly responded with the universal talk of the prairies in the form of sign and then asked the young man if he spoke English or Crow. The boy did not comprehend English but spoke in the Crow tongue. As if on cue, he spoke of the predawn ambush of his people by the hated Lakota and the Northern Cheyenne.

His eyes momentarily misted up, but he quickly wiped them as if embarrassed by his show of emotion. He then spoke of taking his younger brother and running into the willows by the creek for cover, but not before being hit in the leg by an arrow. He continued, "We lay back out of sight under a cut in the stream bank until all the shooting, yelling, and crying had ceased and the two enemy tribes had left. Then you, the bearded one dressed like a buffalo, arrived four suns later.

Afraid, I tried to shoot you with an arrow and missed. I don't remember anything else until now. The rest of my thoughts are with those living with the Cloud People."

"Are you feeling better?" Harlan asked in his broken and rusty Crow language.

The boy broke out into a big smile. Realizing that his Crow wasn't very good, and he may have screwed up and said the wrong thing, Harlan asked him in sign why he was smiling.

"Because," the boy responded, "you said my foot smelled like rotten fish!" Both broke out into big grins, and after that Harlan relied on sign to communicate with the boy until his mastery of the Crow language returned.

The smell of the cooking venison reminded Harlan to retrieve the frying pan and bring it over to the wounded boy. Regardless of the heat of the pan's contents, the young man gobbled down the sizzling, half-raw meat, burning his tongue in the process.

That is good, thought Harlan. If he is hungry, then he is truly on the mend.

———

FOR THE NEXT THREE DAYS, Harlan tended to the boys off

and on as he began cutting timber into logs to make a winter cabin. In the evenings, after the log work and supper, Harlan used his knife and awl to fashion clothing for the boys from his stock of dressed furs by the light of the campfire. Their footwear was good, and he soon replaced what they lacked in the shirt and pants department.

The garments were not Indian-beautiful by any means, but they were hell-for-stout and warm. The boys took to the clothing in a heartbeat because the cool of fall was upon them. By day three, the youth with the thigh wound was hobbling around camp with a makeshift crutch and was now known to Harlan by his Crow name of Big Eagle. The one with the trembles was getting better as well, and Big Eagle told Harlan that his brother's name was Winter Hawk.

Harlan discovered that Big Eagle was fourteen summers in age and Winter Hawk was twelve. The boys had three sisters, twelve to sixteen summers in age, but they didn't know what had happened to them after the raid by the Lakota and Northern Cheyenne.

"They were either killed or taken prisoner," Big Eagle said quietly with a deadly look of vengeance in his eyes.

He had seen his dad, Buffalo Calf, killed in the opening moments of the fight and his mother, Plum Flower, killed and scalped as she tried to flee with her girls to the safety of the brushy creek. After that, he had lost contact in the confusion and had barely managed to escape to the creek with his little brother before they too were killed.

Harlan, sensing the depth of the boy's grief, quietly explained to Big Eagle, "All my family are now dead as well, so I know how you feel."

Big Eagle seemed surprised in light of the many white mountain men he had seen in his young life crossing Crow territory. He figured there were so many that they must all have big families and live forever. When he understood that Harlan was alone, like him and his brother. Big Eagle sat looking into the fire for a long time.

Then Big Eagle said, 'It looks like we are all brothers with a past from the fire of life, and we are now destined to wander together in a time of the unknown."

Harlan's grasp of the Crow language was fast return-ing, and Big Eagle's words stung like a harsh winter wind, especially coming from a young man of just fourteen. But Harlan had to admit that the three of them were now adrift from any family bonds other than those they created themselves.

Yes, Harlan thought, we are destined to roam and live in this great land during a time of the unknown when it comes to the destination of our souls.

The grizzly bear's hams, ribs, and shoulders were smoked to perfection on the drying racks, and the great gobs of fat had been rendered out by Winter Hawk in a large cast-iron pot after instruction from Harlan regarding how not burn the precious contents. Harlan and Big Eagle staked out the great bear's hide and scraped the remaining flesh from it so it wouldn't spoil. Then they salted it and placed it in the sun, fur side down, over an unused smoking rack so that it could cure as well.

This will bring a fair price at the rendezvous next summer for someone wanting a good bear-skin coat, thought Harlan, especially with its twenty long claws still attached.

During that time, Harlan had cut, notched, and placed all the wall logs for their winter cabin. Now, he was in the process of cutting out the windows, front and back doors, and shooting slots for each side of the cabin.

One week later, the roof was a done deal, and everything of value had been removed from the lean-tos and placed inside the cabin. By then, both boys were a great help to Harlan and had learned some words of English. As each day passed, they seemed more and more comfortable in his presence and he in theirs—almost like a family.

Three of us against the wilderness and all its fury, Harlan thought as he watched the young men progress in everything they did around the camp.

Yes, Big Eagle had it right about the three of them adrift in life as a family.

4

A MOVEMENT IN THE WILLOWS

AFTER FINISHING THE CABIN, THEY MOVED IN THE LAST OF their gear, including the pack frames, saddles, and bridles. This was to keep the leather items from being stolen or eaten by the resident porcupines for the salt they had soaked up from the horses' sweat. Then, Harlan and the boys cut their winter wood and dragged it to the cabin with the horses so they'd have plenty of fuel when the winds whistled and the snow drifted up past the eaves of their cabin.

That finished, they turned to the real business at hand: making meat and trapping beaver. The area surrounding the site Harlan had chosen for their cabin was alive with elk, deer, and moose. Soon, hundreds of pounds of drying and jerked meat filled the cabin and the drying racks. Both boys proved their worth at the end of a sharp knife. They took to cutting and smoking the great hoard of meat like a sage grouse takes to exposed black sage leaves on a windswept, barren hillside during the winter.

Observing the boys from a distance, Harlan concluded, *They have done this kind of work before and done it well. It's a real tribute to the training they received from their folks.*

Using two mules in harness to drag back another gutted moose carcass, Harlan realized that their little cabin was now chock-full of deer-skin bags of jerky and salted and smoked meat. He could hardly move inside without banging his head on a low-hanging bag of jerky or smoked bear hams. However, he had to find a means of caching more meat if the three of them were to make it through the harsh Wyoming winter with any meat left on their own bones.

But, Harlan concluded, therein existed a problem. The area they had chosen for their home site was chock-full of grizzlies and black bears! They are everywhere, and I'll have to be damn careful or risk getting chomped in all the wrong places, he thought.

Hanging meat outside in their lean-to or caching it high in the trees was out of the question, at least until hibernation, because black bears could climb trees. He would also have to contend with meat-eating birds if he left exposed slabs of meat hanging on a long-term basis.

Looking up as his mules struggled to drag the 1,100-pound moose carcass back to camp, Harlan saw four closely growing lodge-pole pines next to the corner of their cabin. Within a week, those four trees had a plat-form floor, walls, and roof forming a seven-by-seven-by-four-foot-high cache-house. Sitting back and looking over his latest efforts, Harlan mentally affirmed that its contents would remain dry during the snows and rains and that it was reachable only with the use of a twelve-foot removable ladder.

That sure as hell would be out of the reach of any bear or varmint in the area, including the hated and fearsome wolverine, he concluded with a satisfied smile. Soon, the aerial cache-house was also bursting at the seams with winter provisions of salted meat, jerky, dried onions dug by the boys on the rocky hillsides, and numerous elk-stomach bags full of bear grease.

Sensing that they were ready for whatever Old Man Winter could throw their way, Harlan began planning his fall beaver trapping. He had scouted several nearby streams entering Willow Lake while hunting for their winter provisions and had found all to be loaded with the furry rodent.

He and the boys began smoking his traps (to remove the human scent) and tearing out part of a nearby beaver dam. Setting their traps on the break, the three of them shot another cow moose on the way back to the cabin and hauled the hams and shoulders to their camp for some needed fresh meat. The rest of the moose was left for the critters to enjoy.

Back at camp, Harlan placed generous chunks of the dark, coarse-grained meat in a large cooking pot along with some bear grease and water and set the pot beside the fire but not directly on it so it would simmer while the boys went for some fresh wild onions located on a nearby rocky hillside.

In the meantime, Harlan threw in a handful of salt and pepper and a small sack of dried beans. After the pot had simmered for two long hours, he tossed a pound of rice into the pot, which by now was giving forth many great smells. In the following hour, he placed several Dutch ovens by the fire. Into one holding water went several large handfuls of dried fruit, and into the other went bear grease and biscuit makings. He built up the fire for the warmth it offered, and soon all that could be heard was the sound of three human beings eating after working hard and going hungry all day.

In short, nothing like a celebration, thought Harlan as he surveyed the fruits of their previous weeks' labors with a smile.

It was at that exact time that Winter Hawk suddenly stopped his trembling. It was noticed first by his brother and then Harlan as they consumed their moose dinner. Winter Hawk just grinned with the revelation and reached for another helping of moose stew. But in the hearts of Big Eagle and Harlan, there was Great Medicine that day in the moose stew, along with much happiness. Now they were a healthy family as well.

———

KNEELING by the busted stick-and-mud beaver dam where they had opened a hole earlier, Harlan removed three dead beaver from the water-set traps. Loading them onto their spare pack horse, the three rode back to camp. Dismounting, Harlan took the three beaver and showed the boys how to remove the rear scent glands and save the oily-scented liquid in a small bottle with a wooden stopper. He had six such bottles that had formerly contained spices.

Now, he planned to have one bottle for each of them, with three in reserve in case any got broken. Then they skinned the beaver carcasses, fleshed them out, and properly hooped them with willow branches from a nearby creek. Harlan showed the boys how he wanted the beaver carcasses boned out for the wonderful meat they supplied. As the boys gathered more willow branches for future hooping, the beaver meat merrily boiled away, laced with many spices. With the later addition of several handfuls of rice, it was soon a dinner to be savored.

During the entire process, neither boy said anything, but they carefully observed what the trapper was teaching them. By now they realized that to catch and process beaver along with other furbearers would allow them to procure the necessities of life from something called a "rendezvous."

Neither boy had experienced one of these events, but they quickly understood from Harlan that the rendezvous provided supplies and allowed them to continue living in the wild. That was just fine because, to their way of thinking, this would be their way of life until they stepped across the Great Divide into the Happy Hunting Grounds.

Harlan happily noticed that the boys paid great attention to detail. It would serve all of them well, especially in the immediate future...

Dawn the next morning found the three kneeling by a promising beaver drag, where Winter Hawk made his first set under the watchful eyes and counsel of Harlan. Then it was Big Eagle's turn. Picking a likely place, he made a water set that made Harlan smile with pride. The two young men are doing very well, he thought like a proud father.

During the rest of the day the three of them made twenty- four sets in some of the richest beaver water Harlan had ever seen. The following day, every trap held a dead beaver, and all, but one, were large, blanket-sized animals!

In the process, they had run across eight grizzly bears, including one with three yearling cubs. For once, Harlan was glad he carried the heavy but much-needed Hawken across the saddle of his horse. Even those fearful weapons with their .54-caliber bullets at times seemed almost too small in the face of a fierce charge by an aroused grizzly. All three of them became more and more aware that vigilance would have to be the word of the day if they were to survive a fall of trapping in these beaver-rich waters. As they returned to their cabin, the mules had all they wanted to carry of the day's catch of heavy beaver carcasses.

For the next five days, this routine was not broken. The hard work involved removing and setting the traps, loading the beaver onto the mules, and returning to camp. The first thing they did was save the oil from the castors, placing it into the bottles that hung from each of their necks by a leather thong for easy access when trapping. Next, they skinned the beaver and hooped the skins before getting something to eat. Finally, the three sleepily climbed into their sleeping furs to await another day's work of intense beaver harvest.

As each day came and went, Harlan observed the boys were quickly developing into very good beaver trappers on their way to becoming great mountain men. They set their traps well, read the ground accurately when it came to tracking, could already read the signs of weather, and were skillful with a knife—and Big Eagle was getting better day by day with his bow and arrow. Life couldn't be any better, to Harlan's way of thinking.

————

Roaaaar! Ummmph, ummmph, crash, flooosh, roaaaar. An enormous grizzly boar suddenly burst from the water and willows as Harlan knelt to remove a large beaver from a trap. The bear was just feet away and was on him before he could grab the Hawken lying on the bank by his side.

With the sudden onslaught, the horses and mules carrying the boys and their gear quickly spooked away from the battle scene. Harlan just had time to grab his .79-caliber, single-shot pistol from his belt and shoot the bear under the chin as it grabbed him to give a fatal bite and crushing hug.

Ka-pow went the pistol, but it hardly slowed the enraged bear. Grabbing Harlan in its muscular forelegs, the bear bit down hard on the top of his head, its great canine teeth tearing open an eyebrow and ripping off nearly half of his scalp. Fighting the burning pain and the terror of his assailant's hot, fetid breath, Harlan dropped his now useless pistol.

Grabbing his long-bladed gutting knife from its sheath, he plunged it deeply into the bear's upper vitals. Hot blood spewed over his knife hand and down his arm as the steel found its target. Again and again, Harlan furiously drove the knife into the bear's vitals, trying to keep low as the bear continued tearing at his bleeding head, shoulder, and arm.

Lurching backward, the bear tried to drag Harlan into the deep water of the beaver pond. If the bear was successful, he realized he was a dead man because once in the deep water he would lose his footing on the muddy bottom and not be able to defend himself. With renewed energy, Harlan fought savagely to stay at the edge of the bank and out of the deep water.

Reaching back and grabbing his Hawken from the bank, Harlan cocked the hammer and drove the end of the barrel into the chest of the bear, only to have the gun promptly smashed from his hand. Then, the bear crunched down hard, this time through his left shoulder. The pain and tearing of his shoulder muscles almost made Harlan pass out. But he hung on and kept plunging the long-bladed knife with his other hand into the bear's vitals for all he was worth.

Out of the corner of his eye he saw Big Eagle bravely run right up to the bear, draw his bow, and shoot an arrow into the side of its massive head. Ignoring this new pain, the bear grasped Harlan with the strength of ten men and again bit down hard on his head. Plunging the knife one more time with his fast-ebbing strength upward toward the bear's heart, Harlan quietly dissolved into a quiet, peaceful world of darkness.

5

THE BOYS BECOME MEN

FIRST, THERE WAS THE SOUND OF A WOODPECKER hammering on a dead tree limb in the far-off distance. Then there was the smell of a cooking fire and distant, muffled sounds of talking. Next there was a soft light and blurry visions and shadows of someone walking nearby.

Then, the pain! Oh, God, the burning sensation of pain in his face, head, and shoulder. The throbbing pain coming over him in waves from his shoulder was the worst. Harlan remembered his mauling by a surprised grizzly bear at the edge of the beaver pond just as the lights quietly and thankfully went out once again...

Five days later, Harlan began again to come back to reality from the spirit world. Slowly opening his eyes, he became aware that he was hazily looking through one eye that was still full of blood. It would be another two weeks before that eye would clear enough to see.

He realized it was hard to smile or frown due to the damage done to his face by the grizzly's tearing, six-inch-long front claws. Trying to reach his face, he discovered that his left arm was sore as a boil and would not work. He made an attempt with his other arm and felt a hand grabbing it and stopping him from reaching those damaged places on his head and face.

"Welcome back from the spirit world," came the reassuring voice of Big Eagle.

"Is he gonna be all right?" said another worried voice, that of Winter Hawk in his broken English.

"Yes, he will be fine, but not as good looking as he once was," said Big Eagle.

"Are you hungry?" Big Eagle asked Harlan.

Realizing he was famished, Harlan roared out that he was starved and then regretted his animated talking and movement as the pain returned with a rush like the maddened grizzly. Soon, Big Eagle was spooning the best-tasting thick onion-and-meat soup that he had ever eaten into his mouth. After his third bowl, Harlan asked, "What is this? It's great!"

"Soup from that old griz' you tangled with back there at the beaver dam many days ago," replied Big Eagle with a pleased grin.

That struck Harlan as funny. The bear had come to kill and eat him, and now their fortunes had been reversed. Harlan smiled and then started to laugh, only to regret it as he did. His face burned and hurt like hell, as did his shoulder, with any kind of movement. The top of his head, on the other hand, was totally numb. That he couldn't quite figure out...

———

A week later a wobbly Harlan was on his feet, and what a surprise was in store for him. In the looking glass from the cabin stores, he saw himself for the first time since he and the grizzly had "danced."

His scalp had been almost tom off but had been sewn back on with a needle and thread. It was swollen and had taken on many shades of color, much hair had fallen out, and he smelled like hell, partly from putrefaction and partly from the evil-smelling poultice Big Eagle had squashed all over the damaged areas. His left eyebrow had been almost completely removed but sewn back as well and, aside from being bright red with infection around the edges, appeared to be healing.

His left shoulder was another matter. It had four large canine-tooth holes, two in the front and two in the back, driven deeply to the bone. It was leaking green-and-yellow pus, and he could not move it at all due to its stiffness. In short, he was alive but in one hell of a stinking mess.

But that wasn't his biggest surprise. After receiving an arrow in the head from Big Eagle, the bear had finally dropped Harlan. Then it had turned and tried to kill Big Eagle. However, it had run headlong into a one-ounce slug of lead fired by Big Eagle from Harlan's Hawken, which he had picked up off the ground under the grizzly's very feet. The slug had torn through the bear's heart and spine and eventually landed him in the cooking pot.

The two boys brought Harlan back to the camp and fixed him up as best as they could with the needle and thread they found in the cabin stores. Then they skinned out the bear, cut him into quarters, and wrestled him back to camp for the huge meat supply he offered. As if that were not enough effort at their young ages, they also ran the rest of the trap-line and brought the beaver they caught back for processing.

In fact, the whole time Harlan had been out, they had cared for him and run the trap-line as well. The boys had caught and processed seventy-four beaver in the two weeks Harlan had been under the weather or out of it completely! That did not include the great bear's dressed hide, which now adorned the cabin wall and stretched partly onto the roof. That had been one big and pissed-off bear—a ten-footer, he later discovered.

It was another month before Harlan had regained some of his looks and the full use of the mauled left arm and shoulder. The eyebrow had healed beautifully but left a long scar across Harlan's face. He would live with his signs of battle with the griz' and carry them proudly when among his own kind at the rendezvous and trading posts.

As a surprise, Big Eagle and Winter Hawk had labored long and hard over the grizzly bear's claws while Harlan was recovering. They made the claws into a fine necklace with leather thongs from an elk skin, and the twenty claws looked very distinctive and impressive. When presenting the necklace to Harlan after he had recovered, he was floored by the scope and degree of the gift from a couple of kids who were fast becoming just like the sons he had always wanted.

From then on, Harlan wore the grizzly-bear claws proudly as a reminder not only of the battle but also of the quiet love he now shared with his boys.

His scalp was another matter. It had healed badly because of all the tearing and subsequent infection caused by the bear's slobber. An ugly canine-tooth bite scar ran around the entire top of his head. In fact, it appeared that the boys had sewn the loose scalp on almost backward! It eventually healed, and flattened out in the process like normal skin. But Harlan lost all his hair from the infection! He was now bald as a river rock. But he was alive, and a good wolf-skin cap would keep warm the bald pate that soon came to be known among his peers as his trademark.

———

LITTLE REMAINED of that beaver trapping season; soon the ice became too thick to chop, and the beaver take dropped off. Now was the time to trap other valuable furbearers. Harlan worked hard at those activities as well as instructing the boys in the fine art of forest trapping, including the making of deadfalls and snares. Soon the mink, gray fox, bobcat, northern lynx, gray wolf, and coyote hides began flowing into the camp for processing.

In the evenings, after the work was done and the livestock cared for, the real training began, to the boys' way of thinking. By the light of the fire in their fireplace, Harlan taught them how to handle, load, repair, and care for a Hawken rifle.

Soon both were experts at loading, shooting, casting bullets, and caring for their rifles. Harlan modified one of the older Hawkens by shortening the stock so the smaller Winter Hawk had a rifle of his own that he could easily shoot.

Then came hour after never-ending- hour on how to put an edge on and care for a knife, ax, and tomahawk. That was followed by instruction in how to correctly use a knife for gutting, skinning, and food preparation as well as in defense of one's life.

Those lessons were followed by sessions in the proper use and care of a tomahawk and how to use such a weapon in the self-defense or to defend others. Then, came endless hours of practice with a tomahawk and knife at a throwing target in front of the cabin. They also practiced one-on-one knife combat with Harlan when the winter weather was tolerable.

Last but not least, Harlan worked with Big Eagle on the making of arrow shafts from nearby willows and the knapping of flint and chert arrowheads. They spent hours in bow-and-arrow practice until Big Eagle got quite good—deadly, in fact.

6

A WINTER SURPRISE

LEAVING THE CABIN ONE COLD MORNING TO BREAK THE lake's ice and get some cooking and coffee water, Big Eagle came face to face with thirty heavily armed Snake Indian warriors quietly sitting on their horses facing Harlan's cabin. Without any sign of fear or surprise, Big Eagle summoned Harlan by calling through the open cabin door. Harlan emerged, and Winter Hawk, unseen by the Snakes, picked up his rifle and took up his station at a shooting port inside the cabin, just in case things got out of hand.

Harlan, showing no fear, raised his hand in the sign of peace. For the longest time no one among the Indians moved as they sat on their horses looking long and hard at the cabin and its trappers in their hunting grounds.

Then a tall man, looking every bit the Indian in his

dress, moved his horse forward and said in perfect frontier English, "Good morning, and who might you be?"

Surprised at hearing English spoken, Harlan said, "I am called Harlan Waugh. This is my son, Big Eagle, and my other son, who is inside the cabin fixin' breakfast, is called Winter Hawk."

Big Eagle took a quick glance at Harlan. Harlan had never called him his son before. However, Big Eagle liked the title, and it made him feel proud to be called "son" by a mighty warrior and mountain man like Harlan.

"Who might you be?" asked Harlan.

"I am Joe Meek, the meanest, best-shootin', biggest-eatin', greatest squaw-lovin', knife-throwin', fur-trappin' mountain man in the West. And by the looks of your face and head, you are a great mountain man as well if them be the marks of a mighty unhappy grizzly."

"They be the marks of a griz' all right," uttered Harlan. "A griz' who tried to make me his dinner and stayed for dinner instead."

Meek smiled through a huge growth of facial hair and said, "Care if I light down a bit? Gets a mite cold sittin' up here on a horse in the dead of winter."

"Make yourself at home, and your friends as well," said Harlan. Meek turned to the Snakes and in their tongue advised them to dismount, which they did.

"How we going to feed such a number of people, Harlan?" asked Big Eagle, assuming that a meal was to follow since they had dismounted and were making motions as if to stay.

"Go fill that big pot with water and bring it to our outside campfire. I will have our big meat cooking pot there by the time you return and just fill it half full. In the meantime, Winter Hawk and I will cut some slabs of meat from those grizzly hams in the cache house and start them cooking with a load of dried rice and the beans from last night's supper for thickening."

Big Eagle headed for the lake to get water as instructed. When he returned, a roaring fire had been built and their large rendering pot had been placed at the fire's edge. Into that eventually went five large pots of water, thirty pounds of previously hard-smoked and salted grizzly ham cut into generous chunks, four pounds of dried rice, and the remaining pot of beans from supper.

That was followed by a handful of salt, pepper, and some crushed, dried hot red pepper flakes. Winter Hawk brought out another large cast- iron pot and hung it over the fire on the cooking rod. Into that four-gallon pot went cold water from the lake, and as soon as it was boiling, he added eight large handfuls of freshly ground coffee beans and four handfuls of brown sugar cones.

Soon the talk around the large fire was animated as the cold men began warming up and smelling good things to come. Then one man noticed something on Winter Hawk and brought it to the attention of the group in the Snake language. There was an immediate and abrupt silence, and then the talk really got animated. As Winter Hawk once again approached the fire with two

Dutch ovens for biscuit-making, one of the Snakes grabbed him by the collar and loudly proclaimed something in his tongue, the only word of which Harlan understood was "Crow!"

Winter Hawk tried to pull away, but the man was too strong and had a firm grip on the boy. In a flash Winter Hawk had drawn his knife, twisted around in his shirt, and faced off with his antagonist. Seeing that he was confronted with a determined youth with a knife, the older man went for his tomahawk, only to have Winter Hawk disarm him in a blinding flash.

That move happened so fast that the man was stunned. Realizing he was now disarmed, he drew a pistol from his sash, only to have Joe Meek restrain him at the last moment. It was good that Meek acted so rapidly because Big Eagle had drawn a bead with his Hawken on the man who was about to shoot his brother with a pistol.

"You are a brave one, little man," said Meek with a smile of newfound respect. "Not only brave but deadly as well. Where did you learn to fight like that?"

"I taught him," said Harlan in a cold, flat tone. He also had his Hawken at the ready. At that range, someone would have died had cooler heads not quickly prevailed.

"We didn't come here fer no fight," said Meek quickly with apology in his voice. "We smelled your campfire and, not sure who you were, come a-lookin'. We was headed to make meat on a small buffalo herd in the sagebrush some few miles distant when we came across your campsite. Seein' you appeared to be friendly, we was hopin' for some hot coffee. But seein's you was willin' to feed us, that were even better. Small Buffalo Running here took a look at your young 'un and figured he were a Crow. Them's mortal enemies of the Snake."

"That may be in general, but these here boys are mine and being raised up in a Christian way. Their entire clan was killed some months back by the Lakota and Northern Cheyenne. I am all they have now. They have no tribal enemies unless someone tries to kill them or hurt their loved ones. If that happens, then they will defend themselves like the griz' that danced on my head some time back. Nothing more, nothing less," Harlan stated in a tone cold enough to let Meek know he was ready to be a good neighbor but would kill in a heartbeat if pushed to his limit.

Meek turned to the Snake leader and spoke to him in his language. It was obvious that the Snakes trusted Meek, and soon there were grins all around, especially regarding the issue of one of their own, and a grown man at that, being disarmed by a small Indian boy who was obviously quickly growing into a man. To smooth over that man's feelings, Harlan walked over to the tomahawk still lying in the fresh snow, picked it up, and turned to Winter Hawk.

"Winter Hawk, would you return this tomahawk to its rightful owner?" he asked, realizing that to do so would go a long way toward defusing the uneasy moment.

For a moment Winter Hawk just stood looking at the

extended tomahawk. Then, grasping it firmly, he sheathed his knife and handed it purposefully back to its owner.

"I am sorry I acted so fast," signed Winter Hawk.

Without a word, the embarrassed warrior took his tomahawk and put it back in his sash. The act caused him and the rest of the Indians to nod their approval of the young man's courage. The earlier action now forgotten, everyone gathered around the pot of steaming coffee.

Between Harlan's extra tin cups and those some of the Snakes carried, everyone was soon getting his fill of the scalding, bitter brew. Then the stew pot full of bear meat, rice, beans, and spices was ready, and in a very short time it too was emptied by the fast warming men and Harlan's crew. Afterward, Meek walked over to Harlan, slapped him on the back, and shook his hand.

"Glad to have another white man in these here parts," he happily exclaimed. Then he asked, with a knowing grin, "By the way, what type of grub was in that pot? That weren't no griz furnishin' the meat, were it?"

"That be the same one who intended me as a meal," Harlan answered with devilment in his eyes.

"We couldn't have eaten better'n we tried," Meek replied with a twinkle in his own eyes, knowing his band of Snakes and their total fear of everything grizzly. "By the way, Chief Low Dog wants to know if you and your sons would like to go with us to make meat. He has observed that you have some fine Hawken rifles, and those are better than our flintlock and fusil rifles at bringin' down the buflfler. He says he would be very happy if you would join him in the killin' because his tribe is low on winter grub."

Looking closely at the man he had met just an hour earlier, Harlan decided Meek was a man of his word and not a threat. He turned to the boys and told them to get together their Hawkens, plenty of powder and shot, their gutting and skinning knives, and some jerky.

"We are going off with our newfound friends to make meat," he told them. From the looks on the boys' faces, Harlan could tell they were excited beyond belief.

"Go on, now," he urged, and the boys were off like a shot, eager for a new adventure.

Turning to Meek, Harlan said, "Tell the chief we would be honored, and since we could use some fresh meat ourselves, we will help them kill many buffalo with our rifles."

When Joe advised the chief of Harlan's decision, he got a big smile, and the translation created a ripple of excitement that went through the Indians' ranks at the prospect of having the big Hawkens as an aid in getting some great-tasting winter rations.

7

MAKING MEAT

FROM BEHIND A SMALL HILL THE BAND OF HUNTERS watched a herd of about 150 buffalo feeding in a brush-covered creek bottom some fifty yards away. Harlan, the chief, and Joe Meek conferred about the plan of attack. Soon Harlan returned to the boys to advise them of the plan. The three of them with their five Hawkens would follow the ravine down to a small hill at the bottom overlooking the feeding buffalo.

They would quietly climb the hill and, staying out of sight of the animals, start shooting those at the closest edge of the herd. Once the herd started to move off, the Snake warriors would give chase from two sides, killing as many as they could. By then, the rest of the tribe—made up of mostly women, children, and young men—would have arrived, and the butchering and hauling would commence.

With a wave of the hand for good luck to the rest of the hunters, off went Harlan and the boys. In about forty minutes they were in position and quietly spread out just below the ridgeline. Harlan took three Hawkens, and each boy carried his own rifle as they crawled to a point at the top of the ridge from which they could see the animals below.

On Harlan's signal, they started shooting. Five shots from the Hawkens dropped five cow buffalo right off the bat. Harlan was pleased that the boys had done so well with shot placement, and watching them rapidly reloading made him even prouder. Their training had been well received, and now the proof was in the pudding. After reloading, the five Hawkens barked again in ragged succession. Once again, five cow buffalo struggled with the last of their lives.

Now the herd was getting nervous. But, sensing no danger from the small puffs of white smoke on the ridgeline and the noise of rifles being fired, the animals more or less held their ground. Boom— boom—boom—boom—boom, and five more cows dropped to roam the plains no more. With that, the herd began to nervously drift off to the west, only to run into fifteen mounted Indian riders charging out from the line of willows. The chase was on! The crack of the riders' rifles in the cold winter air put the herd into a full stampede back in the direction from whence it had come.

Seeing the danger while quickly reloading, Harlan and the boys hurriedly moved together as the buffalo roared up the little hill toward them. Their Hawkens barked once again, staggering and then killing three buffalo in front of the charging herd. Harlan then stood up so the stampeding animals could see him and calmly shot the herd leader with his first reserve Hawken. Grabbing his remaining Hawken, Harlan dropped another buffalo, which skidded over the snow-covered earth and came to rest not thirty feet before him.

The inert form looming so large in front of the stampede split the leaders. The boys stood up with their quickly reloaded Hawkens and dropped two more from the herd, turning the animals away from the hilltop on which they now stood, helpless with empty rifles.

The buffalo thundered down off the hill, right into the rest of the mounted warriors on the other side, and the slaughter was complete. Reloading all five Hawkens, Harlan, with a proud heart, and his two boys walked back to their horses and mules, which were tethered in the creek bottom behind them. Over the soft crunching sounds of their moccasins in the snow, they could hear excited talking and laughing from the Snake hunters. Soon the tribe had descended on the fallen buffalo for its first taste in a long time of fresh, hot buffalo liver, soon to be sprayed by salts from the gall bladder.

Walking their horses and mules back to the top of the small hill, they were amazed at what they saw. Dark brown blotches of dead buffalo dotted the snow-covered prairie and sagebrush for a square mile. Scattered throughout the area were thirty mounted riders whooping it up, with another fifty tribal members scattered about, voicing their delight over the harvest lying before them.

Walking over the rim of the hill, Harlan and the boys began skinning and gutting the five buffalo they had dropped in the face of the stampede. Soon their mules were braying loudly over the weighty loads of steaming meat and hides they were being made to carry. That which they couldn't carry was left to the tribe or the scavengers. As was often the case, too many buffalo had been killed even for the Snakes to utilize all the meat, so many prairie creatures happily ate their fill for a few days.

Joe Meek rode up to Harlan and the boys and dismounted. Walking over to Harlan, he said, "The chief is extremely happy over your help on this hunt. He says his people will have much meat for at least another month, and then maybe the deep snow will leave and the hunting will become easier. He asked me to let you know that you and the boys are welcome in his land. Even though the boys are from the hated horse-stealing Crow Nation, they will be welcome as long as he is the chief."

Harlan smiled, wiped his bloody, tallow-covered hands, and said, "It was good to meet one of our own and provide some assistance. Maybe we can meet at the rendezvous this coming summer and tip a jug or two."

"I would like that," Meek said with a grin. "See you there, and bring them sharpshooting boys. I bet they can win some goods from those trappers who think they can shoot better than those young men."

With that and a wave of the hand, he mounted his horse and rode off to mingle with the people whom he called his friends and hosts. Little did Harlan realize that the chance meeting with Joe Meek would later bear fruit of the richest kind...

Loaded with all their groaning pack animals could carry, Harlan and the boys headed back to their cabin and some damn good eating for the next few weeks. Because it was so cold the meat would freeze and keep in their now almost empty cache house high in the trees next to their cabin.

8

THE GREAT WHITE BEAR

IT SEEMED LIKE FOREVER, BUT FINALLY SPRING CAME TO the land in a rush like a charging mountain lion. The wind howled constantly, streams overflowed their banks, the ice went out, and wet spring storms blasted the lands as if Mother Nature had an angry point to prove.

Exposed to the weather in all its moods, the three worked their trap-lines like there was no tomorrow. They had only a few months before the beaver went out of their prime, and this year a trip to the rendezvous would be needed for many essential supplies such as spices, gunpowder, horse and mule shoes, and the like.

Beaver after beaver fell to Harlan and his trainees until little difference existed among the three of them when it came to trapping skills. The boys' prowess with the big Hawkens was also a wonder to behold. If an animal was observed and wanted, they had become accomplished offhand shooters out to two hundred yards. At that range, the big Hawkens saw to it that there was meat in the pot come sundown.

In addition, Big Eagle and Winter Hawk were developing into two very strong and healthy young men. If they had still been living with their tribe, they might have had to suffer through short rations many times throughout the year. But because Harlan and later the boys were so adroit with their outdoor skills and the big Hawkens, not many meals were missed. Those extra calories began to show up not only in the boys' stature but their muscular development as well. Their arm strength was remarkable to behold as they labored mightily alongside their newfound dad.

In fact, Harlan was continually amazed at their strength when the three of them got into wrestling matches over who would cook the evening meal or skin the last beaver. When the boys got hold of him, Harlan discovered that he had to use all his strength and cunning to escape their clutches in order to remain free from the cooking or skinning detail. Harlan was pleased that he had raised such capable and strong young men. That was what life in the West required, and if you didn't measure up, you soon joined the soil forever.

———

AT FIRST, Harlan couldn't believe his eyes. Not forty yards away was a grizzly bear feeding on a fresh moose carcass—a bear of enormous size, pure white in color with pink eyes and reddish-pink claws! Here was a pure albino animal, something so rare that he had heard of only one other having been seen, and that had been only a partial albino.

As if sensing danger, the brute stood up and tested the air with a loud blowing in and out through his nostrils. Then he returned to all fours to feed on the moose he had just surprised and killed in the creek bottom.

My God, thought Harlan, I have been in this country for over five years, and never have I seen such a magnificent creature. That damn bear is at least eleven feet tall and must weigh over fifteen hundred pounds!

The two boys had frozen when Harlan had given the hand signal to stand still, and it was apparent from the size of their eyes that they too had never seen such a creature. Harlan continued to slowly shake his head in disbelief as the boys just looked and looked.

Still sensing something amiss, the great bear rose once again on its hind feet, testing the air, and this time looked directly at Harlan and the boys. Since none of them moved and the bear had such poor eyesight, he detected nothing out of the ordinary. But the look he gave with those bright reddish-pink eyes appeared to Harlan to be almost supernatural. He dropped back down, and all that could be heard was the great tearing sounds that are made when a creature that size dismembers another large animal.

Harlan slowly raised his rifle, although his powerful

Hawken appeared to be only a small popgun in comparison to this monster. He quietly cocked the hammer against his buffalo coat in order to muffle the sound and made sure he had a cap on the nipple. Then he held the sights steady on the area into which the bear had disappeared. The boys, seeing him raise his rifle, followed suit, silently pointing their rifles in the direction of the great bear.

Shuffling his feet loudly in the willow leaves to get the bear's attention, Harlan prepared for what was to come. Woof—woof, snorted the great bear as it once again stood on its hind legs and looked in the direction from where the threatening sound had come. Ka-boom went Harlan's Hawken as his bullet flew straight into the bear's throat, ripping through the spine and killing it instantly.

The bear crashed into a thicket of willows, and a great thrashing and tearing of brush occurred as he danced his last dance. Harlan, trying to reload his Hawken, discovered that his nerves were so rattled that he couldn't do it! Laying the rifle on the ground, he turned and reached for Big Eagle's Hawken in case a second shot was necessary. The brush continued to object to the bear's thrashing, but soon all was deathly quiet.

Returning Big Eagle's rifle and recovering some of his nerve, Harlan quietly reloaded his Hawken. He motioned for the boys to spread out and follow him into the willows where the bear had disappeared, and they cautiously moved in. Within moments the three of them were at the kill, and what a sight it was! There, in all his glory, was the great bear. Even lying down, he was almost four feet high at the shoulder, and his hind feet appeared to be at least twenty-four inches wide! Never in his life had Harlan seen such a creature, and from the looks on the boys' faces, neither had they.

Harlan carefully poked the bear's huge, pink, padded foot with the end of his rifle barrel, but he didn't move. The great white bear was dead. With that, Harlan just sat down and looked over what he had done. The two boys, realizing that something special had just happened in their lives that would probably never be repeated, were lost in the mystical moment as well.

After about twenty minutes of silence, Harlan said, "This ain't getting it done. Let's get to cutting and gutting and see if this here fellow can be loaded on the mules or horses. Most likely we will have to build a long pole travois and have the mules pack it in that-away because of their great fear of anything smelling of bear."

Big Eagle, looking at the moose the bear had killed, said, "Dad, there is a lot of good meat left on the moose; shall we bring that home as well?"

Glancing over and seeing that to be true, Harlan nodded. With that, Winter Hawk commenced dressing out the largely undamaged remains of the moose while Big Eagle and Harlan struggled over skinning, gutting, and quartering out the bear. An hour later, several mounds of meat represented what had once been the mighty moose and the great bear. Off to one side lay the mound of fur, still magnificent in its whiteness against the rich dark brown of the creek bank.

Harlan had been right in his assumption that the mules would refuse to haul anything smelling of bear. A long poled travois had to be constructed, and only Big Eagle's horse would pull the contraption with the load of bear meat and hide. Three trips had to be made before the entire load had been carried back to the cabin.

Leaving Winter Hawk to stake the bear hide and flesh it out, Big Eagle and Harlan finished running and resetting the beaver trap-line they had been working when they had crossed paths with the great bear. Upon their return, everyone fell to fixing fresh moose roast for dinner and processing the rest of the moose meat for the drying racks.

As it turned out, most of the bear meat was not edible because it was too strong-flavored and stringy from its long period of hibernation. After making that discovery, they hauled the remains to the far end of the meadow, where the wolves and other bear made short work of them. But as luck would have it, the hide held its hair because it had been a spring bear and hadn't been much rubbed. It cleaned up beautifully after two days of being washed by the rushing creek waters into which it had been staked down over a riffle.

When they staked out the hide on dry ground after its spell in the creek, it measured over eleven feet in length before final fleshing began. After final fleshing, it was even longer!

Since there were no rub spots on the hide, Harlan proclaimed it more than a fit prize to take to the rendezvous for sale or trade. Little did he realize the real value the hide would eventually bring at a future meeting with a great Crow chief... and the extensive killing it would ultimately cause.

9

THE TRIP TO THE UTAH RENDEZVOUS

SOON THE BEAVER WENT OUT OF THEIR PRIME, AND THE trapping stopped. Then the real work began. Repairing all the horse and pack equipment became the first priority for Harlan and his adopted sons, for without the livestock, they would not survive in the wilds of the frontier.

Then came the bundling and packing of the beaver hides. Since the boys had never seen it done, Harlan had another chance to teach them a necessary part of the fur trade. First, the one-and-a-half-pound dried beaver hides were folded in half, fur side in. Then they were stacked about sixty hides to a bundle and compressed under a long pole. One end of the pole was tied to a large log as the other end was pulled down over the bundle by the combined weight of Harlan and Big Eagle.

Winter Hawk had the job of tying the compacted

bundle in a four-way tie suitable for packing the eighty-
five- to ninety-pound bundles on a horse or mule. Soon,
the cabin was filled with eight fresh bundles of beaver
plews and nine loosely packed bundles of hides from
other furbearers trapped during the months when beaver
trapping was almost impossible because of thick ice.

Rounding out those furs came the eight packs of
beaver hides from the ill-fated Yellowstone expedition.
Next they packed five buffalo rugs, ten deer-hides, eight
elk-hides, and three grizzly hides, including the fur of the
great white bear. As Harlan surveyed the hoard of furs,
he smiled broadly. That cache would make any mountain
man proud, not to mention independent for another year
in the backcountry. Looking over at the boys, Harlan
noticed that they seemed to be smiling with pride at their
accomplishments as well.

Next came the shoeing of the horses and mules,
followed by the repair of clothing and the making of new
outfits so they could make a good showing among their
brethren at the rendezvous. Then the fun work, more or
less, began. Several barren cow elk and four mule deer
were killed and the entire bunch turned into jerky for the
trip to the Utah rendezvous. This place was known to
Harlan, and although it was only a name from the air for
the two boys, it had become a magical one in its conno-
tations.

Then came the serious work: the repair of all the
weapons, the making of bullets, and the sharpening of
knives and tomahawks in case they encountered any

dangers during the trip to the rendezvous. Lastly, any items not needed for the trip were cached in a large hole dug into the ground behind their cabin and lined with fir boughs and dried buffalo hides. Into the pit went their traps, extra axes, pigs of lead, extra knives, sharpening stones, cast-iron gear not needed for the trip, and extra kegs of powder. Now the three were ready for what the world would throw at them on the long trip across country and during the rendezvous.

The time to leave was nearing, and the boys could hardly contain themselves. If they had only known what awaited them, they might have been a little more patient. Then again, maybe not...

———

COME THE MORNING OF DEPARTURE, the three trappers were up early. While Winter Hawk cooked a huge, rib-sticking breakfast, Big Eagle and Harlan packed the two extra horses and six remaining mules. Then the three riding horses were saddled, and to breakfast the man and youths went. Fried moose steaks two inches thick, all slopped up in a rich and peppery heavy gravy, awaited them. With that, were Dutch-oven biscuits by the score, with honey from a stone jar for the topping. A second Dutch oven was merrily boiling a mixture of sugar, dried fruit, and water. Scalding coffee as stout as an angry mule's kick rounded out the fare. The three ate heavily, knowing full well that, because of the

Indian country they had to cross and the danger they would face, their next meal might not be until after dark.

While Winter Hawk tended to the cleanup, Big Eagle and Harlan made another pass through camp to make sure everything was left in order for their return. Returning to the fire, they picked up the cleaned Dutch ovens, frying pans, and coffee pot and loaded them onto several mules standing patiently, ready to go.

With one last look around, Harlan took the lead, posting Big Eagle at the rear of the pack string and having Winter Hawk ride the sides. Moving slowly through the trees with care born from being mountain men in Indian country, the trio headed southwest toward that magical place called the rendezvous.

Harlan headed due west for what are today the Bridger-Teton Mountains, then south down the edge of that mountain range to its southernmost tip. As they continued southwest, the little party constantly marveled at the great herds of buffalo, elk, deer, and pronghorn antelope.

Underfoot almost constantly were coveys of sage grouse, and wherever there was water, hordes of ducks and other shorebirds greeted their eyes. Angling ever south and west, Harlan led them to the southern tip of Bear Lake in the extreme northeastern tip of present-day Utah. The lake had been appropriately named, for everywhere they looked, the moving brown humps of grizzly bear could be seen feeding on roots, tubers, and what water birds and eggs they could gather along the shoreline.

For the boys, these new experiences were pure heaven. For Harlan, who had seen such wonders many times before, it was Mother Nature at her best.

The trio continued southwest over the northern reaches of what is today the Wasatch-Cache Mountains and down into Willow Valley near the present-day town of Hyrum, Utah. Moving toward a large grove of cottonwoods at the confluence of several small streams in the valley, the tired trappers stopped and happily made camp.

After they unloaded the animals and put on their hobbles, they let the livestock out to feed and water. The three then commenced building a small corral among the cottonwoods to hold the horses and mules at night. Immediately adjacent to the corral, they set up camp, building one lean-to for sleeping and another in which to store their gear and keep out the summer rains. In a central spot between the lean-tos and the corral they built a fire pit for cooking, evening warmth, and keeping at bay the ever-present swarms of hungry mosquitoes. It was now June-hot in the year of 1831, and they appreciated the nearness of the cold running streams for bathing and the coolness of the cottonwoods' leafy shade.

———

AFTER RESTING FOR TWO DAYS, Harlan began to wonder

why he had not seen or heard another soul since their arrival in the valley.

That is not right, he thought, concerned. There should be pack strings of eager mountain men and Indians streaming in from all points of the compass to trade and make merry.

When he couldn't stand the emptiness of the valley any longer. Harlan arose early, ate a cold breakfast of fried elk steak, and, telling the boys to guard the camp and livestock, rode off toward the west. He returned several hours after dark. After wolfing down a large dinner of deer steak roasted over the fire and getting a large cup of the evil brew they called coffee, he sat quietly on a log by the fire amid the ever-present swarm of mosquitoes.

"Well, I saw a lot of Indians, mostly Northern Utes and Northern Cheyennes, gathered in several camps awaiting the arrival of the supply trains from back East. I also ran across numerous campsites where trappers were awaiting the supply train's arrival as well. To date, no one has arrived to trade goods from back East for our furs."

WITH THOSE SOMBER WORDS, Harlan took another deep swallow of coffee, then just sat looking into the fire as if the dancing flames had something to say regarding the events at hand.

He added, "I also ran across our friend Joe Meek, in camp with a very famous trapper and old friend named

Jim Bridger over near the west side of the valley. They say to just wait, that the supply train will appear before it is time to return to our cabins for fall trapping. I don't see that we can do much other than to wait as well. We need those supplies for the coming year, so we will wait as the others are doing until just before the snow flies. Then we will have to skedaddle for home so we can gather our winter provisions and make do with what we have."

Both boys were deeply disappointed, but they tried not to show it. They had been waiting and working for months to see this thing called a rendezvous, and now it might not happen. Their faces would have dragged in the dirt if they had let them.

———

SOON THE SIGHT of heavily laden trapper pack strings and great swarms of gaily dressed Indians moving into the valley became an everyday occurrence. People were streaming into Willow Valley by the score in anticipation of the rendezvous and festivities such as drinking, foot races, shooting matches, whoring around, squaw trading, and horse trading. They were also eager for the latest news about who had made it through the winter and who had perished by accident, been eaten by a bear, or lost his hair to hostile Indians.

Soon tepees and lean-tos dotted the valley floor along the many creeks and cottonwood groves in anticipation of being supplied for the coming season. Come the first of July, however, no supply trains graced the valley.

As it turned out, Thomas Fitzpatrick had gone unsuccessfully to St. Louis for backing and supplies for the Cache, or Willow Valley, Rendezvous. Then Smith, Sublette, and Jackson, who were new owners of the company responsible for providing supplies to the current rendezvous, had gone clear to Santa Fe to check out the trapping and trade opportunities in that area and to procure supplies for the 1831 rendezvous.

En route, Jed Smith was killed by Comanche Indians on the Cimarron River. After outfitting Fitzpatrick in Santa Fe, Sublette and Jackson dissolved their partnership because of the loss of their friend Smith.

Realizing that many men depended on the supplies getting through, Fitzpatrick headed north for the rendezvous site with his supply train posthaste. When he met Henry Fraeb just east of South Pass in the current state of Wyoming, Fitzpatrick transferred his supplies to Fraeb. Then he turned around and headed back to St. Louis to make sure the next year's supplies arrived on time. Fraeb, with the supplies, headed for the rendezvous site. But because of the delays, the general summer rendezvous of 1831 was not held. Only a shortened, later version took place because the trappers had to get back to the hunting grounds and prepare for winter camp before the snows fell, making trapping and travel difficult at best.

RETURNING to camp late one evening toward the end of July, Harlan dismounted and, without a word, began to care for his horse. It was obvious from the state of the horse and the tiredness of the man that he had ridden long and hard in his attempts to locate the rendezvous traders.

After caring for his horse and still without a word, Harlan strode toward the campfire. Grabbing his plate, he shoveled a mound of meat and beans onto it and began eating with gusto. It was clear that the jerky he had carried had not kept his big guts from eating the little guts. The boys, because of their Indian heritage and because they knew their dad, remained quiet and didn't ask questions.

Once Harlan had finished his second heaping plate of meat and beans, he took his tin cup of boiling coffee into both hands and stared long and hard into the fire, just as he had on the earlier evening when there had been no news.

Then, as if relishing the moment, he said, "I saw the pack strings and wagons gathered about five miles south and west of here. There must be eighty complaining mules loaded from stem to stern with ever'thing under the sun. They also brought five wagons, heavily loaded by the looks of their wheels sinking into the dirt. Henry Fraeb is leading the pack and advised that he will be ready tomorrow to trade, so be sure to bring your plews and an empty gut because he plans to butcher an ox and load up our drinking cups!"

Harlan gushed out the words with a rush and a twinkle of anticipation in his eyes. Both boys exploded in glee over the long-awaited news, then quieted down as if embarrassed by their un-Indian-like outburst.

The trappers spent the rest of the evening making ready their year's trapping efforts and the clothes they would wear grandly when they rode into the rendezvous.

———

DAYLIGHT FOUND HARLAN, Big Eagle, and Winter Hawk packed and on the move. By ten that morning the rendezvous grounds were in sight. Sitting high in their saddles, the boys searched eagerly with their eyes and ears for the sights and sounds coming from the trading grounds.

Approximately one hundred Indian tepees in two big camps dotted the meadows near a small creek. Around them swirled proud Indian men, brightly dressed women, Indian slaves carrying bundles of firewood for cooking, and scores of children, all interspersed with numerous barking camp dogs.

"Those be the Northern Cheyenne," Harlan stated flatly, deeply aware of the connection between that tribe and the demise of the boys' Crow clan. Both boys looked long and hard at the tribal members they passed, looking as if they might show some reaction to the destruction of their family. They wondered if any gathered there that day had been part of that sad moment from their past.

"Those tepee stands over there are of the Northern Utes," Harlan informed them with a lighter tone. Forgetting the Northern Cheyenne for the moment, the boys looked at the other large Indian encampment that Harlan had pointed out. That camp also swirled with human activity in preparation for the trading to come. Pack strings of trappers with their pelts were streaming into the area from all points of the compass, making the meadows come alive with enough humanity to almost overwhelm the boys' senses.

As they moved closer with their own pack string, the boys could see the trading wagons in a semicircle, with blankets and buffalo robes scattered around on the ground. Laid out in gay profusion were that year's trade items and necessities. There were brass and cast-iron pots, frying pans, Dutch ovens, trade muskets, and a few Hawkens.

Scattered near that assortment of goods were numerous fowling pieces, horse pistols, and kegs of powder. Next were barrels of Green River skinning knives intermixed with bolts of brightly colored cloth and spools of rope and brass wire. The next wagon over was surrounded by piles of beaver traps and barrels of things neither of the boys had ever seen.

Those barrels contained hard candy, an item the boys had never tasted. On the other side of the trading lane were small mountains of sacks of coffee, pigs of lead, more kegs of powder, bags of flints, sharpening stones, fish hooks, and fishing line. Next on several buffalo rugs were axes, tomahawks, blankets from the Hudson Bay fur company, bridles, kegs of rum, and barrels of horse and mule shoes.

That array was followed by mounds of spare rifle and pistol parts, kegs of horse and mule shoe nails, tin pans, looking glasses, and everything else in between. At the end of the trading path were stacked bags of flour, corn-meal, raisins, more hard candy, sugar, dried fruits, coffee beans, and everything else a trapper could want for his next year of isolation.

At the end of this display were five blacksmiths, all with ringing hammers. They were repairing the trappers' equipment or fashioning horse and mule shoes to fit particular animals brought forward by the trappers for specialty shoeing. The boys, never before having seen anything so grand or overwhelming, could scarcely contain their excitement.

Off to one side, Fraeb's buyers were grading beaver plews and furs from other furbearers as trappers stood expectantly by, eyeing the grading process. Much talking was going on as the trappers tried to sell high and the buyers traditionally bought low. The talking got even more intense as the firewater slammed into empty bellies, with predictable results. However, the bottom line always remained the same.

This was the only "store in town," and if you needed supplies for another year, it was either get them here or get them nowhere... Ultimately, transactions were made, and in most cases the trappers found themselves breaking even or in debt for the next year to the trading company. Few got rich other than the merchants bankrolling the rendezvous because of the 70 to 700 percent or higher markup the fur companies were raking into their coffers.

Watching these transactions, Harlan thought, *Living in this beautiful land sure carries a high price... in more ways than one.* To his way of thinking, the price could be found at the end of a speeding lead ball, at the point of an arrow or lance, under the cold steel of a knife or the killing force of a tomahawk, or in the clutches of a mean-ass varmint, including a high-dealing trader.

Many times your own kind saw to it that you died in the traces, he thought as he saw the pelt scalping between buyers and trappers at every processing station.

Then it was Harlan and the boys' turn to move into the active trading zone.

"I don't trade with no stinkin' damn horse-stealin' Crows or their Injun-lovin' kin," growled the fur company representative as he looked up from the pile of furs he had just purchased and stacked off to one side in anticipation of the next seller. He gave Harlan and the boys an angry look as if to emphasize his point.

In one quick, explosive movement, Harlan was off his horse and had his knife at the fur buyer's throat before the man could even blink.

"Them is my boys, and if one is mean-ass to them,

then he is mean-ass to me. Do you read me right, friend?" Harlan asked coldly as the knife began to cut into the man's skin and small droplets of blood rolled down the side of his neck.

"Put that knife away," yelled a nearby fur buyer as he and another buyer quickly hoisted their rifles and aimed them at Harlan.

"Not a good move," shouted Big Eagle as he and his brother covered the two with their own rifles and a look just as deadly as the Hawkens.

"Shoot them damn Indians," yelled another fur buyer, coming to the aid of his buddies with a rifle in hand.

"Don't reckon this needs to get any bigger or bloodier," said a calm voice from the edge of the crowd.

Glancing quickly backward at the speaker of those words, Big Eagle spotted Joe Meek emerging from the crowd with rifle in hand and a killing meanness he had never seen on that man's face before.

A blacksmith stepped forward with his hammer raised as if to strike Meek from behind when another voice said, "This here has gone far enough. Put that hammer down or, my friend, you have hammered the last nail into your coffin if Old Betsy here has her say."

The boys would later learn that this man was Jim Bridger.

"Hold it right there!" yelled Henry Fraeb as he pushed his way through the crowd into the battle zone. "What the goddamned hell is going on here?" he demanded.

Harlan, still not letting go of the offending fur buyer,

said, "Henry, I came here to trade in peace with my two sons. This here piece of buffalo crap had the gall to deny me and the boys from trading. Seems he hates Crows, and as I said, these here'n are mine."

"Damnit, Harlan, I have known you for many years. What made you blow up like that? You usually are calm as the waters of the Missouri in the summer heat."

"Maybe it were losing my brother up on the Yellowstone, or maybe it were being an orphan myself. Or maybe it were the fact these two young'uns saved my life after a griz worked me over. But whatever way, no man is going to insult me or my kin," Harlan said in a killing tone.

"Put down that knife, Harlan. And you, Dan, go collect your wages, take a horse and saddle from my string, and draw the grub and necessities you need to get back to civilization. Now, get out of my sight," growled Fraeb, who could be just as mean as Harlan.

Harlan removed his knife from the man's neck, and the fur buyer scurried away, glad to be out of the clutches of one very angry and apparently crazy mountain man.

Looking over at Meek and Bridger, Harlan said, "Thanks for backing my play."

"Wouldn't have missed it for all the world," Meek answered with a smile.

Seeing that the hurrah was over, the two boys lowered their Hawkens. But never for a second did they take their eyes off the two other fur buyers who had backed up their companion and had hurriedly gathered with the man Harlan had just let go.

"Harlan, you and I will look over what you have to offer, and we will settle on a price," Fraeb said loudly, hoping to defuse the tension in the air. "After all, that hell-raisin' ain't no good for business."

With that, Fraeb started grading Harlan and the boys' furs. He found himself looking at many very well-dressed, blanket-sized beaver plews. After the first two packs had produced only very large plews, Fraeb looked up at Harlan with a big grin.

"You and them boys have done very well if this here sample is representative of what you brought to trade," he said.

Harlan, still mad over the comments by the first fur buyer, just nodded, but he never took his eyes off Fraeb and his fur grading.

"Harlan," said Fraeb, "as I said, you and your'n have really done exceptionally well. I will say this hoard of furs will bring ... about six thousand in trade!" Without giving Harlan time to think over his answer, Fraeb added, "That gives you three dollars for each buffalo hide, four dollars for the beaver, three for your otter, and thirty-three cents a pound for the deer skins. I can only give you twenty-five cents for each coon skin and twenty cents for each muskrat hide, though." Fraeb stood back and intently looked at Harlan for an answer.

"That be fair," stated Harlan after a long moment figuring what they might need for the year and its potential cost. Even at Fraeb's prices, they would have more than enough for all they needed and some left over. Little did Harlan realize at that time how great the need would be for that little bit left over.

"That be fair," repeated Harlan as he and Fraeb shook on the deal.

The boys still kept their eyes on the two fur buyers who had taken offense at Harlan's knife moves on their mouthy friend. They were still in heated conversation with the first offender, and all three were casting dark looks at the boys. Big Eagle had the feeling that they hadn't seen the last of those men.

Harlan and the boys led their horses to the purchasing zone of the rendezvous and began looking over the goods and wares. After getting funny looks from several of the merchants, Harlan walked the boys a short distance away and said, "As long as the two of you wear the markings of a Crow, we will continue to be looked upon with suspicion. However, the Crow to my way of thinking are a noble people, and if you want to show your heritage through the beadwork on your clothing, it is fine with me. Just be prepared for trouble from those who are offended by your race or what your race has done to them in the past."

The three of them turned and walked back to the trading as if nothing out of the ordinary had occurred. However, because their dad had backed the boys' decision to display their heritage, they found their love for the man growing by leaps and bounds after that day.

Before the trading was done, Harlan and the boys had purchased six 25-pound kegs of powder (the mighty Hawkens swallowed a lot of powder) and 150 pounds of lead pigs (the Hawkens ate a lot of lead as well). They purchased two dozen Green River skinning knives for trading with Indians, enough horse and mule shoes for their string for a year (two cents per pound), a keg of shoeing nails (five cents per pound), and 100 pounds of cornmeal in 25-pound sacks.

That was soon followed by two 10-pound sacks of pepper, 150 pounds of salt, 50 pounds of brown-sugar cones, 100 pounds of dried apples, and another 50 pounds of raisins. After the boys had tasted the strange-looking items for the first time, Harlan saw to it that 20 pounds of hard rock candy was also purchased.

Getting serious once again, Harlan purchased 100 pounds of flour, three Hudson Bay five-point winter coats because theirs were wearing out, 10 pounds each of red and blue glass beads for trading, and two dozen fire steels (which were always being lost). He added eight sharpening stones (usually broken or lost), files to float the horses' and mules' teeth, and fancy bridles for each horse and mule.

Then he purchased 5,000 primers for the Hawkens and horse pistols, five nipple picks, two dozen nipples for the Hawkens (always deforming), and four more single-shot horse pistols to add to the four he already possessed.

As the boys toted supplies to their ever-growing pile of goods, Harlan purchased two bolts of calico, one red and the other blue, for trading with the Snakes for furs, as well as sewing needles and thread. Lastly, he added two dozen fish hooks and line, four square axes, twenty assorted iron buckles, eight dozen flints for Indian trading, 30 pounds of top-quality James River tobacco, a new coffee mill, and 100 pounds of beans. As an afterthought, he had the traders throw in 100 pounds of rice in four 25-pound bags.

Harlan had two extra horses, so he proposed to the boys that they sell them to the Indians for their remaining buffalo hides and then sell those hides to Fraeb as well. With that credit, they could buy a dozen or so of the Northwest fusil rifles for resale to the Snakes for more furs. (It is a little-known fact that the bulk of the furs taken during the heyday of the mountain men actually came from Indian trappers.)

Both boys nodded in agreement. Harlan also suggested, because of the Indian's mystic associations with the grizzly bear, that they take their three grizzly hides, including that from the great white bear, and sell those to the Indians as well.

Again the boys agreed, and off the trio went to the first Indian village with their goods and wares for trade. Their just-acquired goods were left under the watchful eye of Henry Fraeb and his partners for them to pick up at later time.

10

"NO SELL UM"

REINING UP IN FRONT OF THE CENTRAL TEPEE HE KNEW would house a tribal chief or important leader, as indicated by the eagle staff sticking up from the ground outside the door, Harlan dismounted. Then he realized his error!

The tepee bore the markings of the Northern Cheyenne. Before Harlan could leave because of the boys' discomfort, out strode the chief in all his finery. Not wanting to create a ruckus by departing now that he had been seen, Harlan made the sign of peace, as did the Indian. In sign, Harlan spoke of wanting to sell his two horses for buffalo hides. The chief grunted his approval and then moved past Harlan to inspect the horseflesh. As he did, the two boys silently sitting on their horses all of a sudden froze as they stared hard into the Indian camp. Not three tepees away was a young woman carrying a large bundle of sticks for the evening's fire. It was the boys' older sister!

Harlan instantly sensed the boys' uneasiness and agitation. Looking past the chief's tepee in the direction of the boys' gaze, he spotted the young woman.

Nothing out of the ordinary other than she is really pretty, he thought as he turned to the boys for an explanation. The words the boys spoke staggered Harlan as if he had been hit by a well-thrown tomahawk!

"Are you sure?" he asked in disbelief. Neither boy spoke, but their stares and tight-knuckled grips on their Hawkens said it all.

Then there was a piercing scream! Before he knew it, the young woman recognized the boys, ran over, and seized Big Eagle's leg, frantically talking and crying at the same time.

The chief, stunned by the action of the young woman, quit examining the two horses, picked up a stick, and started to swing it at the woman to make her get back to her chores. It was obvious to Harlan that she was a slave. However, before the chief could strike the young woman, Big Eagle took the limb away and broke it over his knee in fury and contempt.

The surprised chief stood there for a moment and then let out a blood-curdling yell that aroused the entire tribe. Soon the three trappers were surrounded by howling Indians who didn't even know yet why their chief had called them, but his yell was all they needed.

Harlan, quickly realizing this was a no-win situation,

tried through sign to get control of the rapidly escalating events. What had started out as a simple horse trade was now heading in the direction of a bloodletting.

The chief was having none of the contempt shown by the young Indian sitting on his horse, especially because he now realized from their beaded markings that the two young men with the Hawkens were from the hated Crow Nation.

The ruckus had not gone unnoticed by the large numbers of trappers interspersed among the Indians. The call went out among the trappers that one of their kind was surrounded by the Northern Cheyenne, and soon a hundred or more had gathered alongside Harlan and the boys. A battle was in the offing unless cooler heads prevailed, and once again Jim Bridger strode to the forefront of the action.

"Harlan," he said, "what the hell is this all about?"

Harlan explained the situation, and a cloud of concern spread across Jim's face and those of the trappers near enough to overhear his words. Most of them disapproved of slavery. Squaw- swapping was all right because a business deal was struck in the process, but slavery stuck in the craw of most trappers.

It turned out that the Big Eagle and Winter Hawk's sister belonged to the chief Harlan was dealing with over the horses! Hoping a deal could be struck and bloodshed averted, Harlan asked the chief in sign if he would trade for the young girl.

"No," was his cold reply.

Then trouble came in a double dose! Out from the chief's tepee stepped another young woman to see what the noise was all about. She was younger then the first woman and, from her general appearance, had been badly abused. Winter Hawk jumped off his horse in an instant, ran to the young girl, and wrapped her in his arms before she even knew what was happening. She was another sister of the boys who had been taken prisoner by the Northern Cheyenne during the same raid on their village.

Now Harlan had his hands doubly full of hornets, and so did peacemaker, Jim Bridger.

"What else good do you have to trade for the women?" asked Jim with a hopeful look on his face as he nervously fingered the hammer on his rifle. He knew full well this could blow up in a heartbeat, leaving this rendezvous with a special note in the history books—if anyone survived to describe the bloodbath between the trappers and the Indians over a couple of young squaws.

Harlan, realizing the danger that any spark could set off, told Winter Hawk to let go of his sister and return to his horse. There was a long, heartfelt moment as the two separated, but Winter Hawk did as he was told. Harlan then walked to his pack mule, took off a large tanned grizzly-bear hide, and walked back to the chief with a flourish and show of importance. Laying it on the ground, spread out with the fur side up for the full effect, he bade the chief in sign to sit. After a moment's hesitation, the chief sat down across from Harlan with a scowl that seemed as wide as the mighty Missouri was long, and just as cloudy.

In sign Harlan explained, "The two young girls are sisters to my two boys. These sisters were captured in a fight many moons earlier between the mighty Northern Cheyenne and the horse-stealing, dog-eating Crows."

Those words, deriding the Crows to smooth matters over, brought a flicker of a smile to the chief's face ... but just a little one. Harlan went on to quietly explain that he would like to purchase the girls from the great chief.

"No sell um, " the chief said flatly in a tone of finality.

Harlan continued as if he had not heard the chief, "I will give you one horse for each woman."

For a moment Harlan thought he saw a glimmer of greed cross the chiefs eyes because it was a very good trade in a horse-starved wilderness.

"No sell um," the chief repeated. This time he spoke with a little less certainty.

Rising, Harlan returned to the mule and brought forth an even larger tanned grizzly-bear skin with all its claws intact. He laid it at the chief's feet.

"The grizzly-bear hide you are sitting on and this one along with the horses for the two girls," he bargained once again.

By now one could have heard a pin drop among the Indians and the trappers gathered around the two men seated on the bear skin.

"No sell um," persisted the chief. But Harlan knew he was weakening in light of the more than generous offer lying at his feet. Then, removing his necklace of twenty massive grizzly-bear claws given to him by his sons from the bear that had almost killed him, Harlan laid it at the feet of the chief.

For a moment, the chief just stared at this new treasure. Then he slowly reached for the necklace in a most respectful way, illustrating the full power felt in the bear's magic represented by the claws. As he fingered each long claw, Harlan let him be for the moment because of the magical effect the necklace was having.

Then the chief threw the necklace back down by Harlan's knees, saying, "No sell um!"

Harlan still had an ace up his sleeve. Getting up slowly for maximum effect, he walked again to his pack mule. Removing one of his spare older Hawkens, Harlan messed with the rifle's sights momentarily in order to create a dramatic effect for the chief. Then he slowly walked back, noticing that the chiefs eyes never left the valuable, highly prized rifle. Sitting in front of the chief once again, Harlan cradled the rifle in his arms and then, for show, lovingly caressed it. By now, one could have cut the suspense with a knife, and the crowd of trappers or Indians made no sound that would break the spell.

Then Harlan laid the heavy rifle across the chief's knees, saying, "The two horses, the two grizzly-bear skins, the necklace, and this fine rifle for the two women —but no more!"

The tone in Harlan's voice was not lost on the chief. The chief had bargained hard, and now it was time to make his move—or refuse the more than generous offer for the two scrawny slaves from the lowly Crow Nation. For the longest time the chief fingered the highly respected long-shooting rifle. This rifle was twice as powerful as anything his entire tribe had in its arsenal. Finally, the chief slowly laid the rifle back at Harlan's knees, saying, "A keg of rum in addition to all this, and you shall have the squaws."

Holding back his glee, Harlan, without taking his eyes off the chief's, asked one of the nearby trappers to run and fetch a keg of rum, and he would make it good with Fraeb.

Soon two trappers returned, toting a keg of rum between them, and set it beside Harlan. Harlan took the heavy keg and slowly rolled it over to the chief. Then he extended his hand to close the deal. The chief skipped taking Harlan's hand, jumped up holding the Hawken high over his head, and let out a yell of success.

His tribe joined him in hollering over the good bargain their chief had made with the crazy white man for two scrawny Crow women. When things settled down, the chief grabbed the two women and pushed them down at Harlan's feet. Terror registered in their eyes as they looked up into the grizzly-damaged face, and that of a white man at that.

An even greater surprise awaited Harlan. A couple of Cheyenne women roughly thrust two babies into the Crow women's laps! Harlan realized these babies belonged to the women he had just acquired in the trade.

Turning, he told Big Eagle and Winter Hawk to mount their sisters and their babies on the backs of their horses and return to camp.

The women and infants were gently helped up onto the boys' horses by the surrounding trappers. Both boys waited for a moment, looking at Harlan with tears in their eyes. Then they quickly disappeared in the direction of their camp. Rising, Harlan turned and faced those trappers who had stepped forward to back his hand, sight unseen.

"Follow me, lads," he said. "The rum is on me, and rightfully so."

The cheering crowd of trappers descended on Fraeb's fur company liquor stall, and with some of his remaining credit, Harlan procured four large, uncut kegs of rum. With that, the party began in earnest!

Finally slipping unseen into the night, Harlan left the roaring-drunk party of trappers and headed for his camp. He found the boys on high alert, guarding the two shaken women and their goods.

As Harlan dismounted from his horse, Winter Hawk quickly took the reins and told him he would see that the animal was curried, fed, and watered. Surprised, Harlan walked over to the fire and discovered a pot of beans merrily cooking away and numerous pieces of fresh mule deer roasting on green willow sticks. The smell of freshly brewed coffee flooded his nostrils, and he realized just how tired and hungry he was.

Sitting on a log by the fire, he was again surprised

when the older of the two Indian women served him a plate of steaming beans and several large, choice pieces of deer meat. Smiling, she turned and poured him a cup of coffee. Surprised by all the special treatment, Harlan looked over at Big Eagle with a questioning look.

Big Eagle had a smile a mile wide, and he looked back at Harlan and said, "Enjoy the attention, for it is now part of the way of this family!"

Harlan fell to the chow and ate until he was more than full. Leaning back on his log, he summoned Big Eagle and Winter Hawk over to the fire while the women excused themselves and breast-fed their babies in the lean-to.

"Would the two of you let me know what the hell is going on?" requested Harlan with a big grin matching Big Eagle's.

Big Eagle said, "These are two of our three sisters. We just found out that the youngest of the three was killed after the raid because she could not keep up with the war party after they left the battle site."

There was a sorrowful pause, and then he continued like the man he was fast becoming. "However, we at least have two of our sisters back! The one who provided you dinner tonight is Birdsong. She was named by my father after the morning songs of the birds that brought great joy to my people. She is seventeen summers old, and her baby is from being raped many times by the young men from the Northern Cheyenne tribe."

There was no misunderstanding those words, recounted through tight lips and with hate-filled eyes.

"Our younger sister is named Autumn Flower. She is fifteen summers old and was raped many times by the Northern Cheyenne before and after the arrival of her baby. Despite the abuse they suffered as slaves in that tribe, they are healthy and ready to go with us. As for the babies, they are strong, if not noisy, and healthy. Can they go with us back to our trapping grounds and cabin?" asked Big Eagle as his voice hopefully trailed off into nothingness.

Winter Hawk, who had been quiet throughout his brother's explanation, now spoke. "I will work very hard and never again say bad things about the work I have to do if we can take our sisters and their babies with us. You and they are all the family we have, and we would like to be together once again if that is all right?"

"Well, that poses a small problem," said Harlan. "I just traded our two extra horses for your sisters, and now we have nothing for them to ride. I suppose we can try trading some of our remaining credit from Fraeb for some horses, but that may be hard to do with horses being so valuable and in such short supply."

Continuing to think aloud, he said, "We still have the great white bear hide, which we could try to trade for some horses with the Northern Utes. But that may be a tough trail to follow as well because of the overall horse shortage. They have always been short of good horse-flesh, and I don't think they will have any in excess now."

Big Eagle spoke up, saying, "Harlan, Winter Hawk and I have been thinking and have a plan. We realized when we left the Indian camp that we were short of horses. When we return tomorrow to the rendezvous to pick up our supplies, we will need the hide from the great white bear so we can bargain. We may be able to turn it into some horses."

Harlan looked hard at the boys but was not able to discern from their stoic faces what they had in mind. They had been good commonsense thinkers until now, so on a whim he said, "All right, you can have the great bear hide and let's see just how good you two are at turning the hide into horses. Good horses, mind you. No nags, or you will find yourself riding the nags and the women riding your horses."

The two boys gave each other calculating looks and smiled. Somehow, Harlan thought, this whole thing of letting the boys have their heads could be heading us for one hell of a "horse" wreck.

11

BIG GUNS, LITTLE MEN

THE NEXT MORNING THE NEW FAMILY LEFT CAMP AND headed for the activities at the rendezvous. Harlan rode his horse in the lead, and the two boys gave up their horses so their sisters and the babies could ride. On foot, Big Eagle and Winter Hawk led the six pack mules soon to be loaded down with supplies for the next year's adventurers at Willow Lake.

When they arrived at the main trading camp, Harlan saw many trappers lying on the ground asleep or staggering around trying to get the "rum demons" out of their heads—the demons Harlan had placed there with the four kegs of rum he had purchased for the party the night before. Harlan had to smile and was glad he had left the shindig early.

Over at the wagons, fur buying and the procuring of supplies continued at a furious pace among the more or less sober trappers. After all, it was getting into late summer, and the trappers needed to return to their trapping grounds to prepare for winter by repairing their cabins, especially the roofs; hauling in wood; and cutting hay to feed their livestock when the snows became too deep for the animals to graze. They also had to make meat and trap beaver before the winter winds and thick ice became too difficult to overcome.

The two boys took the pack mule with the great bear hide and headed for the fur traders' wagons. They unloaded the hide and struggled to unroll it until it was spread massively over the top and side of one of the trade wagons. In an instant, all fur buying and procurement of supplies halted as an amazed crowd of Indians and trappers gathered to examine the exceptional white bear skin. For the longest time there was absolute, almost reverent silence. Then a gush of talking ensued among those witnessing the freak of nature before them. The talk was soon interrupted by Big Eagle.

"Sixty beaver pelts against the bear hide if any one of you can outshoot me," he said in a loud, challenging voice.

For a moment, there was stunned silence. Sixty beaver pelts for such a magnificent item was a joke! The rare white bear hide was worth at least one hundred beaver hides, if not more. Soon a throng of trappers pushed to the forefront of the crowd to lay wagers that they could outshoot this pipsqueak of a lad—and a Crow Indian at that. Fraeb opened a keg of rum to encourage the betting, and soon a small target was set up in the field at the one-hundred-yard mark.

A brief scuffle broke out among the trappers as they argued over who would go first—because surely that first man could outshoot a young Indian boy and walk off with the prize albino grizzly hide. Finally, Big Jim Tandy drew the short straw and stepped forward to shoot in the contest.

Still a little wobbly from the party the night before, he settled down and shot— boom! Dirt spewed up from beneath the target, and a laugh as well as a groan went up from the crowd. Tandy and Bridger were considered the best shots in the group, and Big Jim could be a bit of a bully because of his size, so the crowd enjoyed as well as commiserated with his missed shot.

Not believing his eyes but acknowledging the acclaimed judge of the event, Jim Bridger, when he announced a miss, Big Jim just stood shaking his head in disbelief. Big Eagle stepped forward, hefted the heavy Hawken, and in less than a heartbeat sent his shot down range—boom! Jim Bridger declared it a hit, and the crowd went wild with shouts of encouragement for the next trapper to step up to the shooting mark. Meanwhile, Winter Hawk dragged Big Jim's bundle of beaver plews off to one side where he could watch over them.

Next to shoot was Dan "Good Book" Beamer, another excellent shooter, and a religious man at that. He had not gotten drunk the night before, and Harlan began to worry a mite. Dropping his entry fee of one ninety-pound pack of beaver plews in the shooting arena, he stepped to the line, said a short prayer with a reverent look skyward, and fired—boom!

"A hit," declared Bridger.

Big Eagle once again stepped forward and fired in less time than it takes to talk about it—boom!

"Another hit," said Bridger.

Now the crowd was alive with the noise of excitement, gambling, anticipation, and speculation about the shoot's outcome.

"To break the tie, both of you must shoot again," said Bridger.

Dan reloaded, stepped forward, said a prayer once again, and fired—boom!

"A clean miss," stated Bridger.

A groan went up from the crowd, but the men were happy because Fraeb's keg of rum was still gushing forth into their empty tin cups. Big Eagle, taking his cue from Bridger, stepped forward and fired.

"A clean hit dead center, and the winner," Bridger announced, laughing at Dan's embarrassment over being bested by an Indian kid with a good shooting eye.

Six more shooters stepped forward with their packs of plews for the chance to win the albino bear hide, and six times Big Eagle beat them where they stood. Soon, no more takers entered the contest after watching those rounds of shooting by the young man. Big Eagle looked over at his brother and gave him a knowing wink, then stepped away from the firing line as his even smaller brother replaced him.

Now the crowd was excited again. Here was a shooter even younger than the last one, and surely he could be beaten. With renewed interest, five more shooters strode forth to best Winter Hawk, and five more bit the dust. Little did they know that Winter Hawk was an even better marksman than Big Eagle or Harlan—and that was exceptional because Harlan rarely missed! Soon thirteen packs of beaver plews were piled up by the wagon, more than enough to purchase two horses for the women to ride without sacrificing the great white bear skin.

The crowd parted, and up strode the proud Northern Cheyenne chief who had enslaved the two girls, in all his finery. Flinging down a bundle of beaver skins in a challenging way, he pointed an accusing finger at Big Eagle and through narrowed eyes said, "I will shoot against you!"

Big Eagle, realizing that this was a chance to partially avenge the killing of his band, smiled a deadly sort of smile, then nodded his acceptance.

The target was reset in the meadow, and Big Eagle strode up to the firing line and shot—boom! The target was knocked down, and as it was reset, Bridger declared the shot a hit. Next the chief strode to the line and with the Hawken he had just acquired from Harlan took aim and fired—boom! A small plume of dirt flew into the air below and to the right of the target.

"A miss," declared Bridger, beginning to feel

concerned as he realized that something ominous was happening. We may have a trapper-Indian bloodletting after all if this chief flies off the handle at being bested by a Crow Indian and losing face, he thought.

The chief turned and said something in his native tongue to a nearby warrior. In a moment the warrior disappeared and soon returned with the two grizzly-bear rugs and Harlan's necklace from the previous afternoon's trading session.

"This against your beaver pelts," the chief snarled.

Big Eagle, with hatred welling up in his heart and blood in his eyes, stepped forward without a word being spoken and drilled the target dead center once again. That rattled the chief a bit, but he quickly gathered himself up, threw the Hawken to his shoulder, and placed his shot no one knew where.

"Another clean miss," Bridger declared with little enthusiasm now for what was happening in front of God and everybody. "Big Eagle is the winner," he continued after a pause, and with that, a loud roar of approval went up from the trappers for the young Indian shooter. They couldn't help admiring his marksmanship even if they saw him as a stinking, horse-stealing Crow...

The chief blew up, growling threateningly, "We must shoot again! What do you want from me to shoot against all that you now have?"

Without hesitation, Big Eagle said, "Three good horses of my choosing from your herd and that Hawken you are shooting!"

The chief went rigid with anger as well as vain pride, finding himself boxed in and egged on unmercifully by the crowd of trappers.

"It is as you have spoken," he said through clenched teeth.

"Move the target to one hundred and fifty yards," Bridger ordered, and two trappers hurried into the field to move it farther back.

Big Eagle let the chief shoot first. Taking his time, the man slowly squeezed off his shot.

"A clean miss," declared Bridger.

It was apparent that the chief was beside himself with rage as he glowered at the target. Now it was Big Eagle's turn. Stepping forward, he raised his Hawken and fired into the dirt not ten feet in front of the chief! The crowd gasped in amazement at the aggressive gesture. The youth had just wasted his shot.

"A clean miss," slowly declared the wondering Jim Bridger.

Looking over at the chief, Big Eagle said, "I missed. It is once again your turn."

The coldness in his taunting voice spoke of many dark things, and the tone was not lost on the chief. Setting his jaw with determination to whip this young and now hated upstart Crow, the chief took plenty of time preparing for his second shot. It went into the dirt at the base of the target, and a great roar went up from the trappers as Big Eagle stepped up to the shooting line and looked long and hard at the chief.

The message in Big Eagle's eyes was clear. Then, shouldering his Hawken, he drilled the target dead center with such force that it was knocked off the log on which it sat! Another roar went up from the crowd as the chief, realizing he had been bested, threw down his Hawken at Big Eagle's feet in a rage.

"Three of your best horses, and I will be by later to select them," Big Eagle uttered through clenched teeth as he looked the chief coldly in the eyes.

The chief whirled and strode through the crowd of trappers mustering all the dignity he could in light of his defeat at the hands of a mere boy, and a Crow at that.

By now Fraeb's keg of rum was kicking in, and a great time was had by all during the rest of the day of fur buying and acquiring necessities for the coming year. Harlan took the two boys off to one side and looked at them proudly as they grinned at him.

"Never in a hundred years would I have guessed what you two had up your sleeves. You did good, and badly as well," he said sternly.

With those last words, both boys furrowed their brows. It wasn't often that Harlan was critical of their actions. His admonition meant something had gone wrong with their plan, they realized.

"It was not good to rub the chief's nose in buffalo droppings as you did. Especially in plain view of the trappers and his own kind. I only hope we never run across his band in the bush because if we do, there will be a right good killing taking place—and I only hope it ain't us."

The boys, especially Big Eagle, realized the wisdom of Harlan's words now that they thought over their actions. Big Eagle had intentionally made the chief look bad, especially with that challenging shot into the dirt at his feet, but he felt that he had had good reason.

The chief and his band had slaughtered his family and his tribe. Big Eagle hoped they would get a rematch once again, only next time on the field of combat. If we do, he darkly vowed to himself, I will slit the throat of the chief and smear his blood all over myself as a final act of revenge.

Regaining control of his emotions, Big Eagle went with Winter Hawk to the shooting site to retrieve the great white bear hide and pack it back onto their mule. As for the beaver plews they had won in the contest, Harlan quietly told the boys to leave them where they were. That came as a surprise to the two boys, but they did as they were told. After all, their dad had spoken, and he was to be believed in all that he did.

12

THE RENDEZVOUS ENDS, AND A DEADLY EVENT FOLLOWS

THAT AFTERNOON HARLAN, THE BOYS, JIM BRIDGER, JOE Meek, and Thomas "Crooked Hand" Fitzpatrick went to the camp of the Northern Cheyenne chief. To avoid any more embarrassment, the chief had all his horses except his favorite buffalo pony gathered in a small herd close by his tepee. As the men sat on their horses overlooking the situation, Big Eagle dismounted and, after careful review, selected three fine horses as his winnings.

With Harlan's words of caution still ringing in his ears, he approached the chief and in sign thanked him for his generosity. The chief said nothing and with a face still cast in stone glowered at Big Eagle as if memorizing his face for posterity. The party of trappers left, trailing the three horses, with the recent life's lessons ingrained in the two boys as they fast became men.

Having acquired all the supplies their credit allowed,

including some nice bolts of red cloth, iron rings, red and blue beads, and six soft tanned bighorn sheep hides to make dresses for the two females now in their midst, they headed for their camp, but not before Harlan tipped a couple cups of rum with Meek and Bridger while discussing plans for the next rendezvous.

Harlan had returned all the beaver-plew winnings from the shoot-off to their original owners because he knew he had a couple of ringers in the boys when it came to their shooting abilities. Harlan had also quietly returned the two grizzly-bear hides and the claw necklace, but not the Hawken rifle, to the Northern Cheyenne chief.

The chief was still miffed at having been bested by an uncivil Crow youngster, but Harlan hoped the return of these items would somehow take the edge off what had happened that day. Little did he realize that was not to be the case. Harlan decided to keep the hide from the white bear; it had brought such good luck to his new family that he saw little use in trading such a powerful talisman.

On the way back to their camp, Big Eagle wore a huge smile. He had bested many mountain men in a shooting contest and in so doing had won a small fortune in horses and furs. In addition, he had bested one of the hated war sub-chiefs of the Northern Cheyenne, one who had probably participated in the killing of his family and tribe. Enjoying the memory of his performance with the Hawken in front of all those mountain men and

Indian spectators, he found himself brought up short by Harlan during the ride.

Harlan moved his horse over to Big Eagle and, guessing the grand thoughts Big Eagle was thinking about his shooting prowess, said, "Did you ever see such poor shooting as that chief's with one of our fine Hawken rifles?"

Big Eagle grinned and said, "He was a pretty poor shot, wasn't he?"

"Well, just so you keep it in perspective, realize you had a helping hand in his poor shooting ability. You see, when I dragged that rifle off the mule to trade for your sisters, I quickly moved the hindsight so it would be off a mite, no matter who shot the rifle.

I thought that chief would probably find himself at odds someday with some hapless Indian or another mountain man and would use that rifle to exact his revenge. So I knocked the rear sight off its center full well knowing he would never check it and hoping I might be giving some unfortunate a second chance at living.

So don't you get a big head because I had a direct hand in his poor performance. Now, don't get me wrong —you did very well and have learned from our winter training sessions. But in this particular instance, you had a hand helping you make him look like a fool."

Without a look back, Harlan resumed the lead as if nothing out of the ordinary had happened. The matter was never brought up again, but Big Eagle, perplexed by what Harlan had just told him, found himself smiling at his good fortune in having such a great dad and teacher.

Arriving back in their camp, the man and two boys began making ready for the long trip back to their winter site. Goods were stacked according to bulk and weight for each mule or horse to be packed the next day. The animals were curried and grained. In the meantime, the two women assumed the camp duties, and soon the delicious smell of cooking food began to fill the air from the center cooking fire.

This accommodation with the women might not be too bad, thought Harlan with a grin as the smells of cooking other than his own made him hungry.

Harlan's eyes flew wide open, and in that instant he knew he was in danger! That awareness was followed by the braying of his bell mule, Martha. Rolling quietly out of his sleeping furs, he grabbed his tomahawk and Hawken in the pitch dark and silently crawled toward a large cottonwood log near the edge of camp.

Peering into the darkness, he strained for any sight or sound of danger. There was none as the inky darkness quietly kept its secrets. Sniffing hard but quietly, Harlan could not detect the smell of sweat or rancid bear grease of hostile Indians or the rankness of the ever-present grizzly bear.

There was no trace for the longest time. Suddenly, there it was! The smell of stale tobacco, either from chewing tobacco or smoking a pipe. Now he was more than sure that extreme danger was at hand as he silently cocked the hammer of his Hawken against his shirt. Then, he heard the faint rustle of leaves not ten feet from the log behind which he was lying. Silently grabbing his tomahawk, he listened and waited.

The sound drew closer until he could almost sense a form in the dark just inches away. Then came the rustling of leaves next to his log once again, accompanied by the same strong smell of tobacco.

The next thing he knew, a rifle barrel slid over the log not a foot from his face. Realizing that he needed to warn the camp, he grabbed the barrel and slammed it violently downward. Boom went the rifle into the dirt, arousing the camp as Harlan swung his tomahawk viciously where he felt the shooter might be at the butt end of the rifle. There was a thump followed by a terrible screech as something wet and warm splattered Harlan's arm, face, and hand.

Boom—boom went two more rifles in quick succession off to Harlan's right. Memorizing the muzzle-flash locations, Harlan vaulted the log, pulled his knife, and sprinted like a bobcat towards the closest of the shooters. By then the boys had returned fire into the night in the direction of the two muzzle flashes as well.

It had been fortunate that Harlan had managed to hide behind the log before the ambush began. The first shot had gone harmlessly into the dirt, thereby alerting the camp. At the sound of danger, Big Eagle and Winter Hawk had rolled out of their sleeping furs and away from the light of the remains of the camp's small fire, and the two shooters had fired into their empty sleeping furs.

Pow—pow went two pistol shots from the unknown shooters as Harlan continued running toward a dark figure standing to shoot into his camp. Swinging his Hawken like a club, Harlan smashed its cold steel into the human form and followed the blow with a knife attack so vicious that his assailant was disemboweled with one swipe of the blade.

Stabbing again and again, Harlan became aware of Big Eagle wrestling with the other assailant beside the man Harlan was killing. Grabbing his bloody knife to help, he was foiled as Winter Hawk viciously tomahawked the man who was locked in mortal combat with his brother. The blow split the man's skull, and he folded like a sack of flour.

Looking quickly around, Harlan and the boys saw no other threat to their camp. As he made doubly sure, Big Eagle told Autumn Flower in Crow that everything was all right and told her to build up the fire so they could see better. Standing their ground at the edge of the trees in the light of the rebuilt campfire, the three continued to look for any sign of danger.

Finding none, they moved back to the three men they had killed. They discovered that their attackers were the three fur buyers from the rendezvous who had refused to trade with Harlan because of his association with Crow Indians. Harlan found that he had split the first man's skull cleanly from the top of his head to the neck vertebrae.

After disarming the three dead men, they came away with three knives, three good-grade rifles, and four single-shot pistols with accessories. Without wasting any time, they used horses to drag the dead men to the edge of camp and left their bodies for the scavengers.

Looking over their work, Big Eagle thought, I figured back at the rendezvous that these three would be trouble once again, and they were. Now they belong with the ages and the flesh-eaters of the plains.

Back in camp, Birdsong began a low wail. Moving over to her side, Harlan discovered that her baby had been hit by a stray bullet and killed instantly! There was nothing he could do, so he let her two brothers and sister console her for the loss of her child.

Leaving the sorrow back at camp, Harlan took up his unfired Hawken. Checking to see that it still had a percussion cap attached to the nipple, he began a search for their assailants' livestock. It didn't take him long to discover three horses and three pack mules tied in some brush a short distance away.

They must have known we were camping in that grove of cottonwoods and used the smoke from our campfire to find us, he thought grimly.

A quick look at the mules showed all three loaded with supplies from the rendezvous.

Fraeb must have kicked all three troublemakers out of camp, he surmised.

A rustling in the bushes told him Winter Hawk was at his side, and the two of them brought the six animals into their camp for safekeeping. Birdsong continued her low wailing from the shelter of the lean-to while Autumn Flower kept the fire roaring and began cooking a hearty breakfast of Dutch-oven biscuits, deer steak, and boiled dried fruit.

The ever-present coffee was bubbling away over the cooking rod, and soon all could eat. Once chow was ready, everyone except Birdsong sat down to eat, aware of the long ride before them. Birdsong continued to cry over her loss, and the rest gave her the space she needed for her grief.

After breakfast, they began packing their mules, their extra horse, and the three horses and mules the assailants had brought to the ambush as well. Daylight was chasing the dark in the east when they finished packing and were ready to go.

Harlan wasn't sure what to do with the dead baby, but Birdsong settled that issue. Smearing ashes on her face and arms from the now dying campfire, she took the small bundle wrapped in furs and mounted her horse. She continued to cry, but she knew they must move on and was ready to go. Harlan couldn't help but admire her and her stoic acceptance of grief. In fact, he admired her in more ways than met the casual eye.

Retracing their earlier trail into the valley. Harlan led the way, with Big Eagle bringing up the rear. Winter Hawk took up his position alongside the pack string that now included many horses and mules, and the two women rode behind Harlan. Several other changes had occurred. Each male carried a Hawken over his saddle and had another tied on the first animal behind him for emergencies. In addition, they now carried two .79-caliber horse pistols apiece. Last but not least, each woman carried a long-bladed buffalo-gutting knife.

Whoever tangles with this pack string is going to have a hard and deadly time, Harlan thought grimly. As he looked back over his group, his eyes met those of Autumn Flower and Birdsong.

The first opportunity I get, those two women are going to learn to shoot a pistol and a rifle. Never again are they going to be defenseless, he thought with determination.

13

BURIAL, THE LONG TRIP HOME,
AND A HAPPENING

SEVERAL DAYS LATER, BIRDSONG SECURED HER BABY'S BODY
high in a pine tree on the east side of the Wasatch Mountain range so that it could face in the direction of their
winter camp. Once that was done, she mounted her
horse as if nothing out of the ordinary had occurred and
continued the long ride. No one said anything. They rode
silently out of respect for Birdsong's grief and the loss of
her firstborn.

The group frequently rode across the tracks of many
Indians on the move, but fortunately they encountered
none. After cautiously traveling for several more weeks,
they entered the last grove of timber prior to arriving
home.

As they rounded the last stand of timber before their
cabin, Harlan was alerted by the smell of wood smoke
from a campfire. When they came into view of their

cabin, they saw four mountain men unloading their pack animals in front of the door, as if the cabin were theirs.

"Hello, the cabin," yelled Harlan so as not to startle the busy men.

Instantly the men rushed for their rifles and stood grimly to greet the newcomers. As if on command, Harlan and the boys quietly cocked the hammers on their Hawkens in case shooting started. The two women quickly peeled out of the pack string and rode their horses to the rear.

Riding up to the men, Harlan said, "Good afternoon. My name is Harlan Waugh, and these here are my boys, Big Eagle and Winter Hawk. The two squaws are Birdsong and Autumn Flower. Who might ye fellers be?"

For a long moment none of the strangers said anything. Finally, a short man with a massive beard said, "We be the rightful owners of this here cabin."

"How can that be?" exclaimed Harlan with a lightness not betraying the seriousness in his voice or the plain damn meanness rising in his guts at being displaced from his own cabin by these four strangers. "The boys and I built this here cabin last year. We have our cache nearby and claim these here beaver trapping grounds as ours."

"We was here'n first," answered the short, bearded one, "and intend to stay!"

Stepping off his horse as if he were going to a tea party, Harlan strode over to the obvious leader of the group and said, "Look, this is our cabin, and I can prove it. My name is carved on an inside rafter with the year of

Our Lord beside it. Seem' that is the case, I don't see how you folks can claim this property as your'n."

"I wouldn't know, seein' I can't read, and neither can my partners," snarled the short one, in the same breath clutching his rifle even tighter as if he was considering using it.

Suddenly Martha the bell mule let out a bray, and soon the sounds of many horses' hooves could be heard approaching from the timber below the cabin. Joe Meek and about twenty Snake warriors came into view, and the four men in front of Harlan, fearing an attack, broke and ran for the cover the cabin offered.

Reining up alongside Harlan, Meek called loudly, "Welcome back home, you three." Then, looking again, he said with a big grin, "Well, I see you haven't traded off them 'squars' you picked up at the rendezvous yet. We came to see if you and your'n might want to go and make some meat. But I see you have some guests." His grin turned to puzzlement over the presence of four strangers.

"Well, not really," said Harlan. "They are claiming the cabin as theirs even though I told them we built it and it is mine."

A cloud flew across Meek's face, and he quickly dismounted. Boldly walking up to the front door of the cabin, he yelled for the men to come out before things got messy. Soon the four newcomers exited the cabin with their rifles held at the ready.

"You boys is in the wrong cabin. This here cabin

belongs to that man and his youngsters. They built it last year and trapped here all fall and spring. Besides, this is Chief Low Dog's territory of the Snake Nation, and he ain't given any of you permission to trap in this here area like he has Harlan and the boys."

"Who the hell are you, coming in here and giving orders like you belong?" blurted out the short one, pissed at this new intervention.

"I am Joe Meek, the meanest son of a bitch in the valley, part he-wolf and part wolverine. I am the best-shooting beaver-trapping son of a gun to walk these here parts, and if you folks don't move on peaceable-like, these here braves of Low Dog's will have to convince you that to lose your topknot over a cabin that ain't your'n ain't in your best interest!"

Nervously looking over the odds now confronting him, the short one said, "Well, I guess we could move on if'n you put it that-a-way. Come on, boys, let's pack our critters and skedaddle. This here ain't no place for us to touch down if'n we ain't wanted."

With that, the four began packing their animals and a short time later disappeared into the timber heading farther north. Again, Big Eagle instinctively felt as he had about the three fur buyers from the rendezvous: they would see these four skunks again, and the outcome wouldn't be pretty...

"Seems like I owe you and our friends the Snakes another one," said Harlan with a big grin of appreciation for Joe once again backing his play. "I need to pass on making meat with you folks this time. As you can see, we just arrived and need to unload and set up camp in preparation for the fall. If the need still exists in about a week, come on by and if nothing else, we can share some rum and talk about old times."

"Sounds good to me," said Meek. "See you and your'n in a few."

With that and a wave of the hand, off they rode to cause the nearest buffalo some grief.

14

FALL FIXIN'S AND SOMETHING IN THE AIR

FOR THE NEXT TWO WEEKS, LIFE WAS HECTIC AROUND THE cabin, to say the least. First and foremost, another cabin had to be built to accommodate the women. Everyone worked at felling timber, limbing logs, and hauling them with the horses to a site alongside the first cabin.

Then the logs were trimmed to size, notched, and put up to a wall height of seven feet. Once the walls were up, windows were cut out, a front and back door were framed, and shooting slots were constructed along all sides from whence danger might come. The windows were covered with rolled-up tanned deer hides that could be raised to let in a little light and reinforced with log shutters on the inside in the event of an attack.

Log plugs inserted into the shooting slots from the inside allowed the cabin to stay warm but could easily be withdrawn if they needed to run the rifle barrels out and shoot. Last was the roof, which went up in two days and was covered with two feet of dirt for insulation and resistance against fire from the outside.

As soon as the cabins were cleaned out and made ready, the women and Autumn Flower's baby moved into one, and the men occupied the other. Then, everyone worked to make sleeping platforms, chairs, benches, and tables from the leftover materials at hand. In addition, both cabins were used to store the fast accumulating dried meats and freshly tanned hides from the animals they were able to hunt close at hand, along with the contents of the cache that they had left behind when they departed for the rendezvous.

Next they cut dry timber, hauled it to the cabins, and placed it in such a manner that the firewood was readily available for use during the harsh winter months. But they also placed it so that it could not be easily used by outsiders as cover from which to fire on the cabins.

Then the serious rush was on to make the rest of their winter's meat. Harlan, Big Eagle, and Winter Hawk brought elk, mule deer, and moose into camp daily. The two women skinned out the animals, saving the hides, and cut the meat into strips for drying on the racks in front of the cabins. As the meat smoked and dried, Harlan and the boys packed their tree cache house to the roof with the nutritious food in tanned deerskin bags.

They took and prepared over thirty animals in this fashion, with the bones and offal packed off to the end of the meadow for disposal by the critters. Then, the dangerous part of making meat occurred as they went after the ever-present black and grizzly bears for the wonderful sustenance they offered. The straight-shooting mountain man and boys slew six grizzly and nine black bear without incident. All of the bears were rolling with winter fat, which they removed and rendered for its many valuable properties. The fat would be used for cooking oil, rubbed on the body to repel mosquitoes, and smoothed into hair before braiding, along with its many medicinal uses.

The hides were tanned by the women for the fur trade, and the claws were saved in a large deer-hide bag for trading with those wanting a bear-claw necklace, the ultimate sign of power. Last but not least, the shoulders and hams from these animals were smoked and hung from the rafters of the cache house and both cabins. They would be used for deep-winter fare or to feed large numbers of company such as their friends, the Snakes, when they came to visit.

The entire clan took the horses and mules onto the nearby shortgrass prairies and, after a day of searching, located a small herd of buffalo. A successful stalk and shoot by the man and boys yielded fifteen animals, which were cut up and loaded onto the pack animals. Groaning under the weight of the fresh meat, the mules showed their displeasure every step of the way by balking, trying to roll with their loads, braying, and generally being hammerheads as the horses looked on in feigned indifference.

It took many beatings of the mules with switches to convince them to move on, and soon the camp hove into sight. Realizing they were almost home, the complaining mules again tried to roll with their packs or throw them off with a violent shake of their bodies. The whips were once again administered until calm again reigned in the pack string.

Once unloaded, however, all the pack animals, to rid themselves of the meat smell and sweat and needing a good scratch, rolled in the meadow time and time again to show their pleasure at being freed from their loads.

However, for the humans, the work had just begun. Smoky fires were lit, and hundreds of pounds of rich buffalo meat were hung on the drying racks as fast as they could work. They needed to manage the smoking quickly in order to minimize the amount of fly-blown meat. They staked out the hides in the sun, fur side down, and soon were defatting and the skins and scraping off any leftover meat that could cause them to spoil in the drying process.

Soon fifteen buffalo hides were lightly salted and slowly drying in the sun, and the smell of a large pot of buffalo stew graced the air. Then the smell of coffee and hot Dutch-oven biscuits filled their nostrils, announcing dinnertime for the tired but pleased group. It seemed as if so much food had never flown down hungry gullets as fast as it did that evening.

During that momentous feast and celebration of successfully making meat—and rich buffalo meat at that

—Harlan noticed something unusual. During that special meal, Birdsong sat beside him and spooned a succulent piece of meat onto his plate. Then, without a word, she quietly ate her dinner sitting beside him as if nothing out of the ordinary had occurred.

Well, something had occurred that would have life-long consequences. Harlan had admired Birdsong from the very first time he had laid eyes on her. She was tall, lithe, and dark-eyed, with long black hair that fell loosely around her shoulders and over her breasts. She had a winning smile and a personality to match. Yes, Harlan had noticed her—and the gesture she bestowed on him that evening by the campfire did not go unnoticed by anyone!

The next few days continued to be jammed with work. But during that time, Birdsong hardly ever left Harlan's side, or he hers. He enjoyed her company in everything they did, and it was apparent to all that she enjoyed his as well.

Remembering his pledge on the long ride back from the rendezvous, Harlan took time during this busy period to work with the women on the correct use of a knife in self-defense as well as sharpening and general care.

Then came lessons in the loading and shooting of the pistols and the use of the Hawkens. At first, there was some awkwardness for the women, especially with their brothers closely watching their every move. However, Harlan's seriousness made the women realize that when the trappers were away, they would have to fend for themselves. Be the danger from a varmint or a man, they would have to be able to defend themselves without any hope of relief in a land that could kill in a heartbeat.

That seriousness paid off handsomely. The women caught on rapidly, and after two days of intense training under Harlan's watchful eyes, they could shoot the pistols very well and the Hawkens reasonably well. Happy with the results of his instruction, Harlan felt that the women could kill anyone needing killing out to fifty yards with the Hawkens and at close range with the pistols.

In close with the knife, anyone messing around with the women when he shouldn't would be quickly disemboweled. He also discovered that he rather enjoyed holding Birdsong close as he provided instruction with the Hawken. From the way she backed into him during those times, it was obvious that she enjoyed being held by Harlan as well. Those close moments were also noticed by two very happy boys.

The next day was spent in reloading drills for the pistols and rifles, and by noon the women had it down pat. Harlan sat back with a smile and felt confident that the two women could care for themselves if given a fair chance. However, if they are ambushed, well, that could be another story, he thought darkly.

The huge pile of remaining work took his mind off Birdsong, but just for a short while. Preparing for the long fall trapping season, the group shod the horses and mules who needed it, repaired the tack, and cast many bullets for the big Hawkens from their stash of lead pigs.

Then clothing was repaired and winter clothing fashioned, and the women made heavy winter coats for the men from buffalo hides.

Finally, dense fires smoked the beaver traps to rid them of any human scent. As in times past, they opened a gap in a small nearby beaver dam and set four traps to catch the beaver hell-bent on fixing the dam. The next day, the man and boys skinned and hooped out the four beaver caught at the breached dam. Into the small glass bottles that hung from their necks went the valuable oil from the beavers' castors. This oil, placed on a stick near a trap, would lure unsuspecting beaver to their final moments in a steel trap before they drowned attempting to escape.

Next, the three began scouting to see where they would begin their trapping season. The streams to the south had been almost cleaned out of beaver during their first year of trapping. Knowing the few remaining animals could not sustain their trading needs, they traveled a few miles north of their camp, where they soon discovered many more dams and streams loaded with the furry creature.

They decided that was where they would start their fall trapping season, with all three of them trapping together for safety. They returned to their camp to make final preparations for the many rewards and close calls, not to mention a small mountain of furs, of the upcoming 1832 rendezvous.

———

AFTER A HEARTY BREAKFAST, the three men left for the first day of their fall trapping adventures. They left behind two heavily armed women who could now shoot and defend themselves, along with a baby who represented new hope for the group. The day has dawned well, thought Harlan as he and the boys began another adventure together as a family in the sometimes deadly wilderness they loved.

Kneeling by a small beaver dam in order to set his trap, Harlan noticed the track of a very large grizzly. Quietly pointing it out to the boys, he signed for them to cock the hammers on their rifles in case he got ambushed as before. Once was enough, he thought as he skillfully set his last trap, all the while keeping a sharp eye peeled on the brushy areas alongside the beaver pond.

That particular day he and the boys set out eighteen traps. Any more than that and the mules would be overloaded with beaver carcasses and the men would have to work far into the night skinning and hooping their catches. Quietly and carefully, the three moved farther north, scouting out new trapping territory for the morrow. What they saw pleased them greatly. The land was alive with game, and the beaver ponds and streams were crawling with the sought-after furry rodents.

"With a little luck we should be able to take at least two hundred beaver this fall," calculated Harlan with a wide grin.

On the way back the three discovered that over half of their traps already contained beaver! Removing the trapped animals and resetting the traps, Harlan smiled as the boys skillfully provided cover against any bear attack.

ROUNDING the spit of trees prior to entering camp, the men observed the women tending the last of the meat-smoking fires as they starting cooking the evening dinner. As they came closer, they could see that in addition to carrying a long-bladed buffalo- gutting knife in her sash, each woman now wore a pistol as well.

Harlan grinned back at the boys over the successful instruction in how to stay alive in a beautiful but dangerous country. The return grins from the boys showed their pleasure with Harlan for training their sisters and giving them the chance to defend themselves against being killed or captured again.

Dismounting in the area set aside for skinning the beaver, the men greeted the women and started untying the beaver carcasses from the mules. Birdsong came over to help, and as she walked by Harlan she gently brushed her hand across his shoulders. Without any thought, Harlan reached out and gathered her into his strong arms.

Facing her, he gently kissed her lips, feeling the firmness of her breasts through his shirt and a trembling of her entire body. After the kiss, she moved back a few inches and looked into his gunmetal-steel-blue eyes. In her black eyes, Harlan could see a thousand years of wisdom. In his, she saw strength yet gentleness, courage governed with wisdom, and a will to survive and experience life such as she had never seen in any man. It was at that moment that the two of them quietly dedicated their lives to each other. It was also a happy moment for the others because now they would be a real family once again.

———

FALL TRAPPING WENT as Harlan expected. They caught over two hundred beaver, not to mention killed another five rolling-fat grizzly bears before the snow flew. There was another happening as well.

Autumn Flower moved in with the boys, and they delighted in being that close once again to their younger sister and her baby. Harlan and Birdsong moved into the other cabin and began life together as man and wife.

15

ANOTHER DEADLY SURPRISE,
FOLLOWED BY A SURPRISE OF A
UNIQUE KIND

WINTER CAME WITH A VENGEANCE. MANY A NIGHT IT WAS so cold that the trees, especially the aspen near the cabins, popped their bark! Hearing the baby fussing one morning, Winter Hawk rose, dressed, and rekindled the fire in the cabin fireplace.

Satisfied that it would last until he returned, he left the cabin to greet the day. It was just getting light as he positioned the ladder against the cache house. Climbing up, he unlocked the door, reached in, and took out a large chunk of moose meat. Closing the door and latching it so the crows, ravens, and magpies couldn't get in and eat the meat, he climbed back down the ladder and removed it so no land-based varmints could climb into the cache house.

Laying the ladder to one side, he returned to his cabin and headed for the cooking pot so he could put the moose meat into it. Seeing that it needed more water in order to make a large stew for the family, he grabbed the water pail, opened the cabin door, and stepped out. Quietly closing the door so he would not wake the others, he headed down the trail from the cabin toward the lake.

Something made him instinctively stop and look toward the lake. Boom—boom went two rifles in unison. Winter Hawk spun around from the bullets' impact, flying into the snowbank next to the cabin! A bright-red stream of blood splattered the snow where he came to rest. As he lay there in the snow, the blood began to pool beneath his inert form.

Harlan and Big Eagle, hearing the report of heavy rifles close to their cabins, scrambled out of bed, grabbed their rifles, and threw open their front doors at almost the same time.

Boom— boom went two more shots from the hidden rifles. Harlan felt hot lead pass alongside his cheek, just breaking the skin and cleanly taking off the lobe of his right ear. The bullet meant for Big Eagle was off its mark, smashing into the front door and tearing it out of his hand. Both quickly slammed the doors shut, but not before Harlan had spotted Winter Hawk lying in a crimson- stained heap by the other cabin.

Knocking out a shooting-port plug, Harlan chanced to see a man out in front of his cabin about thirty yards away, lying prone behind a small log used for pitch-wood. He was lying on his side, hurriedly reloading his rifle, when Harlan raised his rifle and snapped off a shot at the arm and shoulder showing above the log.

Boom!

"Ahhh-eeeeow," screamed a human as Harlan's shot smashingly found its mark. That sound was quickly followed by the whimpering of a man in abject pain.

A hand or arm wound, thought Harlan as he quickly grabbed his reserve Hawken from its pegs over the front door. Birdsong, already out of bed, bolted the back door and, grabbing her pistol, stood at the ready. Still looking out through his shooting port, Harlan saw movement behind the horses and mules in the corral, but the nervous horses were moving around enough to make a shot in their general direction a poor choice unless he wanted to kill his livestock. He knew it would be a death sentence in that country to lose his means of transportation.

Boom! went Big Eagle's rifle, and Harlan saw snow and dirt spew by another log at the edge of the timber off to one side of his cabin. Watching that spot for any sign of movement, Harlan finally saw some. He quickly raised his rifle, but the movement disappeared from sight almost as fast. During the next few moments, Harlan and Big Eagle spotted at least three armed men shooting at their cabins, not counting the wounded one who just lay behind his log, still crying out loudly in pain.

Three against two, but no way to get at them and no way for them to get at us, Harlan thought grimly. I need to wait until night and then break out and kill them one by one. But if I wait that long, Winter Hawk, if still alive, will bleed or freeze to death.

Big Eagle was thinking the same thing. Here they were trapped while his brother, if still alive, was lying out there dying or freezing to death. Tears rose in his eyes as the frustration almost overwhelmed him.

Zip—thunk went an arrow into the left eye of the shooter behind the horse corral, exiting through his right ear. The man was dead before he hit the frozen ground. Hearing his partner fall with a muffled crump off to his left, another shooter behind a log at the edge of the forest chanced a quick look in that direction. In that glance he saw an arrow heading for his face a microsecond before it sank deeply into his nose and continued into the base of his skull. He never felt his body hitting the frozen ground.

Seeing his remaining partner fall with an arrow to the face, a short, bearded individual lying by another log rose and bolted for their horses tied in the timber behind him. Boom—boom went a Hawken quickly fired from each cabin.

The two heavy slugs hit with such force that it slammed the runner into a tree fifteen feet before him, splitting the front of his skull on the stub of a tree limb. The wounded one, now realizing his mortality was upon him, tried to rise on his remaining arm, only to have Harlan's tomahawk explode his head like a melon. He never felt another thing.

Quickly looking around now that he was out in the

open, Harlan saw an Indian walking toward him from the corral, holding his bow high in the air over his head in a sign of peace. By then Big Eagle was out the door, covering the Indian, who still held his bow high in the air as he walked toward Harlan.

The Indian quickly signed that he was from Low Dog's tribe of Snake Indians once he saw the looks of extreme killing anger on the trappers' faces. Continuing to sign, he said, "I heard the shooting while hunting and decided to see what was going on. I thought it might be some members from my tribe hunting, but soon I saw the four white men shooting at your cabin. Low Dog and Joe Meek consider you friends, and since that is my clan, so do 1.1 tried to help as fast as I could, but it appears one of your friends is hurt."

Realizing the Indian was a friend, Harlan ran to Big Eagle, who was now bending over the bleeding Winter Hawk.

"He is still alive, Harlan! Help me move him inside before he freezes or bleeds to death," yelled the frantic Big Eagle.

The two men grabbed Winter Hawk, carried him into the cabin, and laid him gently down on his bed. Autumn Flower and Birdsong quickly pushed the two men aside and began to wipe the blood off Winter Hawk to see where he had been hit. One shot had left a dark, ugly purple burn across his ribs. The other had grazed his head from the crown all the way across the side above his ear.

"Bloody but no brains," said Harlan with a sigh of relief.

The two women continued to tend the groaning Winter Hawk while Harlan and Big Eagle realized they had left the Indian who had helped them standing outside. With that realization, they moved rapidly out the door. The Indian man had not moved, and his bow was still held high in the air as a continuing sign of peace.

Harlan strode over to the man, held out his hand in friendship, and said, "The boy still lives. He has a bad head wound, and the women are working on him to see if they can save him. Big Eagle and I wish to thank you for your help. Without it they had us trapped, and we couldn't use the back doors because we feared they had those areas covered as well."

They walked over to the man who had been shot by Big Eagle and Harlan as he tried to escape. It was obvious that he was dead. The bullets from the two rifles would have killed him before he hit the ground, but the final fling into the tree with the impact of those two hits had more than done it. Rolling him over with his foot, Harlan recognized the bearded trapper who had tried to claim their cabin some months earlier. Big Eagle just grunted and then thanked his instincts for showing him this man in a true light.

The three disarmed the four shooters and stacked their bodies by the corral. Saddling his horse, Big Eagle dragged the men one by one across the snow to the boneyard at the end of their meadow until all the evidence of the fight was left to the dead men's God and the always hungry wolves and coyotes.

They returned quickly to the cabin to check on Winter Hawk. He was very pale, was breathing very shallowly, and looked as if death was just around the door. Sick at the sight, the men went outside to the fire pit and kindled a roaring fire.

As they warmed themselves by the fire, Harlan asked the man who had saved their lives to tell them about himself. At first he was reluctant to talk about himself, but he soon opened up, especially after a scalding cup of coffee had been thrust into his hands by Autumn Flower.

What he had to say dropped like a mad bear on Harlan and Big Eagle. His Snake name was Dog Eater, but his Crow name was Runs Fast! He had been captured as a young man of fifteen summers, had been adopted into the Snake tribe, and belonged to Chief Low Dog.

Harlan and Big Eagle were stunned. Autumn Flower, who was bringing the man another cup of coffee laced with lots of sugar, dropped the cup into the snow at her feet upon hearing those words from another Crow Indian. The only sound heard for a long time was the crackling of the pine limbs in the fire.

Then Autumn Flower regained her composure, picked up the empty coffee cup, and fled back into her cabin. Runs Fast never took his eyes off her until she disappeared inside. Shortly thereafter, and with more composure, she returned with another cup of coffee, and this time she managed to get it into Runs Fast's hands with a smile that was more than returned.

Turning to Harlan, she said, "Winter Hawk's eyes are open, but he doesn't see anything and still does not talk."

Jumping up, Harlan and Big Eagle left their guest sitting on the log by the fire and returned to the cabin to see for themselves. The women had Winter Hawk bundled up in a buffalo robe and had bandaged his head wound. They had left the ugly purple wound along the rib cage as it was because there were no broken ribs and there wasn't much they could do to alleviate the pain of that kind of wound.

Painful? Yes. Was the rib injury life threatening? No, thought Harlan. However, a look into Winter Hawk's staring but unseeing eyes led him to fear that death was not far from the cabin's doorstep. Winter Hawk was mumbling words that could not be understood, and it was plain that he was struggling to live through what must be a terrible concussion. Laying his hand on his son's shoulder, Harlan became aware of the coldness it projected. Tears came into his eyes, and he had to turn away before the others saw his pain.

Stepping back outside and leaving Big Eagle to sit by his brother, Harlan returned to the Indian on the log by the fire. Sitting down by the man, he turned to him and said, "Runs Fast, you are more than welcome at my campfire any time you desire. You single-handedly saved us from those buzzards lying at the end of the meadow waiting for the varmints to finish the job. I will be forever grateful for your prompt action in joining the fight and helping us win. What can I do for you in return?" Runs Fast sat for a moment and then said, "Nothing, Harlan. Just the right to join you anytime I am free to do so would be reward enough."

"Done," said Harlan as he extended his hand in the sign of peace and deep thanks to the young Crow Indian who was a Snake slave. "Now, let us go and see if we can find those fellows' horses and mules. They have to be getting kind of lonesome out there by now and fearful of the wolves."

Joined by Big Eagle, they backtracked the culprits who had shot Winter Hawk and located their animals within an hour. There were nine horses, five of which were fully packed with camp gear and beaver plews.

There were also four mules carrying several tepee skins and the rest of the party's camp gear. It was obvious that the men had been living in tepees, and when the weather got harsh had decided to take over Harlan's camp when the Snakes were not nearby to help. However, they had not counted on the deadly shooting of Runs Fast when they had made plans to wipe out Harlan and his clan.

They brought the animals back to camp and unloaded them. There were four packs of beaver plews, which Harlan and Big Eagle took into one of the cabins for safe storage. Then there was camp gear and provisions for a party of four for a year's trapping. Harlan quietly sorted out the goods and then loaded two of the pack mules back up with powder, lead, food items, traps, knives, beads, coffee, sugar, and two Hudson Bay five-point winter coats, previously unworn.

Strapped to the outside of the packs were coffee pots, Dutch ovens, and frying pans. He cut out one of the horses from the dead men's string and tied it in with the mules. In short, he set apart everything valuable to an Indian living in the wilderness. Then Harlan took the best of the rifles from the dead men along with two pistols and a gutting knife. Walking over to Runs Fast, he handed him the items.

Harlan figured that since all the man had was a bow and arrow, he could use a good rifle. He was surprised when Runs Fast recoiled at the presentation of the rifle and other firearms.

"What is the matter?" asked Harlan.

"I do not have full status as a tribal member but am still considered as having come from the outside, since I am a Crow. I am not allowed to have firearms but only bows and arrows," Runs Fast replied quietly.

"Well, then, you shall have much treasure to present to Low Dog when you return in celebration. Big Eagle, why don't you and Runs Fast ride over to the end of the meadow and lift those four varmints' scalps so our friend also has the trophies of the fight to bestow even more honor on Chief Low Dog?"

Turning to Runs Fast, Harlan said, "Please advise our friend Low Dog that we appreciated the brave assistance from one of his clan in our fight. Also tell him that I will provide a big feast for his clan just as soon as the ice goes out because of your help in saving our lives."

Those words brought a huge grin to Runs Fast, whose head was spinning with what had just happened and the many goods from battle he had just acquired.

Just imagine, he thought, what it will be like when I return with much treasure for Low Dog and the tribe. That plus the scalps from the four men who tried to kill their friends. The big grin continued to spread across his face when he pictured the honor he had earned, especially in the eyes of the tribal members who still considered him a second-rate warrior.

The grin got noticeably wider when Autumn Flower once again brought him a cup of scalding coffee loaded with much brown sugar—and in her hurry forgot to bring any to Harlan and Big Eagle.

———

A WEEK LATER, a still somewhat confused Winter Hawk pulled out of his partial coma. The two women made much of him as if nothing else mattered, and soon he was sitting up in bed, eating a little, and talking. A week later he was up and moving around, still a little wobbly and having bad headaches when he stood up too fast, but on the mend. If the slug to his head had been one- quarter inch closer, he would have been killed.

During that time, Winter Hawk had a frequent visitor in Runs Fast. They talked a great deal, but it was obvious that Runs Fast was there mostly for the attention he received from Autumn Flower.

Their affection was not lost on anyone else in the little group, especially Harlan, who realized that if those affections became an issue, he, a guest of Low Dog, would have to cross the lines of hospitality to see what he could do. Harlan was still keenly aware of what he had had to do to get Autumn Flower and Birdsong from the Northern Cheyenne chief.

I really don't need that kind of problem in my own backyard if I can possibly avoid it, he thought. Then, with a grin, he remembered his dad's old saying: Life doesn't always wait for the waters to calm.

Finally, Winter Hawk was well enough to assume his role around camp, and that in and of itself brought much joy to the group. In fact, Winter Hawk hit the ground running just in time for spring trapping, and trap they did.

The men were able to trap over three hundred beaver before the animals went out of prime. In the process, they about wiped out the beaver population in their valley. That made Harlan aware that this must be their last year in this location if they wanted to survive in the fur trade. They would have to move elsewhere after the summer rendezvous… and where he knew not.

Dismissing that thought for the moment, Harlan decided he would face that issue when the time came. In addition to the five hundred-plus beaver they had trapped, they had more than two hundred beaver from the men who had tried to kill them during the winter. In addition, they had twenty-one dressed wolf pelts, fifty-nine coyote pelts, a dozen river-otter skins, eighteen deer-hides, and twelve elk hides. Rounding out that complement, they had sixty-two muskrat hides from inadvertent catches, twenty raccoon hides, and fifteen pelts from both grizzly and black bear.

After the beaver went out of prime, they traded with their friends the Snakes. Here they unloaded most of their fusils (cheap flintlocks), red and blue beads, Green River skinning knives, extra flints, some powder and shot, and several kegs of uncut rum. In return, they received over sixty buffalo skins that had been tanned by tribal members during the winter months. All in all, aside from the shoot-out with the renegade trappers and the wounding of Winter Hawk, it had been an exceptional year, especially considering the affection Autumn Flower and Runs Fast were now openly showing for each other.

And it was about to get better—in fact, a whole lot better...

16

A CELEBRATION AMONG FRIENDS,
AND A WHOLE LOT MORE

HARLAN AND THE BOYS PEEPED OVER THE RIDGELINE AND down into the draw some fifty yards below. About three hundred unwary buffalo were grazing there. The three of them took their shooting positions, and the killing began.

In about five minutes it was over, and twenty buffalo lay dead or dying when Harlan raised his hand to signify "enough." From behind their shooting positions, the women brought the horse and mule string, now grown with the addition of the dead trappers' animals to an almost being unruly number. The rest of the afternoon was spent in salvaging the best cuts of meat for the long trek back to the cabin in preparation for the next day's feast and events to follow. What remained was left for the critters. After all, there were always more buffalo just over the next ridge...

Daylight the next morning found Harlan and crew

busy around the cabins with three large roaring camp-fires. Their largest cast-iron pots were filled with generous chunks of buffalo meat and beans and set at the edge of the campfires to simmer. Smaller pots were also set around the fires to simmer with huge chunks of buffalo, spices, and rice to be added later.

Around the remaining two fires hung huge slabs of fresh buffalo meat staked on green willow limbs to roast slowly. Alongside the slabs of meat hung huge racks of ribs, skewered and sizzling in their abundant fat juices as well. Into their last two big pots went ten pounds each of dried fruit, sugar cones, and water to slowly simmer. This high-mountain concoction would soon provide a thick, sweet fruit compote that was a favorite among Indians and mountain men alike.

Last but not least, three large coffee pots were filled with water, and handfuls of coffee grounds were added to boil when the rest of the participants arrived from the Snake Indian village for the spring celebration that Harlan had promised after their shootout with the four renegade trappers.

About noon, Harlan heard the sounds of horses' hooves breaking limbs and twigs, excited talking, and laughter along with the barking of dogs as Low Dog and his clan of sixty-plus Indians approached the trappers' cabins. Harlan turned and faced the horde, giving the sign for welcome and peace. The sign was quickly returned by Low Dog, Meek, and others.

Telling Meek and the others to light down, Harlan

welcomed them to the feast. There was little fanfare as the Indians unceremoniously dipped into every pot with their tin cups and plates. Then they commenced eating with their fingers, a few spoons, and their knives, accompanied by appreciative slurping and belching sounds. Great slabs of buffalo were stabbed from around the fires and gobbled down even when sizzling sounds were made as the roasting meat met their tongues and lips.

More meat was quickly added from their fresh meat stores, and just as fast as it cooked, it too was gobbled down as if the Indians hadn't eaten in a month! Harlan and company were hard-pressed to keep the fires and pots supplied, but they had one hell of a cache of fresh meat, and it just kept coming until everyone had their fill.

Then, great cups of the sticky-sweet fruit mixture were ladled out and consumed with the same gusto as had the beans, rice, and buffalo meat. The camp dogs also feasted on the leavings. After a solid hour of gorging, Harlan brought out the "topping" as everyone lounged around the campfires, pleased with the feast and too full to move or even wiggle.

A barrel of two hundred stout Virginia tobacco cigars and a keg of rum rounded out the fare, to the delight of the Indians—especially the men and boys. Meek, on his third tin cup of rum, walked over to Harlan and said, "Harlan, you are a man of your word. This here get-together is one of the best I have ever been to. Hell, this is almost as good as our annual gatherings at the rendezvous."

"I am glad you are happy, and I hope Low Dog is as well because I have a proposition for him," Harlan said very seriously.

Meek, catching the tone, said, "I hope it is good news for the chief, Harlan, because he can be a son of a bitch if something catches him wrong."

"Well, I hope so as well. Bail me out if I get in too deep, my friend," said Harlan.

Meek's answering look was satisfactory as far as the support thing, so Harlan proceeded.

Harlan raised his hand, and Big Eagle brought forth a beautifully tanned grizzly hide and placed it in the center of the group of Indians for the effect such a beast and the presentation had on them. The general noise and chatter began to diminish as the Indians realized something serious was in the wind. Harlan walked over to Low Dog and in his best Snake and sign beckoned for the chief to sit on the hide. This Low Dog proudly did with little fanfare, and Harlan sat across from him with a serious look on his face.

"Chief Low Dog," he began, "for two years you have allowed me and my family to trap beaver in this beautiful valley under your protection. My family and I have prospered as a result of your generosity. This dinner has been my way of thanking you, in part, for that generosity."

He raised his hand once again, and Winter Hawk entered the arena carrying twelve new beaver traps and a keg of powder. Following him was Big Eagle with several pigs of lead, a large bag of flints, and ten pounds of red glass trade beads.

By now the assembly of Indians had grown reverently silent over the developing ceremony. The boys returned again and placed at Low Dog's feet the last of their Green River trade knives, several sharpening stones, fish hooks and line, and several axes. Low Dog's eyes were as big as dinner plates at the stack of gifts before him.

"Now," Harlan continued in a serious tone, "I would like to buy the one you call Dog Eater and add him as a member of my family!"

There was a stunned silence among the Indians, even more so than before. Meek's jaw dropped and stayed there. Autumn Flower, still serving coffee to those who wanted it, dropped the pot, coffee and all, and stared at Harlan with fear in her eyes. As for Runs Fast, he stood frozen in time. No one but the two boys had known what Harlan had up his sleeve. As for the chief, he sat stunned by Harlan's words.

Harlan went on, "I know how valuable this man is to you, but he would be of even more value to me. He could be the husband to Autumn Flower, a brother to my boys, an extra gun to help protect us, and a son to me."

With those words, Harlan sat back and looked at the chief as if he had just asked him about the weather. The chief sat there and stared back. Finally, Low Dog said, "You are right. He is like a son to me, and for me to sell him to a trapper is not right. I will need him in my old age."

Harlan knew he had lied about Runs Fast's value and closeness to the chief. He caught a glint of greed crossing the chief's eyes in a moment when Low Dog felt that Harlan was not looking closely at him.

One does not live long in the wilderness without the eye of an eagle and the quickness of a snake's strike, Harlan thought smugly regarding the sly look Low Dog had just given him.

Autumn Flower had picked up the coffee pot and headed off to fill it again with water, coffee, and cones of sugar and set it by the fire to heat. She dared not look at Runs Fast for fear of collapsing in terror at Harlan's bold approach to the powerful Snake chief.

Runs Fast found that he could hardly even breathe over what was being said between the two men. The proposition had caught him cold as well, and now he stood in terror at what the mighty chief's words might be. Yes, he was in love with Autumn Flower, but he was a slave to the Snake chief, and as such his life was one of drudgery, subjugation, humiliation, and hard work.

"Before the great chief Low Dog makes up his mind, let him see what I have to offer to such an important man for one who is so lowly," Harlan suggested, not wanting to let the chief off the hook.

He waved his hand again, and Big Eagle brought forth four horses! A ripple of surprise went through the assembled Indians at the wonder of such a gift in exchange for a lowly Crow Indian captured long ago.

Winter Hawk and Big Eagle also brought saddles and

all the other tack belonging to the horses. Without fanfare, they then brought forward the three deceased trappers' rifles, more powder, flints, and lead, laying them at Low Dog's feet. Sitting in front of the chief was a small mountain of riches, far more than anyone could expect as the purchasing price of a human being!

Harlan raised his hand one more time, and the boys brought forth shiny brass pots, iron rings, a ten-pound bag of blue glass beads, and a mule loaded with tack! By now the chief was overwhelmed, and Harlan could see it in his eyes. To make matters worse for the chief, his two daughters and wife had seen the bags of beads and shiny pots. They were closing in on Low Dog and quietly offering their opinions on the matter.

Rising, the chief continued to look sternly at Harlan, but Meek was smiling because Harlan had overwhelmed the chief with more gifts than the old man had ever seen. Looking over at Runs Fast, the chief gestured that he should come forward. Runs Fast was frozen in place until someone pushed him from behind to get him moving in response to the chief's request. Maintaining a stoic appearance, Runs Fast approached the chief and stood at his side as any obedient son would do.

"He is yours," uttered the chief in clipped words as he pushed Runs Fast toward Harlan.

Sticking out his hand, Harlan said, "Then it is a deal. Runs Fast for these goods and the livestock."

"It is a deal," said the chief and then uttered in the same breath, "is there any more rum?" Many of the tribe squealed with delight as Harlan ordered his last keg of rum opened for his friends and in honor of his new son. Runs Fast just stood there looking at the smiling Harlan Waugh. Autumn Flower, on the other hand, was in her sister's arms crying with joy.

Yes, this is becoming a rather substantial family, Harlan thought happily.

It wasn't until late in the evening that the last Indian left the celebration. After the trade, Low Dog spent the next hour distributing his newfound wealth to other members of the tribe, in so doing showing all what a great chief he was. However, the glass beads, shiny brass pots, and iron rings stayed with his family at the insistence of his wife and two grown daughters.

As the fires died down and they were once again left to themselves, Autumn Flower threw herself into Harlan's arms, crying and talking all at once. Harlan smiled at this first showing of emotion since she had been purchased from the Northern Cheyenne chief. It felt good to get that kind of attention from his quiet daughter. The attention he got from his wife later in the evening was of a different nature, but it felt good as well...

As for Runs Fast, he was given several sleeping robes to sleep in outside the cabins and just told. "Good night."

The following morning at daylight, Runs Fast had a roaring fire going and a quantity of buffalo meat roasting on willow sticks. The smell of roasting meat roused Harlan from his bed, whereupon he dressed and strode out to be with his new son. The two men sat quietly by the fire and were warmed by its flames.

Then Runs Fast spoke: "I am not sure what to say. Yesterday you surprised and honored me at the same time. Today I have a new life, an honorable one, and for that I thank you and the Great Spirit. You were right. Autumn Flower and I do have eyes and hearts for each other. I wish to make her my wife and her child my child as well. Autumn Flower feels the same way. My only hope is that you will let this union happen so we can live happily forever."

Harlan said nothing as Runs Fast spoke to his true nature and from the heart. Then Harlan said sternly, "If you two become man and wife, that will be up to her, for she is her own woman in this family. I have no problem with what you propose, but again that is up to her. But I do welcome you to our family for many reasons. The main one is for you to become one of my sons."

The other cabin door opened, and out walked a smiling Big Eagle and Winter Hawk, closely followed by Autumn Flower. She kept her eyes to the ground in a typical Indian sign of respect as she prepared coffee and Dutch-oven biscuits and helped her sister with the meat.

Yes, thought Harlan, today is going to be a good day and the start of a new future for this family.

The rest of that day was spent getting Runs Fast settled into the regimen of the family. First he was provided with one of their reserve Hawkens, primer caps, nipple picks, nipples, powder horn, bullets, and wadding.

Then the training in the use and care of weapons began because he had not been allowed to use firearms in his life with the Snakes.

By the end of the day, he could hold his own in shooting, reloading, and caring for the big Hawken. Harlan realized the young man was a natural frontiersman and as a result poured the training into him. In the interim, the boys cut and limbed a dozen lodge-pole pine saplings that were fifteen or so feet long. Taking one of the tepee skins from the two they had obtained from the dead trappers, they assembled Runs Fast's first home, placing it next to their cabins with the opening facing to the east.

Next Harlan broke out the "possibles" any good mountain man would need to carry in order to survive. That included a powder horn for Runs Fast's Hawken and another for his two pistols. Tins of caps, extra nipples, nipple picks, bullet molds, bullets, a gutting knife, and several skinning knives came next. Those were followed by a sharpening stone, steel and flint for fire making, twelve beaver traps, a tomahawk, and two .79-caliber horse pistols. Runs Fast sat there in awe, looking at the small fortune in goods being placed before him.

"Now," said Harlan, "take good care of your gear, and it will serve you well." He continued, "The women are, as we speak, supplying your tepee with those sleeping skins and other goods you and Autumn Flower need. Anything that is missed can be procured from our supplies in the cabins."

Runs Fast just continued to sit there in a daze. Having

come from a life of slavery to one of equality and eventually to that of a free trapper was without a doubt a heady yet humbling experience. Then Autumn Flower, without a word, arrived and took all her man's possibles and gear, removing them to their tepee.

Yes, thought Harlan, life sure is going to change around here—and surely for the better!

17

LEAVING THEIR VALLEY AND THE 1832 RENDEZVOUS

Swinging around in the saddle, Harlan took one last look at what had been their home for the past two good years. For the previous month, the family had prepared for this day, and now that everything was in order, they were on the move. A pack string of ten horses and ten heavily loaded mules was strung out behind Harlan, carrying the family's goods and stores. At the end of the string of livestock rode the ever-alert Big Eagle.

Riding alongside the string were Winter Hawk on one side and Runs Fast on the other. The two women and baby rode directly behind Harlan for the protection he could offer in the event of an attack. Harlan grinned widely as he surveyed the scene. They had had a good trapping season and now had more than enough goods for trade for another year in the wilderness.

My family has grown to a total of four men, and woe

to anyone tackling this pack string with ill intentions, he thought. His eyes scanned the two happy women as they rode behind their dad and husband. Both were armed with pistols and their own knives, and, though one cradled a baby, they were ready for the day.

Traveling northwest into the magnificent Absaroka Range, Harlan's group came into daily contact with herds of buffalo, the grand moose, elk by the score, and the dainty mule deer at every turn in the trail. Every night the party feasted on whatever they desired of animal species, and only the choicest cuts of meat.

The waters were clear and cold and the mountain grasses high and nutritious. Soon the horses were not pleasant to follow because of all those rich grasses being turned into foul-smelling methane gas. The trail they followed became clearer and clearer because of the numbers of mountain men and Indians who had gone before en route to the upcoming rendezvous. However, because they were now in the country of the deadly Blackfoot, their vigilance remained high.

Up they climbed, using the many animal and recently made human trails over the Togwatee Pass and down its steep back side. In front of the group in all their mountain majesty lay the spectacular Tetons, spiritual home to the mountain men. Skirting the south side of present-day Jackson Hole, they camped at the edge of the great valley in a large stand of timber.

By their second day in the valley, Harlan's family was joined by several groups of friendly Flathead Indians and trappers, all heading for the rendezvous several days away. This larger group continued up over Teton Pass and down its steep back side into Pierre's Hole, which to a mountain man was another most beautiful place.

Geographically speaking, Pierre's Hole was about twenty-five miles long and anywhere from one-half to fifteen miles wide. One side of the valley was rimmed by the majestic Teton Mountains and the other by the Snake River Mountains. In between was grass belly-deep to a buffalo, watered areas streaming from the mountain ranges full of trout, and camping places aplenty. Even though the trappers lived in God's paradise on a daily basis, they always appreciated another one of His masterpieces, and Pierre's Hole fitted that bill. Its beauty was topped off by soft blue skies and pleasant evenings so full of stars that Harlan found it hard to close his eyes because of their numbers and magnificence.

Sublette and Campbell's fur companies were there to supply the trappers at the 1832 rendezvous with supplies for the coming year. As usual, they and their American Fur Company didn't arrive until the rendezvous was basically over. For once, however, that proved to be a small thing. Traders from Hudson's Bay and the Rocky Mountain Fur Company happily showed up on time, as did several independent traders such as Gant, Blackwell, and Nathaniel Wyeth.

Entering the valley, Harlan and his group were greeted by the sight and sounds of many Indian tepees, barking dogs, running and playing children, and proud warriors riding about. Interspersed throughout were numerous trappers' camps of every kind, with most utilizing the shade from the many cottonwood groves along the edge and center of the valley floor.

Heading toward an unoccupied grove of cottonwood with a stream nearby, Harlan pointed and exclaimed, "That site will be our home for the next few days."

The animals were unloaded, curried, and tied close to camp to feed and water. Covering the camp goods with a tepee covering, the men began making several lean-tos with animal-skin tops to keep out the afternoon rains and the morning dew.

In the meantime, the women dug a fire pit, lined it with rocks, and soon had a merry fire blazing away. They soon had great strips of elk back strap taken the evening before cooking, to the delight of four very hungry men. The meat was accompanied by a bubbling pot of rice and bear fat, salt, pepper, and dried hot red pepper flakes. Last but not least, a large pot of coffee was left to boil as it hung over a cooking rod.

With camp made, the men sat around the fire with their backs against a cottonwood or a pack of beaver plews, waiting for the meal to be ready. Soon everyone was partaking of the evening meal in God's country.

About a quarter mile to the west lay the camps of the fur companies that had arrived earlier and were setting up for the business of trading. Already, there were mobs of fur trappers and Indians swirling around to trade, drink, and share the news known to them regarding who had survived the winter and who was becoming a part of the soil.

"Mobs" was the best word to describe them because this was the greatest gathering of fur trappers and Indians in the history of such rendezvous. Over four hundred trappers and more than three hundred Indians from a handful of tribes showed up to make it a gala affair for all concerned.

Looking over at the huge crowd of gaily dressed humanity mobbing the fur traders, Harlan said, "We will wait a day or two until they 'get all the hair off' before we begin our trading. There are plenty of supplies, from the looks of it, so we shouldn't have any problems getting what we need for the coming year."

The rest of the men, used to the peace and quiet the backcountry offered, just nodded. None were too keen on mixing it up in a crowd like that and were glad Harlan backed them off from the madhouse of trading for the moment.

Two days later, when the crowds had thinned somewhat and the drinking had begun in earnest, Harlan quietly told the boys, "Pack 'em up; we are going trading." It took the four men, with help from the women, about an hour to load all their trappings onto the mules and horses.

Seeing that the women wanted to go as well, Harlan told them with a grin, "Get your finest on, and we'll all go to the show."

———

QUIETLY RIDING by and looking the traders over, Harlan said, "We will trade with the Rocky Mountain Fur Company. Their prices are about the same as the others, and they seem to be doing a better and fairer job of grading the furs."

Walking the pack string over to that fur company, Harlan awaited his turn. While he waited, Birdsong and Autumn Flower dismounted and, with the baby, began looking over the trade goods offered that year to the trappers and Indians.

"Harlan, you old rip. How the hell are you doing?" shouted a fur buyer grading furs for the American Fur Company.

Before Harlan could respond, an old friend, Gavin Hatch, beckoned him over to trade in his buying area for the American Fur Company.

"Gavin, you old scudder, what the hell are you doing working for a trading company? I thought you was free-trapping in the Bighorns," said Harlan.

"Couldn't make my keep. The damn Indians kept my head down most of the time, and when I could run and trap as I needed, they kept raiding my campsite. I lost just about everything but my hair. Then when this offer came along, I jumped at it. After all, it still allowed me to remain in God's country," he responded with a grin as the two of them shook hands.

Dismounting, Harlan introduced his sons to Gavin

and pointed out his daughter and wife as they merrily examined the trade goods laid about them in profusion.

"How the hell did you throw such old'uns out so fast? The last time I saw you, you were free and single, trapping with your brother and a couple others up on the Yellowstone."

"My party was killed up on the Yellowstone by the Blackfoot. Me, I escaped and in running to the south out of their territory ran across an Indian massacre. Picked up these two boys there. Their parents had been killed, and they had hid out from the savages killing their kind.

Then, at last year's rendezvous, I traded for those two squaws who just happened to be captured sisters to these here two boys. In the case of Runs Fast here, I bought him for the extra protection his rifle offered, as well as my daughter's husband and another son. I kinda like these here ready-made families, if'n you get my drift. They sure are a lot less hassle," Harlan said with a grin as he doffed his wolf-skin cap.

"My God, Harlan, you certainly had a run of good and bad luck since I saw you last! It is good to see you, my friend, but what the hell happened to that lovely head of hair you had back in '28?" Gavin asked, looking at Harlan's scarred bald head.

"Griz, and a damned big one at that. In fact, those two boys I saved turned around and saved me," Harlan replied proudly. "Don't look none too good as a result but am still alive and roaming the backcountry without a hitch in my giddy-up."

"Well, let's get to tradin' and see what you have," Gavin replied. "We can always palaver as we trade and get caught up on the news."

With that the trading began in earnest, and Harlan's three sons looked on keenly at the process. For about an hour, Gavin disassembled the packs of furs and hides and carefully examined each one with the practiced eye of a trader and former trapper. Finishing his grading, he stood up and stretched out the kinks in his tired back from so much bending over to study the quality of the furs lying at his feet.

"I can give you four dollars for your beaver hides, three for them buffler hides, a dollar and a half for the wolf and coyote hides, and three for your otters. I can give five each for them griz hides because there is a market back East to mount them for display as well as bear-skin coats, two dollars for them deer and elk hides, and fifteen cents apiece for the muskrat and raccoon hides." He looked over at Harlan for his friend's reaction to his grading and pricing of the furs.

After some long figuring, Harlan arrived at a total figure of about three thousand five hundred dollars (at the time, three hundred to five hundred dollars a year was the average salary of a man working back East). Figuring again to calculate what the group needed for the next year in goods, Harlan realized that amount would more than carry them through another year.

"You have a deal," Harlan replied, "just as long as you throw in a keg of uncut rum."

Gavin grinned and said, "You have a deal. That is more than fair."

The two old friends shook on the deal, and Harlan and his kids went shopping for what they needed for the next year from the American Fur Company's stockpiles of goods.

At the top of the list was 150 pounds of salt, 20 pounds of black pepper, 10 pounds of red pepper flakes, 200 pounds of red beans, and 200 pounds of fine corn-meal. Harlan went heavy on the cornmeal because Bird-song and Autumn Flower favored stews made with cornmeal and meat.

Next, looking to gain acquisition for defense, they purchased 100 pounds of powder, 150 pounds of lead pigs, and 1,000 primer caps for their Hawkens.

They purchased 100 pounds each of rice and pinto beans for the hearty meat stews they would prepare during the winter. Next came 20 pounds of red and blue glass beads, 4 fusils, and a dozen Green River skinning knives for trade with the Indians. They added four sharpening stones because they were always getting lost or broken, a bolt each of red and blue calico for the women, 75 pounds of coffee beans, and several more kegs of rum.

Wondering whether he had forgotten anything important, Harlan conferred with the women, and they pointed out the need for flour! That oversight was quickly rectified with the purchase of 150 pounds.

Good thing the women remembered the flour, thought Harlan with a grin. Not having fresh biscuits from a Dutch oven most mornings would lead to disaster.

The purchasing of goods continued until their credit was exhausted. Harlan believed those acquisitions, coupled with what they still had in reserve from previous years, would be more than enough to hold them through the year.

Pleased with their trades, Harlan had the boys bring up their mules and horses, and the packing for the return to their camp commenced. They hadn't been packing for more than ten minutes when word spread throughout the camp that the Blackfoot were en route to the rendezvous with blood in their eyes.

Within moments hundreds of trappers and Indians mounted their horses and headed toward the danger. Harlan never blinked but just kept loading his horses and mules as if nothing out of the ordinary was occurring. Finally, after many questioning looks from his boys as to why they didn't go after the dreaded Blackfoot with the rest of the trappers, Harlan said, "Trouble will find us soon 'nough. No sense going a-looking for a killing when the Good Lord will find us in his own good time."

The men continued loading their pack animals and made ready to return to their camp.

"Keep what is left of that ugly topknot, you old bat," said Gavin with a large smile.

"That I will, and you do the same," replied Harlan with a wave of the hand.

Once back at their campsite, the men unloaded their

supplies into a lean-to, making sure the goods were covered against the afternoon rains. They left the women in camp to guard their goods and returned to the rendezvous for some hell-raising with old friends and to make some new ones.

When they arrived back at the rendezvous, they learned that the Indians had not been Blackfoot but their kissing cousins, the Gros Ventre—Indians who were equally deadly. The trappers currently had the war party cornered in a stand of timber, and a lot of lead was being wasted by both sides without much killing to show for it.

"Harlan, come and tip a cup with us," shouted a voice off to Harlan's left.

Looking over his shoulder, Harlan recognized his old friend Jim Bridger. With many greetings and much back-slapping, Harlan introduced his boys all around. Several tin cups full of rum were produced, and after Harlan had cautioned his sons to drink only one cup each, the men set to drinking and yarning.

When the boys finished their rum, they excused themselves, as their dad had instructed, and began walking around camp, taking in the sights. Harlan continued to drink with his buddies, laughing loudly at the many pratfalls spoken of as they described their previous year's experiences.

About an hour later, Harlan and the men he was drinking with heard a ruckus off in the distance. At first they ignored it, assuming it was just another fight between a couple of drunken trappers, and the rum in their group continued to flow. Then Harlan saw Big Eagle running toward him as if a hive of bees were in his buckskins.

"Dad, you need to come quick. A trapper tried to take Winter Hawk's Hawken, and he is defending himself. Runs Fast tried to help, but several other trappers beat him up and are now holding his arms so he can't help. They tried to catch me, but I got away," he exclaimed breathlessly.

Grabbing his Hawken, Harlan sprinted toward the noisy gathering pointed out by Big Eagle. He broke into the circle of men and found Winter Hawk, knife drawn, holding a burly trapper at bay. The trapper was Patrick Bosco de Gamma, whom Harlan knew to be a bully and a drunkard. From all appearances, he had not done so well against the smaller Winter Hawk. Bosco had a cut across his right cheek clear to the bone and a rip across the front of his shirt that was bleeding heavily as well. Winter Hawk had a blackened and closing left eye but other than that was faring well in the exchange with a grown man and an experienced trapper.

"Hold it right there!" Harlan bellowed.

Startled by the loud shout and his appearance, both fighters hesitated.

"Drop your knife, Bosco, or by God I will put a ball through you, sending your miserable carcass into the next world," Harlan uttered quietly with a look of impending death in his eyes if his words were not heeded —and fast.

The two men holding a battered and bruised Runs Fast let him go and grabbed their rifles as if to aid their partner against this intruder giving out orders.

"That be far enough, gentlemen," came a quiet voice from the edge of the crowd. "Any further actions on either of your parts will result with a ball in one of you and my tomahawk in the other." It was Jim Bridger, and behind him stood another dozen men who had been drinking with their friend Harlan moments earlier.

The dangerous moment had passed with the addition of Harlan to the fight and the appearance of Jim Bridger and his pals.

"What the hell started all this?" demanded Harlan.

"This here young'un, and a Crow at that, has a Hawken. Few of us can afford such a weapon, and to my way of thinking, he stole it off some white man. More than likely a fur trapper like us," Bosco de Gamma growled as he wiped the blood off his cheek with a rag offered to him by his friends in the crowd.

"That Hawken be my dead brother's," Harlan said with steely coldness. "He were killed in '30 by the Black-foot up on the Yellowstone. I got it back from his killer and brought it with me down to my camp on Willow Lake. I picked up this here boy from an Indian massacre site and have been raising him as my own. I gave him that rifle because he earned it.

"Since he is one of mine, you have also picked a fight with me," Harlan continued calmly. "Is that your wish now that you know the facts behind the rifle, or do you want to continue this fight with a man instead of a young boy. although a better man than you?"

Being a coward and now confronted by a man whom he knew to be capable of killing if riled, Bosco de Gamma begin to have second thoughts about continuing the business at hand with Winter Hawk.

"Bein' that you put it that-a-way, Harlan, guess I don't have any bone to pick with this here Injun. If'n he is agreeable to let it ride, I guess so am I," replied Bosco de Gamma with a sneer on his bloody face that said this event wasn't over by a long shot.

"Then let it be a lesson learned. Not everything appears as it is," Harlan advised sharply. "Now, as long as it lasts, I have a keg of rum that will go a long way toward healing up your wounds, if you and your friends be agreeable." Harlan's voice became quietly soothing now that he had made his point.

The keg, once brought into the appreciative crowd, didn't last long. However, Bosco de Gamma is not a man to easily forget something like this, thought Harlan, keg of rum or no.

Back at camp, Autumn Flower patched up Runs Fast as best as she could. Winter Hawk had only the black eye for his troubles and had moved one more step closer to manhood. Big Eagle and Harlan just breathed sighs of relief. If Big Eagle hadn't gotten to Harlan in time, their camp and family might have held two fewer individuals that beautiful summer evening.

The following morning the family prepared to leave

Pierre's Hole forever. Harlan figured it would be best in light of what he'd heard about Bosco de Gamma's nasty temper and his penchant for getting even, even if it meant back-shooting someone from ambush.

Standing quietly in the sun's warming morning rays, Harlan shook his head. Tangling with Bosco de Gamma was not wise on any man's best day. The man was not large, but he was strap-steel tough and hardly afraid of anything, especially if he had his equally mean pals with him.

He was an odd duck. First and foremost, he stank to high heaven. Bosco de Gamma didn't believe in bathing because he said it would make his body hair fall out, and that and the occasional squaw were all he had to keep himself warm in the winter. In addition, he was a killer of the worst degree. He never forgot a slight, and even for the smallest disagreement the offender had to watch his back because a knife thrust or rifle ball was waiting for him somewhere down the road—especially if an attack could be made when Bosco de Gamma's chosen victim was not looking.

William Bent, a mountain man and fur trader located on the Arkansas River, told a story of an occasion when the Comanche Indians had caught Bosco de Gamma trapping beaver. After torturing him for several days, they had staked him over an anthill and left him for the Apaches. Somehow Bosco de Gamma survived and lived to kill every man in that twelve-man Comanche war party, and it was said that he ate their raw hearts after each kill. After that, he bragged that his bad smell killed the ants' appetite.

Yes, thought Harlan, Bosco de Gamma is one to avoid at any cost, but if you did tangle with him, he needed to be killed because only then could you live in peace. Otherwise you'd be looking over your shoulders for the rest of your life!

He had learned at the rendezvous that Captain Bonneville was en route to the Green River Valley at that very moment. Bonneville would eventually choose to locate his trading camp at Horse Creek for the 1833 rendezvous. His route to that area would take him via South Pass in the present-day state of Wyoming.

It was rumored among the traders at the current rendezvous that he was bringing more than a hundred men, many pack animals, and at least twenty wagons full of trade goods, as he planned an overwinter stay.

Like many other trappers, Harlan did not know the exact location of Horse Creek, but he knew the general lay of the land in the Green River Valley, which was many days south of their present location.

Once there, thought Harlan, it is just a matter of talking to the local Indians or other trappers regarding the exact site of the rendezvous. Failing that, a bit of riding in the general area will allow us to locate the traders' site.

Even with the land almost empty of civilization, the West still had its own set of ears and eyes for those who know how to hear and see.

18

THE BIGHORN MOUNTAINS
BECOME A NEW HOME

STILL CONCERNED WITH THE MISCHIEF BOSCO DE GAMMA and his party of hardened trappers could create, Harlan figured his group needed a faraway place to trap during the coming season. Another winter would give the boys time to gain some age, experience, and meat on their bones. Those gains would also allow them to better defend themselves if they ever crossed paths again with Bosco de Gamma without Harlan to lend a hand.

Plus, the distance would let Bosco de Gamma cool off —or maybe get his hair lifted. In his conversations with Gavin, the trader had spoken of the riches of furs beyond compare in the Bighorns as long as one could keep the Crow or Blackfoot Indians from lifting one's hair, stealing one's horses or plews, or putting an arrow into one's carcass.

Heading southeast from the rendezvous, Harlan's

party began by retracing their steps from their original route to Pierre's Hole. Once in the area of present-day Bondurant, Wyoming, they headed northeast over the beautiful Wind River Mountains.

Continuing northeast, the group finally arrived at what is today Thermopolis, Wyoming, site of the world's largest hot springs. Camped there in gay profusion were many groups of Snake and Northern Cheyenne Indians enjoying the waters' healing properties. By chance, Harlan and company located Low Dog and his clan, and a great celebration was had by all. Low Dog, in honor of the event, threw a big feed that lasted two full days, and at the end most participants swore off gorging for at least a month.

The only troubling event that occurred during the three-day stop at the hot springs was that Harlan and company ran across the Northern Cheyenne sub-chief whom Big Eagle had bested in the shoot-off at the earlier rendezvous. The sub-chief instantly recognized Big Eagle, and the look on his face showed that he had not forgotten the embarrassment the young man, and a Crow at that, had caused him.

To avoid further problems, Harlan had his brood packed and on the road before daylight the next morning. Heading due north, Harlan pushed his little band until they arrived in the vicinity of present-day Greybull, Wyoming. They frequently ran across the trails of unshod ponies and travois from many Indian groups out hunting buffalo.

Worried about encountering the dangerous Lakota, Harlan headed his group due east into what is today the Cloud Peak Wilderness Area. Once into the timbered area, he relaxed because most Indian tribes would be out on the shortgrass prairies chasing the buffalo herds.

Climbing ever higher, they soon ran into numerous mountain streams loaded with beaver dams and the dam-building rodents. They all had to smile at the furred bounty before them. Gavin had been right—the country had not been touched except maybe by a few Indian fur trappers. (During the height of the days of the mountain men, the best records show only about one thousand of their kind trapping in the backcountry during any given year.

Of that number, roughly 25 percent never returned or disappeared before the trapping season ended for the year. As stated earlier, most trapped furs sold to white traders came from the many tribes of Native Americans.) And those Indian fur trappers, as far as Harlan could see, had made no real dent in the beaver population in this new area.

Harlan also smiled at the other possibilities in the fur-trapping arena. The area was full of coyotes, wolves, lynx, and river otter. Surprisingly, there were also a fair number of buffalo in the wooded areas they now trod. Not great herds but many instances of single animals enjoying the coolness, the excellent feed, the lack of biting insects, and the quiet isolation the forests offered.

Near present-day Burgess Junction, Harlan called a

halt by a small creek adjacent to the edge of timber with a grassy meadow full of ducks, geese, and little brown cranes. It had been days since they had seen any fresh Indian sign, and the surrounding creeks were full of beaver ponds just waiting to be trapped. Looking over the area for its defensive characteristics and nearness to the trapping grounds, Harlan was satisfied with what he saw.

"This will be our new home for at least the summer, fall, and coming spring trapping season," he declared.

In nothing flat, the pack string and riding horses were unloaded, hobbled, and let out to pasture. Then the work began in earnest. By late afternoon, a very strong livestock corral had been built in the trees out of casual view at the edge of the meadow.

After Autumn Flower had fed her baby, she and her sister built a central fire pit after discussing where to site their cabins with Harlan and the boys. Soon dinner was cooking and filling the air with pleasant smells. The men took their shovels, cleared a large area for the cabins, and built two large lean-tos next to the cleared areas.

Under those lean-tos went all their gear, tack, and sleeping furs to protect their belongings from the almost everyday occurrence of afternoon thunderstorms. With that completed, the crew fell to the chow. They all sat around on the logs by the fire and drank in the sights and sounds of what God had created just for them at their new home site. Those moments were accompanied by the melodious croaking of the cranes and the whistling wings of many waterfowl moving to and fro in the wet meadows.

Daylight the next morning rang with the sounds of chopping axes and horses hauling cabin logs. By the noon meal, a mound of lodge-pole pine logs had been cut, trimmed, and laid by the new cabin sites. Soon those logs were laid in position, notched, and stacked until a long and wide set of three adjoining cabins began to take place. By the third day, all the walls were up, doorways and windows were cut out, and numerous covering firing ports had been chiseled into the standing walls.

Two days later, the roofs were in place and the men were making the doors, shutters, firing plugs, sleeping platforms, benches, tables, and the like while the women chinked the cabins with mud and grasses from the meadow. By the end of that week, the three cabins were finished and all their gear had been moved inside the protection of the log walls. Then dry logs were cut from the surrounding forest and moved into a nearby, central place so the trappers could have a ready supply of wood no matter the depth of snows to come.

There was a serious need to make meat because autumn was coming quickly, so the killing began in earnest. Most of their meat came from moose, elk, and mule deer, with the addition of the occasional forest buffalo. They also took eight grizzly bear for the fat and ham meat they offered. Soon whatever wasn't curing in brine was smoked or jerked and hanging inside the three large cabins, which collectively were twenty-six feet long, seventeen feet wide, and six feet high. Now the married couples and the two boys would each have a home of their own but would still be close in case of danger.

Harlan had to smile at the progress made when four men and two women put their minds toward their survival. Yes, I have the makings of a good family, he thought with a satisfied look.

While smoking their beaver traps to remove the human smell one morning, Harlan thought he saw a whisper of a glint of metal off in the timber below their meadow. He strained his eyes, but the glint was no more. He continued to look until his search caught the eyes of the boys, and they all stared at the same area but saw nothing.

Dismissing it as a will-o'-the-wisp, Harlan shrugged it off and continued the task at hand. By noon, the traps were finished, and he and the boys tended to all the other work that needed to be done before they could begin the trapping season. Big Eagle and Runs Fast opened a nearby dam and set four traps in order to collect the castor oil needed to lure beaver while Winter Hawk and Harlan spent the afternoon casting a small mountain of bullets for the ever-hungry Hawkens. They also refilled the powder horns and prepared bags of other needed items.

Tomorrow they would start their fall trapping season, and the men could hardly wait. They hadn't seen the numbers of beaver they had in the Willow Lake area, but they knew the animals were there aplenty. With a lot of work, they would be able to fill their store with more than enough plews to trade at the next year's rendezvous.

————

THE NEXT MORNING, the men stood around the outside campfire while the women cooked their breakfast. It was decided that Harlan and Winter Hawk would trap the waters to the east, and Big Eagle and Runs Fast would trap those to the west. Finishing breakfast, they packed their horses and mules and with a wave of the hand went their separate ways.

Harlan set his last eight traps as Winter Hawk sat on his horse and watched for danger. Easily swinging back into his saddle, Harlan said, "Your turn, Hawk, and I will stand guard."

Winter Hawk dropped effortlessly from his saddle, withdrew a trap from the sack on the mule, and walked a short distance upstream until he found a fresh beaver run. Setting his trap at the end of the run in the water, he walked back and retrieved another trap from the sack. Continuing his exploration of the beaver pond, he walked forward about one hundred feet until he came to another likely run.

Harlan rode his horse and led Winter Hawk's horse and the mule along behind the young trapper. Bending over, Winter Hawk again set his trap at the end of the run and made sure it was anchored well so the beaver, once in the trap, could not drag it away.

This routine continued until Winter Hawk approached a very large beaver dam at the foot of a huge pond with several beaver lodges located out in the middle of the water. Turning and grinning, he took another trap and set it below the top portion of the dam near a clump of willows, a place where a beaver was sure to investigate the smell of Winter Hawk's castor oil, which had now been daubed on a twig over the water set.

"YEH-YEH-YEH-YEH!" yelled an Indian as he ran from behind the cover of the willows toward Winter Hawk with an upraised tomahawk. Winter Hawk just had time to duck the swing and draw his pistol as the two collided. Pow went his pistol into the Indian's midsection as the force of the collision carried the two of them over the bank and out of sight in a cloud of dust.

"Yeh-yeh-yeh-yeh!" yelled three more Indians, rushing from the cover of a fallen tree toward Harlan, who was still surprised by the explosive attack on Winter Hawk. Not having time to await the outcome of his son's battle, Harlan sprang into action while his horse and mule crow-hopped wildly at the surprise onslaught.

Boom went the big Hawken, spewing the guts of the closest Indian all over his buddies. Pow went Harlan's first pistol into the face of the next Indian in line, flinging him backward as he tried to tear Harlan off his horse.

Grabbing his tomahawk, Harlan just had time to swing it to block the tomahawk swung by the Indian now at his side. With a whack, the two handles snapped as they met with explosive force. Harlan stuck his fingers into the man's eye sockets, and the two of them hit the ground as the terrified horse jumped to one side. Jerking out his knife, Harlan plunged it deeply into the Indian's neck as his assailant tried to use his knife as well.

A gurgling as breath escaped through an opened windpipe was Harlan's reward. Scrambling to his feet, he was bowled over by the impact of the fourth howling Indian smashing into him from behind at a dead run. Over the bank the two of them hurtled at a high rate of speed, landing in waist-deep cold water. The Indian landed on a sharpened willow stick from a previous beaver's meal that was still anchored in the bottom of the pond! He died there, gurgling his life away with the stick deeply embedded between his ribs and into his lungs.

Scrambling back up the bank, Harlan was confronted by a fifth Indian drawing down on him with his rifle at a distance of less than ten feet! Boom went Winter Hawk's Hawken. That man breathed his last as he spun around at the bullet's impact, folding like a sack full of rocks.

Scrambling over to his mule and using it as a shield, Harlan removed the spare Hawken just as five shots were fired in his direction from the nearby trees. All five smashed into the side of the mule, killing it instantly.

Had Harlan been standing on the other side, his fate would have been the same. Harlan ran back to the creek bank and jumped below it for cover. Up the bank to his left, he could see Winter Hawk reloading his rifle and pistol. However, they were pinned down and in a very poor position to shoot back because the Indians held the higher ground in the timber.

"There are at least five more still up there in the timber," yelled Harlan to Winter Hawk.

Winter Hawk just nodded, never taking his eyes off the tree line. No movement could be seen that would allow the sharp- shooting trappers a target. For the next hour, a standoff ensued. The Indians couldn't flank the trappers because of the width of the beaver pond, and the trappers couldn't address their problem of the Indians' good offensive position in the timber.

Zip—thunk, zip—thunk went arrows into two of the five Indians lying behind logs confronting the trappers hiding below the creek bank. Rising to their feet to flee the attack coming from behind, the three Indians ran for their horses.

Winter Hawk and Harlan, seeing their chance, quickly picked off two of the escaping Indians with their rifles. The remaining Indian from the war party continued running toward the place where he and his friends had left their horses. For a fleeting second, Harlan thought he recognized the man, who was now being hotly pursued by Big Eagle and Runs Fast.

A blood-curdling screech soon came from the darkness of the timber, and then nothing. For the longest time, Winter Hawk and Harlan stood below the bank, waiting to see what had happened.

Big Eagle and Runs Fast returned, both terribly

smeared with blood. Fearing the worst, Harlan ran to the two young men to ascertain the extent of their injuries. As it turned out, both were smeared with the blood of the last Indian from the war party. When Harlan looked into their eyes, both young men had the wildest killing look he had ever seen, nothing short of absolute blood lust.

Harlan had been right: the fleeing Indian he thought he had recognized had been none other than the Northern Cheyenne sub-chief from Thermopolis, the man Big Eagle had bested in the shooting match at the rendezvous. True to his promise to himself, Big Eagle had met the man on the field of battle, killed him, and smeared himself with the chief's blood!

The blood on Runs Fast had come from pulling his frenzied brother off the butchered remains of the Indian chief. Apparently seeing Harlan's group at the hot springs had made the chief's blood begin to boil again, and he had put together the small war party in the hope of settling the score and capturing the trappers' gear and horses as spoils.

Damn, thought Harlan, now we have another problem. All the chief's kin will come looking for him and in the process locate our new camp. Those are not good odds, no matter how one figures it. Well, the damage is done, and we'd best make the most of it.

Returning to the mule and his horse, Harlan was surprised to find both of them dead from the Indians' gunshots. But that gave him an idea of how to partially cover their trail.

"Winter Hawk," he said, "bring your horse to me."

Riding up to the dead Indians, Harlan threw a rope around them one at a time and dragged them to where the dead horse and mule lay. Seeing what he had in mind, Big Eagle, Winter Hawk, and Runs Fast stacked the other Indians' bodies with their brethren. Out of deference to Big Eagle, the Northern Cheyenne chief was left in disgrace where he had fallen.

Big Eagle and Runs Fast returned to their horses and, along with Winter Hawk, located the Indians' tied-off horses and brought them back to Harlan. In the meantime, Harlan had been backtracking their beaver sets, pulling their traps. When the boys found him, they helped pull the remainder of the traps. Then all of them returned to camp with Harlan proudly riding a big buckskin from the Indians' remuda.

Harlan hoped his strategy would work to cover up the killings. The trick was to stack so much meat in one place that it would quickly attract a large number of hungry scavengers such as wolves, coyotes, and bear. They would make short work of the carcasses. Before the feeding frenzy was over, the men's bones would be scattered far and wide to the four winds.

Harlan and the boys had removed the horse and mule shoes from their dead animals, not only because metal was valuable on the frontier but because if any Indians happened upon the scene, they would think the livestock had belonged to the Indians rather than the hated white man. In that case, they would figure their friends had run into some of the ever-present meat eaters and had lost the showdown. If they refrained from trapping in that area, then even if the bones were found, the trappers might not be blamed for the disaster...

When they arrived back in camp, the women knew something was wrong. The men had returned early without any beaver, and Big Eagle and Runs Fast were smeared with blood! Sitting down by the outside camp-fire, Harlan asked Birdsong for a jug of rum and four cups, which she promptly provided without question. Harlan then poured all the men a full cup, sat back, and asked Big Eagle and Runs Fast for their side of the story.

"Not much to tell," said Big Eagle. "We heard the shooting and figured the two of you were under attack. Finally locating where you were, we dismounted and discovered the Cheyenne hiding behind those logs.

Saving our powder and shot, as you have often told us to do, we returned to our horses, retrieved our bows and arrows, and killed two of them. When the remaining three jumped up to run to their horses, you and Winter Hawk killed two of them. Runs Fast and I took off after the runner and killed him in a knife fight. That is all there is to say." Big Eagle finished in a tone so flat that it was as if he had been asked how to dig wild onions.

Good old Big Eagle, thought Harlan, always long on words when it comes to complex, life-and-death explanations. Yes, my boys are now mountain men.

Harlan said, "We still have a problem. How do we make sure we have really hidden the whereabouts of the raiding party and their chief? That is not the only thing we need to worry about. The raiding party more than likely left a clear trail clear to where we live.

That means the rest of the tribe is probably following their trail as we speak. Soon they will be here and in time will figure out what happened and come looking for us, especially if the critters haven't had the time to eat all the meat and scatter the Indians' bones. Looks like we might have to move, and fast. I doubt the rest of the tribe is more than a week behind the ones we killed."

He went on in a disappointed tone, "Well, let's not dwell on the matter. What is done is done, and that is that. We can pull up stakes tomorrow and ride far enough away and across enough other Indians' tracks to lose them, and that is what we will do."

The boys nodded in unison at his decision and then fell to the delicious dinner the women had prepared. Afterward, they sat around the campfire late into the evening, smoking their pipes and talking about the morrow. When a cold wind heavy with moisture came up from the north and began to rattle the treetops, they took it as a sign to go to bed.

The next morning Harlan left the sleeping furs early to go outside, take care of the call of nature, and bring in some firewood to warm his cabin. Stepping outside, he stumbled into a foot of fresh snow, and it was still falling heavily! They had been hit with an early winter storm in the high country, and a knowing, wide smile crossed his face.

"So much for the rest of the tribe tracking their kin to this place!" he exulted.

"Boys!" he yelled. "Get your butts out of bed. We have some trapping to do before this stuff gets any deeper than it is!"

19

KILLING THEIR OWN

THE REST OF THE FALL TRAPPING SEASON WENT LIKE THOSE before. The men successfully trapped many large beaver and when the ice on the beaver ponds became a problem turned to the trapping of other furbearers. Soon their three cabins were full of wolf, beaver, coyote, gray fox, lynx, and pine marten hides. There was even a respectable pile of deer, elk, and buffalo hides from their travels to trap other furbearers. It looked like the beginning of another good year, and that made for smiles all around.

The braying of Martha, Harlan's ever-loyal bell mule, carried through the cold, early-morning air. Harlan awoke and was out of bed like a shot. Martha didn't like Indians; it was that simple. Even the boys, when they were around her, would get a nip in the hind end if they didn't step lively.

Grabbing his Hawken, Harlan noticed through the open hallway between the adjoining walls that the boys in the next cabins were scrambling for their shooting irons as well. Peering through a shooting port, Harlan could see their pack string being hurriedly led away from the corral by a number of crouched and darkened figures.

It was too late to go after them at that moment without chancing heavy rifle fire from an ambush. With that realization, the men quickly dressed in their winter gear, grabbed extra powder and shot, and took off after the horse and mule thieves when the coast was clear. Realizing from the trail in the snow that the animals were more than likely being led to a small valley over the ridge behind their cabins, they took off at an angle to intercept the stolen animals and their captors.

Rounding a small copse of dense standing timber, the men noticed in the brightening daylight six horses tethered to a stand of willows along the frozen creek.

That is good, thought a slightly winded Harlan. The horse thieves haven't made their getaway yet.

Spreading out, the men formed a single line abreast behind some trees on their intercept course and waited. Pretty soon, six winded Indians could be seen trotting and leading the horses and mules stolen from the men's corral. They were so intent on reaching their horses and escaping that they did not see Harlan step out from behind a tree, raise his Hawken, and cleanly drop the first man in the line of horse thieves.

Boom—boom—boom went the boys' Hawkens in

quick succession, and three more Indians dropped like sacks of flour dumped from the back of a bouncing wagon.

The remaining two men dropped the reins of the stolen pack string and sprinted for their horses, only to have the one in the lead dropped deader than a stone by a shot from Harlan's reserve Hawken.

The other man abandoned his horse and took off across the country with Big Eagle and Runs Fast in hot pursuit as they reloaded their rifles on the run. Minutes later, a single shot rang out, and soon the two boys could be seen returning through the trees. In the meantime, Winter Hawk and Harlan had rounded up their stock as well as the raiders' mounts. Harlan realized that the markings on the six horses belonged to Indians from the Crow tribe! That raised an immediate concern because he and the boys had just killed a number of his sons' own people.

When the boys returned, Harlan quietly pointed out that the horses were from the Crow Nation to the north. There was a moment of silence, and then Runs Fast said, "A skunk is a skunk. Stealing a man's stock out here is like a death sentence for its owner. Their deaths were deserved."

Big Eagle and Winter Hawk nodded at the wisdom of Runs Fast's words, and not another word was said about killing their own kind. To everyone's way of thinking, a wrong was a wrong, and this one had been taken care of.

As he thought over the raid, a frown crossed Harlan's

face. Indians don't go on the warpath or on raids during the winter. In all my years in the wilderness, I have never heard of Indians venturing away from their winter quarters except to move to better horse feed or to kill buffalo, he thought. That could only mean we are close to a Crow Indian encampment, and our horse and mule herd were discovered by the dead men as they hunted for meat.

Sensing that something was bothering his dad, Big Eagle asked Harlan what was wrong.

Harlan explained his concerns and said they would now have to be more alert if his thoughts were in any way true, especially if another party of Indians came looking for those they had just killed.

———

As it turned out, the next thirteen days were filled with blizzard after blizzard and temperatures so low the aspen bark exploded off the trees near their cabins. When decent weather returned, Harlan and Big Eagle rode north and discovered the remains of a Crow Indian encampment that had been abandoned after the weather had cleared.

It was apparent that the Indians had moved on to seek a location with more firewood and better horse feed. There were no signs of anyone coming south toward their cabins to look for the six horse thieves Harlan and his clan had killed.

That is twice now the weather gods have intervened

when it came to actions in which Indians should have come looking for their kinfolk after they disappeared, thought Harlan. He questioned just how long his luck would last if another like situation arose. Thank goodness I don't have any hair to lose, he thought darkly.

Little did any of the men realize this episode would come back to haunt their lives a long way down the trail.

2 0

SPRING BRINGS NEW LIFE, FOLLOWED BY AN UGLY TRIP TO THE RENDEZVOUS

WITH ICE OUT IN THE SPRING, THE MEN WENT BACK TO their trapping, and soon their cabins were filled with many rich plews. However, it was painfully clear that the streams and ponds could not take the trapping pressure they were now facing and would be empty when the fur went out of prime. But now was now, and the foursome trapped as hard as they could because their existence depended on it come the next rendezvous.

Sitting by the fire one morning, waiting for the coffee to boil, Runs Fast quietly said, "Autumn Flower is going to have a baby."

"What?" said Harlan, jumping up as if that would allow him to hear better.

"Autumn Flower is going to have a baby," said a calm Runs Fast with a big grin.

"Holy cow; did you hear that, Birdsong?" Harlan exclaimed.

"Yes," she said with a knowing smile as she tended the fire. "And you will have a child about the same time," she quietly whispered in his ear.

Harlan just stood there in stunned shock and then sat back down on his log, saying, "Holy cow, I am going to be a dad and grandpa all at the same time!"

After that revelation, Harlan began to wonder if this kind of rough-and-tumble existence would be right for his children and theirs. Life can be cheap out here, especially if the right Indian, varmint, or drunken trapper catches a man just right and not looking, he thought.

Then those dark thoughts quickly departed as he thought more rationally about the situation. This is our home and our way of life, he thought with conviction. This being our way of life, we will meet whatever comes our way and hope for the best. If our destiny is not to live long, then so be it. As I thought so long ago, if something bad happens, then I will have a chance to meet my family once again across the Great Divide and tell them about all that I have seen. Yes, if we are to have new life, let it be here in God's country.

"Birdsong," he yelled, "break out the rum. The boys and 1 have something to celebrate!"

———

LEAVING their campsite and the now beaver-depleted

waters with hardly a backward glance at the end of trapping season, Harlan headed the crew southwest. Several days' ride brought them to what is today the area around Cody, Wyoming.

They spent a day in the area to let the horses feed heavily in a lush meadow, then embarked in a southerly direction toward the modern-day small town of Meeteetse, Wyoming. It was there on the banks of the Greybull River that their luck ran out. Crossing the Greybull and moving up its southern bank one morning, they ran headlong into a small war party of about twenty-five Northern Cheyenne!

The Cheyenne, just as surprised as Harlan's group, sat frozen on their horses, not believing their luck at encountering a fur trappers' pack string of sixteen horses and ten mules, fully loaded, with only four mountain men to defend it while they numbered in the twenties!

Harlan, not missing a beat in the face of this new danger, yelled, "Make for that cottonwood grove to the west along the river!"

The pack train lumbered into a full gallop out of desperation. Cast-iron pots, pails, and sleeping furs spun wildly off the running pack animals, clanging and scattering onto the shortgrass and sagebrush plain in front of the war party. The Cheyenne, amazed at the booty being dropped in their presence, rode along the drop line examining what had fallen onto the ground during the trappers' flight.

They knew the trappers could not outrun them, so

they took their time. They believed the killing was not far away, nor the looting that would take place shortly thereafter—not to mention the raping of the two young women in the trappers' group.

Racing into the cottonwoods, Harlan quickly jumped off his buckskin. Slapping it on the ass, he ran to the edge of the trees to cover the remaining animals in the pack string as they entered the grove in a cloud of dust.

Big Eagle had sailed off his horse as well and was kneeling behind a huge cottonwood for the cover it afforded as he faced the still surprised Northern Cheyenne. Runs Fast and Winter Hawk took the pack string and riding horses into a small gully in the grove of trees where they would be partially safe from flying arrows and bullets, then stripped the extra Hawkens off the mules.

Running to the edge of the grove, they took up defensive positions in case the Indian attack came from that side as well. Dismounting, Birdsong quickly removed two reserve Hawkens from two other mules and ran one back to Big Eagle and the other to Harlan. Then, she ran back to the pack string to hold and defend it if necessary with her pistol. Autumn Flower had already taken cover, had hidden her child under a bush, and with pistol in hand was preparing for the worst. Both women resolved they would not be taken prisoner again by the Northern Cheyenne, "not without someone dying first!"

Bear Comes Running, the raiding party leader, could not believe his luck. The little band of trappers had run into the trees and brush looking for cover and had formed a defensive position. A smile slowly crossed his weathered face. The trappers were surrounded and outnumbered; it would be a short fight with only one possible outcome, to his way of thinking. Looking back at his warriors, he yelled, "Hi-yeh-yeh-yeh," and charged the trees to overrun the small band of trappers before they could get set.

In the face of the full-frontal charge, Big Eagle and Harlan had only a moment to cock the hammers on both the Hawkens and their two horse pistols before the rushing horsemen were upon them. Using the trunks of the trees for cover, they began shooting into the front ranks of the onrushing horde.

Boom—boom—boom—boom went the four Hawkens in quick succession. Four Indians sailed out of their saddles to ride no more, including Chief Bear Comes Running. But still they came, crashing into the brush at the edge of the trees, hoping to trample the trappers with their horses and split their skulls with their wildly swinging tomahawks.

Pow—pow—pow—pow went the trappers' pistols at point-blank range, with deadly results. That shooting was so close that smoke poured from the entry wounds of the Indians hit by the huge pistol balls, some struck just inches from the ends of the barrels!

Next came a surprising boom—boom—boom—boom from Winter Hawk's and Runs Fast's Hawkens. Observing that the Indians were charging in a single group, they had quickly abandoned their rear positions and raced to the front line of the battle with their weapons at the ready. Arriving just as the Indian's charge broke past Harlan and Big Eagle, Runs Fast and Winter Hawk stopped it cold with four accurate shots from their rifles into the surprised faces of the attackers.

Dropping their rifles, into the fray they sailed with both of their pistols firing, killing four more Cheyenne warriors at point-blank range and splattering those riding behind with what was left of the breakfast of the rider ahead! Then, swinging tomahawks, rearing, panicked horses, and flashing knives ruled the violent moment. The women, witnessing the fury of the battle, bravely ran to the edge of the fight with their pistols and killed two more warriors who had not expected to be shot from behind.

They ran back to the pack string to reload their pistols out of the line of fire, then came back once again, killing two more swirling Cheyenne warriors at the edge of the battle by shooting them in their backs.

Much was at stake for them—not only their honor but also the lives of their men. Knowing nothing but misery awaited them if they lost the fight, they found themselves driven to the same level of desperation as their men. The white clouds of black-powder smoke were now so thick in the brush line that they could hardly tell friend from foe! Adding to that din was the racket of more than twenty panicked and rearing horses, trampling the living and dead beneath their flailing hooves.

Swinging wildly with his tomahawk and slashing with his knife in the other hand, Harlan killed one big, fat Indian when he axed him square in the forehead, splitting his skull. Next his knife found the soft underbelly of another Indian. The thrust was so powerful that it swept the raider off his horse and under the hooves of his friends' horses.

Big Eagle threw his tomahawk at one man, missed, and killed the rider behind him when the ax struck him full in the throat! Then an Indian jumped off his horse, right onto Big Eagle and his flashing knife. By then Harlan and Winter Hawk had each axed another Cheyenne in the confusion as they tried to ride off and escape the bloody scene of unimaginable fury they had not anticipated.

Runs Fast savagely brained the last Indian with his pistol. The man had fallen from his madly rearing and terrified horse and, in the process of trying to remount, died in his tracks.

Then there was nothing but the quiet that comes after desperation, savagery, and bravery in a land where such acts could be commonplace. As the smoke, noise, and struggle died away, the men looked at each other to see who was still standing. On the ground in bloody profusion lay twenty- seven dead and dying Cheyenne warriors who just moments before had been looking forward to the battle.

However, they had not anticipated the straight-shooting trappers armed with double sets of weapons.

Now they would forever roam the Happy Hunting Grounds looking for their souls.

As for the trappers, it would take several weeks before all were healed from the battle. Harlan had an eight-inch gash wildly bleeding on the top of his head. Blood was running down his shoulder and chest where a tomahawk had struck and glanced off, but not before ripping open a large wound in his already damaged scalp.

Big Eagle was missing the last two fingers of his left hand from trying to block a vicious swipe of a warrior's knife. In addition, his right cheek was ripped open to the bone, and he had lost two teeth in the same blow from an unseen tomahawk strike.

Winter Hawk had a deep knife wound on his left forearm that went clear to the bone and another across both shoulder blades. Runs Fast had a ten-inch gash in his thigh from a spear thrust. Other than that, they had survived.

Making camp right there in the cottonwoods where the battle had occurred, the women set about caring for their men. Birdsong cleaned Harlan's head wound with some rum and then sewed it shut with needle and thread.

While the other men were being tended to, Harlan mounted his horse and slowly began dragging away the Indian dead before the buzzards and other varmints gave away the trappers' position any more than they already had. There was a steep-sided gully a hundred yards from camp, and soon the dead warriors shared a common hole in the ground— but not before each had been scalped by Harlan.

Then Harlan cut branches from the trees and dragged them across their tracks and into the gully to cover the morning's violence. However, the hiding of the bodies turned out not to be necessary. One hell of a prairie thunderstorm blew up that evening, and as the lightning crackled all around, the gully full of dead Indians filled with a torrent of water and mud.

The next morning Harlan and Winter Hawk went to rebury the dead, figuring they would have been washed out by the storm, only to find that the torrents of water running down the gully had washed all the dead into an even deeper hole and neatly buried them under tons of alkali silt.

Fearing more roving bands of Indians and now with an additional sixteen horses collected from the dead as a potential target, Harlan and his band headed slowly due west for the Wind River Range, seeking the coolness of higher altitudes for those suffering healing wounds. The mountains were home to the trappers' friends, the Snakes.

If they could reach that sanctuary, the chances of more Northern Cheyenne following them by tracking the escaped horses were small. Harlan had learned early on that one way to lose pursuers was to make liberal use of opportunities to walk in creek and stream bottoms in order to erase one's tracks. He used that tactic with great effect in the small streams of the Wind River Mountains.

The next day found the band of trappers and their new horse herd deep in the covering timber in the mountains of the Wind River Range. The second day of travel after the battle found the tired and sore little band at a welcome place—their original cabin site near Willow Lake! The horse corral was still there, and into that went the Indians' horses after being fed and watered. Their own stock was then unpacked, hobbled, and let into the nearby meadow to feed and water because the corral could not hold any more animals.

As the women cleaned out the old cabin, the men rehung the front door and hauled in some wood for the evening fire. Then, as dinner was cooking, they all sat around the fire and tried to relax without falling asleep in case they had been followed. After dinner and the events of the previous days, emotions came crashing down on them as they retreated to their sleeping furs in the cabin. There they were quickly lost in the deep sleep that comes from running on the edge of bodily reserves.

———

FOR THE NEXT few days the men tended to the livestock, enlarged the corral, and hunted the ever-present moose for fresh meat. The women kept tending their wounds with rum and clean coverings to avoid infection. Then the men set to work on the horses belonging to the Northern Cheyenne and removed all the painted markings relating to that tribe. That would make the horses easier to sell at the upcoming rendezvous without arousing any suspicion if they ran across bands of friendly Northern Cheyenne en route to the same get-together.

During that time, Harlan began thinking of moving on to safer climes. He had had enough of the angry Lakota and Northern Cheyenne seemingly lurking at every turn in the trail.

Crossing their hunting ranges to get to the beaver-trapping grounds is someday going to be a one-way trail to the Happy Hunting Grounds for all of us! he thought.

He had to find a good beaver-trapping area surrounded by friendly Indians. With that idea, he had a quiet yet surprising plan for the survival of his family at the upcoming rendezvous if he was given a chance to get there safely.

21

THE 1833 RENDEZVOUS

THE UPPER GREEN RIVER VALLEY WAS THE HISTORICAL crossroads of the Old West. Surrounded by the Wind River Mountains to the east, the Gros Ventre Mountains to the north, the Wyoming Mountain Range to the west, and the Uinta Mountains far to the south, it was a natural high plateau where the ancients and early Native peoples gathered. Loaded with wildlife of every kind and number, the area extended over one hundred miles from north to south and over fifty miles from east to west. Bisecting the length of this unique ecological and historical area was the mighty Green River.

From 1825 until 1840, the Upper Green River Valley was considered home by the mountain men and the traders from the various St. Louis fur companies, so much so that eight of the fifteen summer rendezvous took place in the area. Six of these rendezvous were held in the vicinity of the present-day town of Daniel, Wyoming, at the confluence of Horse Creek and the Green River.

Harlan remembered hearing from the trappers at the last get-together that the rendezvous of 1833 would be held at this confluence. That area was but a few days' ride southwest from their current location at Willow Lake and across territory that was fairly friendly unless they ran across buffalo-hunting or war parties of the dreaded Lakota or Northern Cheyenne.

It is good that the next rendezvous is so close, he thought, because that will give my party a few more days here to heal before we have to make that trek.

———

THE TRAVEL to the rendezvous site was uneventful, taking only five easy days, which pleased Harlan and his party. Arriving, they discovered about one hundred trapper encampments scattered about the site. Those numbers were augmented by about three hundred Snakes, Arapaho, and a group of Crows camped five miles north of the rendezvous site.

Trading will be good, thought Harlan, and this is working into my plans perfectly.

Finding a place in a small grove of trees about one-half mile from the rendezvous site and away from other trappers, the men quickly set up camp. First they made a temporary corral, using several ropes wrapped around a ring of trees to form an enclosure. Then, using rope hobbles, they hobbled every Indian horse within the corral. That way, if someone wanted to steal some of their horseflesh, they would have to work at removing the hobbles from a passel of horses while under fire from the clan's straight-shooting Hawkens the whole time.

While the boys unloaded their horses and mules, Harlan took a short ride around the rendezvous site. Present was the American Fur Company and his friend Gavin. The St. Louis Fur Company and the Rocky Mountain Fur Company were posted in the same area. However, there was some bad news: the price of beaver fur had gone way down, from nine dollars in the eastern markets for a large hide or "blanket" to no more than three dollars at rendezvous prices, with most bringing less than that.

It seemed that something called silk from a worm had taken over the fashion market and replaced beaver fur in the making of hats. However, buffalo hides were bringing a premium price of four dollars, and Harlan's crew had over one hundred hides they had acquired in trade from the Indians over the year. As Harlan watched the fur buyers, it was apparent that they were buying low and selling their goods for very high prices—that was, except for the smaller St. Louis Fur Company.

They seem to be reasonable in their fur grading, and with them I will trade, thought Harlan.

Three days after their arrival, Harlan and the boys moved their pack strings into the trading arena. True to his word, Harlan bypassed the rest of the fur companies, even his friend Gavin, for the St. Louis Fur Company. After the trader spent an hour examining the quality of the furs, the deal was cut. They did very well with their furs, mainly because the women had done a great job preparing and tanning them. When Harlan and the boys walked away from the trading, they had over four thousand dollars in credit for their labors!

———

"Now," said Harlan as they sat around the campfire that evening, "when we go back to pick up our goods, I want each of you to think ahead. We may not be back to the 1834 rendezvous, which the word is will be on Ham's Fork of the Green. That area is south of us by about fifteen sleeps.

We may just stay up in the high country for two years before coming back, and I am thinking farther north than we have ever been. North in the land of the Crows instead of in the land of the mean- ass Lakota and Northern Cheyenne. I am tired of having to fight for my life at every turn in the trail over beaver that have dropped in price to where they are almost not worth catching. And certainly not worth risking one's topknot, especially with one youngster in our midst and two more on the way.

"I would also like to go north in order to let all of you experience living with your own kind under natural conditions," he said with a twinkle in his eyes, knowing full well that revelation would catch everyone unawares.

Harlan could see that those words had created a ripple of careful thought and excitement among his clan. He wasn't sure if his thoughts were received favorably by the whole group because some were so quiet. But it was a carefully thought-out plan that he had stewed over ever since the battle with the Northern Cheyenne in the cottonwood grove. Now the weasel was out of the sack, and his group would have to chew on it for a while.

"As I understand," he said, "there is a small band of Crow just north of us who are here to trade with the fur companies. I propose to go talk with their chief, and if he is a good man and one I can trust, I will ask him if we might be allowed to travel with his clan back to his land as friends," Harlan said.

He spoke slowly so his words' importance would not be lost in the excitement of the moment. "There will be extra protection traveling across this land with a larger contingent of fighters, especially with the addition of our guns. Plus, they will know the way, will be our friends, and in the end will give all of you a chance to live happily among your own people. Now, does anyone have an objection or concern over what I am proposing?"

For the longest time no one spoke. They all sat in deep thought. Then Big Eagle rose as if to emphasize his point and said, "I would like to see what it is like to live among my own kind and hunt buffalo for a living. I am also tired of wading in the cold water all the time for beaver." With that, he sat down and quietly stared into the fire.

Runs Fast rose and said, "I too would like to return to the land of my kind and see what is there. Maybe I can find some of my own family there as well." Like his brother, he abruptly sat back down as if to finalize his words

Birdsong rose and said, "I would like to go with my brothers, and Autumn Flower would like to go with her husband."

Looking over at Winter Hawk, all Harlan could see was a man still sore from the recent battle with the Northern Cheyenne. But his youngest son also possessed a big smile at the possibility of returning home and seeing what it would be like to live among his own kind.

"Then it is done," said Harlan with a tone of finality. "Tomorrow I will ride up and meet with the Crow chief and see what kind of a man he is. If he is a good man and a leader, I will ask him to take us in as brothers and show us his land so we might live in peace with a greater degree of safety. Then, if he agrees that we can go with him to the land of the Crow, we will come back to the rendezvous and, using our credit and some of the captured Northern Cheyenne horses for trade, procure what we will need for such a journey.

If not, I propose we move south to hunt buffalo and continue our trapping as long as we can make a living. There are trading posts as far south as the St. Vrain and Arkansas Rivers as well as west to Taos and Santa Fe. If necessary, we will trade our goods there instead of at the rendezvous," said Harlan as if laying out their future in stone. Looking around, Harlan could see everyone was in deep thought at what had been said that evening.

"Boys," he continued, "tomorrow I want all of you to remain in camp and protect the horse herd. I saw lots of covetous eyes looking them over among the trappers and the Indians because good horseflesh is so hard to come by. So be alert and on the lookout for trouble."

All the boys looked at him in unison with the realization that the trading of those horses might very well be their ticket back to their homeland and allow them to purchase enough supplies for two years of life in the backcountry.

Woe be to any horse thief not correctly reading the meaning behind their eyes, thought Harlan with a smile.

22

THE CROW CAMP

DAYLIGHT THE NEXT MORNING FOUND HARLAN QUIETLY sitting on his horse at the edge of the Crow encampment. The camp was a fairly large one, consisting of thirty-two tepees. It likely held about one hundred twenty-five men, women, and children as near as Harlan could determine from his past experiences with Indian-camp layouts.

Behind him was a mule carrying a few gifts for the Crow chief if everything went according to plan. If not, he, the mule, and his horse would have a long, disappointing ride back to his camp.

As the Crow camp awoke and smoke from the cooking fires in the tepees rose lazily into the chill morning air, hardly anyone stirring paid much attention to Harlan sitting on his horse at a little distance. Then a Crow warrior noticed that the lone rider was a white man and paused to stare long and hard.

Without haste, the warrior walked to the center of the village to a tepee marked by a long staff of eagle feathers stuck in the ground out front. Standing outside, he said something to the tepee's occupants. Shortly thereafter, the door flap was thrown back, and out walked a magnificent specimen of a man. Bare-chested, at least six feet tall, and wearing only long deer-skin pants, elaborately beaded moccasins, and a double-train war bonnet made from eagle feathers, he listened to what the warrior had to say.

After a short conversation, the warrior trotted off and began visiting a number of other tepees as if alerting those inside. Soon the camp began to swarm with armed warriors as the chief stood in front of his tepee looking at the lone white man sitting on his horse overlooking their camp.

About thirty warriors gathered at the chief's tepee, and they too quietly watched the man sitting outside their camp. Then the chief raised his hand in the sign of peace and beckoned Harlan toward him. Harlan made the sign of peace and slowly walked his horse and mule into the Crow camp, right up to the chief. Stopping about ten feet from the chief, he sat looking at the man while the chief and his people quietly looked back.

Then the chief beckoned for Harlan to dismount, which he did. Harlan stood six feet two inches in his moccasins, which was big for a man in his day. It was obvious that the chief noticed his stature and bearing as well as his badly scarred head and face.

The two large men stood for another moment looking at each other.

"Do you speak Crow?" asked the chief.

"Very well," replied Harlan in the man's native tongue, which seemed to surprise the man.

"What do you want, white man?" asked the chief.

"I come to parley with the great Crow chief," said Harlan not outlining his needs any further.

The chief stood looking at Harlan, and Harlan never took his eyes off the man in his attempt to read who he really was.

With a flourish of his arm, the chief opened the flap of his tepee and beckoned Harlan to enter.

"I ask the great Crow chief to protect my animals and goods," Harlan requested in a respectful tone.

Again the chief looked long and hard at Harlan, and Harlan did the same right back. Turning, the chief asked a warrior to hold the reins of the two animals and beckoned once again for Harlan to enter his tepee.

Ducking, Harlan entered the tepee. Inside, a small cooking fire burned, and two women scurried off to one side and stood with their eyes downcast in a sign of respect. Entering the tepee, the chief moved to the right of the campfire and sat down. Then he beckoned for Harlan to sit, which he did. Once he was seated, one of the women brought the chief a brightly beaded leather bag and then scurried off to one side of the tepee again.

Harlan noticed that the other woman standing near

her, probably a daughter, was young, possibly in her late teens, and very beautiful like Birdsong.

Reaching into the leather ceremonial bag, the chief took out a sacred pipe, stuffed it with tobacco, removed a small stick with a burning end from the fire, and used it to light the pipe. He took several long pulls on the pipe and then pointed it to Mother Earth and the sky, blowing out smoke, which he brushed back into his face with his hand.

Then he handed the pipe to Harlan. Harlan correctly took the bowl of the pipe in his left hand and the stem with his right. Taking several deep puffs on the pipe, he too pointed it to Mother Earth and the sky, blowing out the smoke and then pulling it gently back with a cupped hand over his face and head for the blessings it brought.

The Crow chief smiled at the good manners of the white man, took back the pipe, laid it by his side, and said, "What is it the white man desires from Chief White Bear?"

Harlan, shocked by the name of the Crow chief, smiled widely.

"What does the white man find so funny?" asked White Bear, letting a flash of anger race across his eyes at these apparent bad manners.

"The chief has a great and strong name," replied Harlan in a convincing tone meant to relax the chief and reduce his doubts about the man sitting before him.

The chief sat back against a backrest and studied this bold yet calmly surprising white man closely. He discerned that Harlan was a man of strength who lacked fear, and his instincts said the man before him was not two-faced, like many white men, but honorable. He appeared to be gracious and learned in the ways of the Crow, among other things understanding the meaning behind the sacred pipe ceremony. His many scars spoke to his ability as a fighter. Truly, this is a man to be reckoned with and respected because he knows and lives "the way." thought the chief.

Harlan had already discerned that this chief was a noble man. He began to explain the reason for his visit in the Crow language.

"Chief White Bear, I have an adopted son, a daughter, and a wife, and the two women are each now carrying a child. They are all from the great Crow Nation, having been captured by the Northern Cheyenne and the Snakes in years past and made into slaves.

I also have two younger sons from the Crow Nation whose parents were killed by the Lakota and Northern Cheyenne several years ago. I discovered the last two young men after the battle as the only survivors and have raised them as my own.

The first three I spoke of I purchased from the Snake and Northern Cheyenne. I purchased the two women because they are the sisters of the two young boys. The other young man I purchased last year from the Snakes because he saved my life and the lives of the rest of the family from bad white men. He, like all my boys, is a great warrior.

The two women are also brave fighters, having already killed Northern Cheyenne warriors in battle, and will bear many strong children. It is because of them that I come with a request. All of them would like to return to the great Crow Nation to live with and learn about their own kind."

Harlan paused in his story to try to read Chief White Bear's reaction to he had just said. It was obvious that the chief was listening carefully if the look in his eyes meant anything.

Harlan continued, "My family and I have been in many battles over the years with bad white men and enemies of the Crow, the Northern Cheyenne."

He left out the killing of the six horse-stealing Crows the winter before, for obvious reasons. "We are small in number, and there are many around us who would like to kill us and take our furs and other goods. It is with those thoughts that we would like to join up with your band and follow you north to the land of your ancestors.

We would like to trap beaver and kill buffalo as well as trade and live in peace among your people. Your band is strong and would be made even stronger by the addition of my family and our straight-shooting Hawken rifles.

If it pleases you, at the end of the rendezvous, we would like to become part of your band and move north to live quietly with you in the land of the Crow."

Finished, Harlan sat back, looking long and hard at

the Crow chief for any sign of his feelings regarding what had been said.

"You are a brave and strong man, white man. How are you named?" abruptly asked the chief.

"My name is Harlan Waugh, mountain man and friend to the Crow," Harlan answered.

"Well, friend to the Crow, you may join my band as we go north to our homelands after the rendezvous. I would be happy to have four more brave warriors in my band with their long-shooting Hawkens," Chief White Bear replied with a big grin.

Rising, he extended his hand in the sign of peace to Harlan, and Harlan rose and accepted. Harlan noticed that the chief's handshake was almost crushing in strength, reminding him of the grip of his friend Tom "Iron Hand" Warren, keel boatman who was an ex-mountain man, and also a man-mountain of considerable power and courage.

Yes, here is a real man, Harlan thought. "I have some gifts for Chief White Bear," he announced.

Before the chief could respond, Harlan strode outside to his waiting horse and mule. The warriors were still gathered in front of the tepee, as were now about a dozen curious women and children. Unpacking the mule, Harlan brought forth a Hawken rifle, a keg of powder, five pigs of lead, and accessories to service the rifle.

Turning, he handed the prized items to Chief White Bear, who had followed him from the tepee. The chief stood in amazement at the precious gifts of deep meaning. None of his tribe could afford such a weapon or would be allowed to purchase one from the traders at the rendezvous because they were the hated Crow.

They were allowed to trade only for the poorer-quality Hudson Bay fusils of flintlock fame. Before he could recover from the receipt of such a gift, Harlan reached for the item he had luckily brought along as a present. Unpacking a large roll from the mule, he brought forth the massive hide of the great white bear and rolled it out fur side up in the grass in front of the chief, to the sheer amazement of all who had gathered around.

In a second, all backed off several steps at the revelation of the power the albino grizzly hide represented! The look on the chief's face showed that he was awe struck at receiving such a magnificent gift.

"This is for the great chief of the Crows, White Bear," Harlan announced. Now the chief would know why Harlan had smiled when the chief had revealed his name.

The chief just stood before the bear hide, then finally knelt down and touched it reverently. Harlan could tell he had a friend for life.

"When will my Crow brothers leave?" Harlan asked to break the spell and let the chief understand no gifts were expected from him in return.

Looking up, the chief said, "We will return to our land in two days. If the great bear killer and his family wish to ride with us, we would be pleased to call them our own."

Again sticking out their hands in a sign of friendship,

the two men shook like both of them meant it. With that and the sign of peace, Harlan rode back to his brood with the news of the meeting. Looking back over his shoulder as he rode off, Harlan could see the Crows still gathered around the great white bear hide in awe over such a gift presented to their chief.

Yes, Harlan thought with newfound hope in his heart, we have a new family and a friend for life! A new beginning, that is for sure. Now we have safety in numbers and a new land to explore.

If Harlan had only known what would face his little family in the land of the Crow...

After he returned to camp with the news about traveling north with the Crow in two days, the family was abuzz with talk about the chance for a new life among their own kind. It had been a long time since Harlan had seen everyone so animated.

Perhaps it is a good sign for what is to come, he thought.

Riding up to the St. Louis Fur Company traders the next day, Harlan announced that they were there to claim their credit in the form of goods for the coming year. Soon they were piling up kegs of powder, primer caps, flint for trade, fire steels, and two dozen sharpening stones, which they would soon need because they were going into buffalo country.

The stones would be greatly needed because the great beasts' wiry hair always dulled their knives during skinning. They also acquired bolts of brightly colored calico for the women, pigs of lead, and a dozen fusil rifles for trade. They added the always needed and hard-to-get horseshoes, horseshoe nails, and mule shoes. Then Harlan and the boys began selecting bags of brightly colored beads, 100 pounds of coffee, 200 pounds of flour and cornmeal, salt, cones of brown sugar, and two 25-pound bags of peppercorns. As an afterthought, Big Eagle selected several sacks of dried spices, including red pepper flakes. When their credit was exhausted, Harlan, true to his word, brought forth six Northern Cheyenne horses for trade. The traders, eager for any horse or mule flesh to pack back their bundles of hides, swarmed over the horses.

Soon a bargain was struck, and more goods were then selected from their stores, including four new Hawkens and all their fixings. Lastly, Harlan and the boys purchased eight ready-made pack saddles and much leather strapping that could be made into more packs if needed.

As they headed back to their campsite, almost every horse and mule was loaded to the gunwales.

It is a good thing I kept back ten of the horses gathered up from the fight in the cottonwood grove, Harlan thought, because they will be needed to distribute the weight of these loads for the long-distance travel to the Crow Nation, and for bringing many buffalo hides to the next rendezvous we attend.

Since they were leaving the next day, much haste was made in preparing for the loading of the pack string and the trip to the Crow camp and beyond. Possessing twenty horses and ten mules, Harlan divided the pack string up among the boys and himself. It would be easier to move them across the country as several smaller pack strings rather than one that was long and hard to control, especially when moving through timber and deadfalls.

Each of the women would trail a horse with a travois holding two tepee skins, camp gear, and sleeping skins. The men would be responsible for the pack strings carrying the valuable merchandise for trading and goods for living during the next year.

Finally, everything was set for the morning's labors in readying the pack string. A final meal of fresh moose and buffalo cooked in bear grease graced their plates, as did many Dutch- oven biscuits slopped heavily with honey from one of the many stone jars for which they had recently traded.

Life was good.

23

THE START OF A NEW LIFE

DAYLIGHT FOUND HARLAN AND HIS FAMILY SITTING quietly at the edge of the Crow Indian encampment, which was being tom down to make ready for travel. As they waited on a hill at one side to be out of the way, Harlan was pleased to see Chief White Bear riding their way.

Making the sign of peace, the two men approached each other and shook hands like brothers.

"I am glad you made it, my friend," said White Bear.

"Wouldn't have missed it for all the world," said Harlan with a grin.

Harlan introduced his kin to the Crow chief, who seemed pleased at what he saw, especially the strapping young men and all the trade goods on the horses and mules.

Soon the Crow village was on the move, along with

Harlan and company. The line straggled out over half a mile in length and was a laughing, happy mixture of people and barking dogs on the move back toward their home. On the perimeter of this horde rode many alert Crow warriors, Harlan, and the boys.

If anyone wants to wreck this happy gathering, they will have to run a gauntlet of arrows and hot, flying lead bullets, Harlan thought comfortably.

Over the next several days, camp life consisted of travel all day and breaking early in the afternoon for dinner and making camp. The tribe moved north across what is today the eastern side of Yellowstone National Park towards Red Lodge, Montana, the summer home of Chief White Bear and his people.

By the second day, the Crow people had warmed up and begun to welcome Harlan and his family into their clan. Much visiting took place between the young warriors and the boys, especially concerning the firearms the boys carried. As for the women of the family, they were soon swamped with a million questions from the Crow women regarding who they might be, who their parents had been, when were they had been taken prisoner, and the like.

The Crow women were amazed that Birdsong and Autumn Flower openly owned and carried their own pistols. The two women responded to questions about their firearms with the statement that they would never again be taken prisoner without a fight to the death.

Harlan could see that there was a genuine interest and

liking by the Crow people for the members of his clan. From the looks of it, the favor was returned, especially by Big Eagle for one tall young woman who was the daughter of Chief White Bear. She was the beautiful one Harlan had seen inside the tepee the day he and the chief had first spoken about traveling north together to the land of the Crow. There were no overt gestures outside cultural bounds, but Harlan saw the girl and Big Eagle frequently looking at each other and smiling. He watched with fatherly concern, as did Chief White Bear.

But he would make a fine suitor, Chief White Bear thought, smiling, with all his goods and many horses. Yes, he would make a fine husband and strong addition to my family.

Finally making camp just west of present-day Red Lodge, Montana, the Crow set up living quarters for the summer in a small wooded valley with lots of grass for their pony herds and wood and water aplenty.

Harlan and his family set up camp on the north side of the main Crow encampment in a large grove of cottonwood trees by a small but lively cold running creek. Their two large tepees were soon erected and corrals built for all the stock, and then the men began cutting logs to build two large cabins to live in and protect their many supplies from the weather and theft.

In ten days the cabins were ready, with Harlan and Birdsong residing in one cabin and Runs Fast and Autumn Flower in the other. The tepee stores were transferred into the cabins for the greater protection they offered. Big Eagle and Winter Hawk occupied one tepee, and into the other went all the tack from their livestock. Soon life began to run smoothly for the clan as Harlan began scouting the country for signs of beaver and other furbearers.

Chief White Bear came visiting one day shortly after the establishment of the two camps. Sitting with Harlan after they had smoked the sacred pipe, he asked if Harlan's group would like to go with his people to make meat from "much buffalo." Being short of meat and jerky for the winter months ahead, Harlan answered that they would very much like to accompany the tribe.

"Then it is decided. Tomorrow we go to the Little Greasy Grass Valley, where many buffalo are living," White Bear exclaimed, with anticipation running high in his voice. (This is the area where General Custer would be killed in 1876.) He rose and without a word other than a firm handshake, strode out from the cabin, mounted his horse easily and rode back to his camp.

"Well, boys, we have a mountain of work to do before tomorrow. We best get cracking," said Harlan with a look of anticipation as well.

They spent the rest of morning casting many bullets, filling powder horns, checking rifles, honing knives, and packing extra sharpening stones with the gear to be taken. When that was finished, the boys rode into the dark timber and cut enough lodge-pole saplings to make five new travois.

Dawn the next morning found the tribe and Harlan's

band on the move to the east. Except for the very young, the very old, and a few warriors left behind for the protection they offered, the entire tribe was on the move. Hours later, a herd of buffalo was located in a creek bottom interspersed with numerous cottonwoods.

Reining up out of sight so as not to spook the herd, the tribal elders discussed the best way to approach for the largest kill. Then White Bear strode away from the elders and approached Harlan, who was sitting off to one side with his family, waiting for their hunt instructions.

"My brother,'7 he said, "will you join us and help make plans for the hunt?"

"I would be happy to join my brother," Harlan replied, pleased that he had been asked. He followed White Bear back to the council.

Returning shortly, he said, "We have been given the place of honor in killing the buffalo. They respect our Hawkens far more than their flintlocks and bows and arrows, so we will position ourselves downwind, sneak up, and kill as many buffalo as we can. When the buffalo finally break, the warriors led by White Bear will charge from the downwind side and kill as many as they can before they leave the valley. Hopefully, we can kill several months' worth of meat for ourselves and our friends.

"Now, boys, before we left, I handed each of you an additional Hawken to act as your reserve in instances like this. It is also at times like this that I expect you to shoot, and shoot straight. Much depends on us to kill as many as we can before they spook and scatter all over the prairie. So shoot the cows, and make one-shot kills if possible. Above all, stay out of sight because once the buffalo wind or see us, they will be off and gone."

An hour later, Harlan and the boys were behind a slight rise, some forty yards downwind from the herd of buffalo, which numbered about five thousand animals.

As buffalo are wont to do, they are feeding in numerous scattered bunches across the prairie. But once the shooting starts, they will bunch up and mill about in confusion, and that is when the real killing can begin, thought Harlan.

Making sure everyone was set and there were enough small cottonwoods behind them so that they could run and climb to safety if the herd stampeded toward them when the warriors struck, Harlan gave the signal. The big Hawkens spoke thunderously as if in chorus, and seconds later eight fat buffalo cows were kicking their last at the edge of the herd. By the time the telltale clouds of white smoke had drifted away on the ever-present prairie wind, the rifles had been reloaded.

Eight more shots were quickly fired, and another eight cows lay dead or dying. Some of the herd began to get nervous over the smell of blood and wisely started to move away from the noise and smoke coming from the hillside. They were the next eight to die.

Soon, the men had the buffalo at their mercy as the animals just stood in confusion, allowing themselves to be killed one by one. Within half an hour of careful, selective shooting, sixty-five buffalo lay dead or dying.

By then, the rest of the herd had had too much of the smell of the recently spilled blood, and they nervously began moving to the south, away from their dead and dying brethren. It was then that White Bear and his warriors struck, and bedlam ensued! Small herds ran every which way, and one group that came by Harlan and the boys lost seven more to carefully placed shots. One of the Hawkens misfired, allowing the eighth buffalo sighted upon to escape.

Soon it was over, and the rest of the tribe, along with Birdsong and Autumn Flower pulling a pack string of five travois plus the two attached to the horses they were riding, moved onto the killing field. For the next hour or so, all one could hear was the excitement and laughter that comes from a good kill of a favorite meat animal.

Then the field got quiet as everyone pitched in with the butchering and loading of the meat onto the travois. Come nightfall, many huge bonfires were lit in the trees next to the creek, and great slabs of meat and ribs were set about the fires for cooking. When the meat was done, the tribe gathered around for a great celebration and feast. Around midnight, people started heading for their sleeping robes because they knew tomorrow would be another long, hard day of butchering.

Come daylight, the huge fires were rekindled, and everyone ate fresh buffalo meat until they could eat no more. Then out onto the prairie they went to butcher the remaining buffalo left from the day before. Those animals that had not been gutted the day before were somewhat bloated, but a little ripe meat didn't faze the Crows, and it was all collected, green-looking or not.

Harlan and his family had loaded their animals with all they could carry, and, like some of the other Indian families, they began to drift homeward so they could begin processing their valuable stores before the meat was fly-blown or spoiled.

Harlan thought, *How wonderful to be able to just leave and wander across the Crow Nation without the fear of running into a hostile tribe. Yes, we made the right decision to make the Crow Nation our new home.*

About an hour from the buffalo killing field, Harlan heard the sound of a horse's hoofs coming up behind him at a gallop. Turning, he saw White Bear fast approaching.

Reining in next to Harlan, the chief said, "My brother, your shooting was straight and deadly. You and the boys have killed many buffalo for my tribe. I am grateful to have such a brother and his sons in my band!"

Harlan smiled proudly and said, "It is also great to be your brother and to be among the mighty Crow Nation. I cannot remember when I have felt this safe and happy since I came west to this great land so many years ago."

White Bear grinned and said, "As long as I am chief, you and yours shall have a home among your Crow brothers and sisters."

With that and a flourish of the hand, he rode off to visit a nearby group of Indians dragging home their winter meat supply.

Back at camp, the exhausted people still had a mountain of work ahead of them. Drying racks had to be built and smoking fires lit. Then great mounds of meat had to be reduced to sizes that would smoke and harden quickly before it spoiled. For the next two days and nights, the fires were tended and the meat processed. Soon the cabins bulged at the seams with deer-skin bags full of rich dried buffalo meat, hanging from the rafters and walls on wooden pegs.

Once the buffalo had been processed, the men moved to the west of camp, and shortly thereafter moose, deer, and the occasional buffalo were hauled back to camp on the travois to be made into more jerky and smoked meats. Soon, there was no more room in the cabins for meat. However, Harlan decided they still did not have enough meat to carry the family of seven people, with two more on the way, through the fast-approaching winter.

As they sat around the outside campfire one evening, Harlan said, "Tomorrow I want you, Big Eagle, along with Winter Hawk to go back to the mountains and see if you can kill some more moose. We have a need for additional meat to last through the winter safely.

From what White Bear tells me, we can still hunt buffalo in the winter when the plains are blown free of snow, but I don't want to depend on that for our food. You two take four pack animals and go back to where we were several days ago because the game is still plentiful there. Kill and load the animals with as much as they can carry, especially with ham, back strap, and shoulder meat.

In the meantime, Runs Fast and I will build another smaller cabin with pegs and shelving just for storing extra winter meat."

Big Eagle and Winter Hawk nodded in agreement, and by daylight they were long gone. Harlan and Runs Fast began cutting and trimming nearby lodge-pole pine logs to build another smaller cabin just for storage of winter meat, and when the women had time, they assisted as well. However, both were beginning to show that they were carrying babies, and Harlan restricted them to lighter duty than the men.

Three days later, the two boys returned with the pack mules loaded with many hams and shoulders of rich moose meat. Moving next to the smoking racks, Big Eagle unloaded all the meat except one very large and choice moose ham for the women to section and start the smoking process.

Without a word, Big Eagle took the pack animal carrying the moose ham and, saying nothing to anyone in his family, walked the animal across the meadow straight to the tepee of Chief White Bear. Watching from a distance, Harlan saw White Bear come out of his tepee and talk to Big Eagle. White Bear then turned and said something to those inside the tepee, and out came the two women. After a brief conversation with White Bear, the two Indian women removed the moose ham and struggled with its weight as they carried it to their drying racks.

With that, Big Eagle turned and headed back to camp,

while White Bear reentered the tepee and disappeared. Meanwhile, the two women commenced cutting up the huge moose ham for smoking and drying.

When Big Eagle returned, no one said a thing, as if nothing out of the ordinary had happened. What Harlan had hoped for in returning to the Crow Nation was now beginning to happen. The men finished the new cache cabin just in time for the women to store the newly smoked and jerked moose meat away from the weather and critters.

24

FALL TRAPPING

THE RITUAL FOR FALL TRAPPING AND ALL ITS ADVENTURES now began. The honing of skinning knives, smoking of beaver traps, casting of bullets, horseshoeing, and equipment repair led the list. Soon the men were almost ready as the women filled their powder horns, topped off their possibles bags, and stuffed their saddlebags with jerky. By daylight, they were gone, leaving the women to fend for themselves under the watchful eyes of their Crow neighbors. However, each woman still carried a very sharp knife and a loaded pistol, just in case.

Traveling due west, the men soon found good beaver waters, not like those they had found in the Bighorn and Willow Lake areas, but still sufficient numbers to make the trapping pay. Harlan and Winter Hawk continued due west a few more miles and started trapping other beaver-rich waters they discovered as Runs Fast and Big Eagle set up camp. Once camp was made, the latter two headed north and soon discovered beaver waters to trap themselves.

That evening, Harlan and Winter Hawk headed toward the small dot of light ahead of them in the pitch-black forest. The traveling was made easier because horses, even in the darkest of night, can see the faintest of trails and bring their riders home. Soon they were all gathered around Big Eagle's roaring campfire, horses and all. Around it were slabs of roasting deer meat, along with a boiling pot of coffee casting its wonderful smells to the heavens.

Bailing off his horse, Harlan said, "How did it go for you two fellas today?"

"Not bad, Dad," Big Eagle sang out proudly. "We set out all our traps and had four beaver and a river otter in them by the time we had scouted out tomorrow's area and returned. How did the two of you do?"

"Not bad either. We caught five, but there isn't a whole lot of good beaver water left out our way. We will look in another direction tomorrow after we run our traps," replied Harlan.

Runs Fast said, "Dinner is ready if you two are hungry." With that, the four hungry men wolfed down great gobs of partially cooked venison and sipped their scalding cups of coffee in silence. After dinner, the four mules and four horses were hobbled and let out into the small meadow to feed and water. The men still had work to do. They had nine beaver to pelt out and hoop, and soon that was accomplished.

Finished with their day's work, the men bedded down in their lean-to and soon were asleep with their rifles close by. After all, they had a forest full of varmints at hand who could be attracted to their camp by all the good smells, especially the livestock.

For the next five days the men trapped hard and lived off the land. Every day's routine was the same: up at daylight, trap beaver, and return to the camp to skin and hoop out the day's catch by dark. By day five and the time they planned to return home, they had fifty-seven beaver plews to load on the pack mules. However, the beaver in the waters they had trapped were no more. It was time to move on to better trapping grounds farther north. Harlan chose north because the Yellowstone River and what it meant in the earlier loss of his brother was to the south...

Returning home, the men rode into a camp containing two happy women and a mean-ass-looking dog of huge proportions! They were afraid to step off their spooked horses, and Harlan yelled, "Someone get that barking damned dog under control!"

Autumn Flower, laughing all the way, ran and grabbed the dog, which she told them was called Timber.

Once the animal was under control, the men dismounted and Harlan asked, "Where the hell did that damn wolf-dog come from?"

Running Fawn, Chief White Bear's daughter, stepped out from inside Harlan's cabin. She looked embarrassed at being present when the men came home from trapping. Seeing the chief's daughter, whom he was sweet on, Big Eagle flew out of the saddle, slipped, and damned near fell on his hind end in front of her.

Quickly composing himself, he sternly walked back to his horse and mule, leading them to the corral as if nothing had happened. But the rest of the group had seen what had happened and chuckled inside. The two young people were fond of each other, and the process of new life on the frontier would soon begin.

As it turned out, Timber was part trapper's dog of many mixes and part prairie wolf. He had been a present from White Bear to help in protecting the two women while their menfolk were out trapping. With that information, Harlan's feathers were somewhat smoothed out, and he accepted the gift. It took about a week before Timber took to Harlan, but when he did, he was a friend for life. Timber had really taken to Autumn Flower's little daughter, and woe to anyone causing her to cry.

For the next two days, the clan was happy at being together once again. But preparations were already under way for another trip into the western forests in the quest for beaver and other furbearers before the winter snows flew.

In the meantime, Big Eagle had time to be with Running Fawn, but only under the ever-present and watchful eye of her father, mother, and several cousins.

By the second day after leaving the camp, Harlan and his sons had ridden far to the north, then headed west once more into the deep of the forest and high mountain valleys. They discovered lots of watered areas but few beaver. Apparently the area had been trapped out by White Bear's band of Crow trappers years earlier. Continuing deeper into the forest, they chanced upon what is today the Stillwater River. It was not as loaded with beaver as the waters around Willow Lake had been, but the animals were there in large enough numbers for the trappers to be encouraged.

Setting up camp in a small meadow adjacent to the river, the men began trapping. Soon the number of beaver coming into camp was so great that at times two of the men had to stay behind and spend a day skinning and hooping out the skins instead of trapping.

Wanting to avoid repeating the long ride home and back to their current trapping area, Harlan decided they would stay for two weeks instead of the usual one and continue trapping. Soon the hoops of beaver dominated their camp, and although tired, the men were happy with their success. As they moved farther north on the river, the beaver continued to be plentiful.

Finally, the men had caught all their pack animals could carry. Loading up their animals, they began the long trek home. That trek was made all the better by the thought that they had caught and hooped one hundred and thirty-seven beaver in just two weeks' time!

Coming out of the forest near present-day Nye, Montana, Harlan turned the group southeast toward home. Two days of hard riding put them just north of their campsite when they crossed a pony trail of about thirty unknown riders. All the ponies were unshod, which told Harlan they were Indians. But what nation? he asked himself, worried that they might be the dreaded Blackfoot.

Off to one side, as if they were riding with the Indians, were the tracks of eight other horses, and they were shod! Stopping, Harlan got off his horse and closely examined those tracks. Four days, five at the most, he deduced as to the age of the tracks. Maybe other trappers ... but maybe not.

In the meantime, the boys sat rigidly in their saddles, alertly looking all around. This was the land of White Bear, and he had not told them of other trappers or Indians in the area, so caution was in order.

MOUNTING UP, Harlan said, "Let's go, boys. Them is old tracks, and we can't do nothing about them now."

Hours later, they pulled into their camp just ahead of a winter storm boiling off the mountains to the west. The two women came flying out of Harlan's cabin with strain written all over their faces. Birdsong started to say something to Harlan about their being a week later than they had expected but decided against it when she saw the clouded look on his face.

She had seen it before when he got into a killing mode or went into a "do-or-die" battle. Something was on his mind, and she decided she would get it out of him later in bed. In the meantime, Timber the dog was happy to see everybody and showed it by nipping the trappers' rear ends for attention.

"Boys, would you unload the furs and cache them away? I am going over to White Bear's to discuss those pony tracks," Harlan said quietly.

Turning his tired horse toward the Crow camp, he rode off to see his friend and talk over what was bothering him. It was bothering him enough to make it an issue, and that raised the concern of the boys as well. Our dad is not one to run at the first whiff of gunpowder, they thought, but when he hunkers down like h' s doing now, a fight is not long in the offing.

Sitting around the fire in White Bear's tepee, Harlan discussed the shod ponies with the chief. Harlan told him the location and direction the band were going. He said they acted as if they owned the place and were not in a hurry or concerned that they were in Crow country. More importantly, the eight shod ponies were carrying weight like that of riders and traveling gear.

For the longest time, White Bear just looked introspectively into the small fire crackling away at his feet. Then he began, "It is not good. I feel that the Blackfoot or the Gros Ventres may be ranging below their country, either hunting the buffalo or looking for places to raid. I have heard such things from other nearby clans of Crow but did not think they had ranged this far already. Tomorrow I will lead a war party to look into those tracks, especially the ones of the shod horses being ridden by maybe whites."

"Do you want me or the boys to go with you?" asked Harlan.

"No," replied White Bear. "This is the country of the Crow, and we will find out who the strangers are and take care of the problem if there is one. I know the trail is cold, but my warriors can trail fast, and with our fresh horses, we will do so."

The chief then stared even more deeply into the fire, which was his way of saying the talking was done for now. Harlan got up, bade him good-bye, and left for his cabin, a good meal, and a warm bed. The chief and his band of twenty-five warriors were gone before daylight the next day.

———

THE STORM that finally blew in the next evening was rain that eventually turned to heavy, wet snow. Lying in his sleeping furs, Harlan wondered whether the chief would be able to follow the cold trail in light of the newly fallen snows. He received his answer several hours later when the war party returned, stymied by the lack of tracks now covered by snow.

Making ready, the trappers left the following morning to follow the trail they had blazed on the trees when they had had left the forest after trapping the Stillwater. Two days later found them on the Stillwater trapping in decidedly colder weather.

Winter was on its way earlier than usual, and with it came a sense of urgency to trap hard in case they could not make it back because of the weather that far north. In the first week, they had to move their camp twice to accommodate the distance they were traveling north on the river to trap the beaver.

But the trapping was good, and despite the foul weather, they managed to catch another forty-three beaver and sixteen river otter. Realizing another week might be all they had before bad weather set in, the men continued trapping with a fury they had never applied before. However, the long days wading in deep, icy waters to set their traps and working late into the night hooping the skins finally took their toll.

One morning Harlan called a halt to the hard work and asked Big Eagle to kill a deer so they could cook the whole thing that night for dinner instead of eating jerky. Big Eagle complied, and even though they were big meat eaters, the men could not finish the whole deer. There was just enough left for breakfast the following morning.

Fixing their gear, packing the furs into loose bundles, and repairing their clothing and tack, the men spent a busy day in camp. The partial week had gone well. By Harlan's rough calculation, they now had almost three hundred beaver skins in total, which, if the price held, would be worth about nine hundred dollars at the next rendezvous. That amount was two or three times what most men made per year in those days.

They still had the winter trapping of other furbearers such as fox, wolf, coyote, and lynx before them, and those furs they could trade with the Crow. They could also trade the buffalo hides from the hunts with the Crows. Things are looking good for the next year, Harlan thought as he hooped the last beaver, and they still had spring beaver trapping ahead of them.

Harlan had never been happier, especially with his firstborn due sometime in February.

———

WINTER FINALLY ROARED out of the north, almost catching Harlan and his group on the open plains as they returned home from their beaver-trapping excursion. They had hit the northern reaches of the Stillwater and cleaned it out of beaver on this last trip. They had another fifty-nine beaver plews for their efforts, but they had earned everything they had caught.

Big Eagle had taken a spill in deep, fast-moving water and almost drowned. Harlan had caught a branch in his left eye while on horseback when he was not looking and damned near lost the eye. A week later, he was still seeing double with it.

As for Winter Hawk, he had run into a grizzly feeding on a dead moose carcass who had instantly charged and managed to slash his right leg with four large claw marks an inch deep before he could escape. Only Runs Fast had escaped damage of any kind.

Turning south from the dense forest, all the men were relieved when their cabins hove into sight, along with the thirty or so tepees of White Bear's clan.

The usual homecoming awaited them as the men tended to their worn-out stock. The smell from the cooking fire was overwhelming, and the entire clan fell to moose and rice stew with biscuits.

As he finished his second plate of food, Harlan noticed White Bear walking across the dried grass meadow toward him. Getting up, Harlan greeted his friend. They spoke of the latest trapping trip and of going hunting together soon for more buffalo. Then White Bear told Harlan that the clan was breaking up into three smaller groups and moving off into different winter quarters so there would be enough grass throughout the winter for their pony herds. He said his clan would be moving the shortest distance away, about five miles to the east into the Bear Creek Valley.

"There will be much grass, water, and firewood, plus cover from the north winds in the draws of the valley. However, before we go, my group wants to trade our buffalo hides and beaver to you, my brother. With those, we hope to get additional winter supplies," White Bear said with his characteristic smile. There was no talk about the mysterious shod and unshod pony tracks discovered earlier.

Harlan said, "Have them come tomorrow, and we will

trade. Now, my brother, how about some very fine moose meat and rice stew?"

The following day turned out clear but cool. Surrounding Harlan's cabin was a gaily dressed crowd of Crow Indians trading various furs and deer, elk, and buffalo hides for the supplies the trappers held in their cabins.

At the end of the day, Harlan had acquired ninety buffalo hides, one hundred and fifty-two beaver plews, sixty deer- hides, and twenty-four elk hides, all beautifully tanned by the Crow women. They still had a vast treasure of supplies for spring trading, and Harlan knew his group would do very well at the next rendezvous or nearest trading post regardless of beaver-plew prices.

The day following the trading session, the Indians broke into smaller bands and, after many good-byes, left for their winter camps several miles away. Hardest hit was Big Eagle because with the clan breakup went the woman who was becoming the love of his life.

Walking up to Big Eagle and putting his hand on his shoulder, Harlan said, "There is nothing stopping you from riding over and visiting them when your work here is done."

Big Eagle turned and said, "I will visit her many times, Father, for I love her so."

The two men continued watching the last Indian caravan disappear into the river bottoms to the east.

25

DESTINY FROM BEYOND THE NORTH WIND

THE WINTER SNOWS SEEMED TO BE HOLDING OFF FROM covering the land that December in Montana, unlike many years past. In fact, many warm winds blew, and the buffalo herds were everywhere, making killing easy for the trappers and Indians alike. Numerous community roasting fires that winter supplied many meals of the rich buffalo meat and joyfulness among the various visiting Indian families, but it couldn't last—and wouldn't.

"We should be back in no more than three days," said Harlan, as he and the boys made ready to run their trapline of snares, deadfalls, and leg-hold traps in the forest to the west.

"Please be careful," said Birdsong. "I have had bad feelings from the evil spirits ever since you and the boys discovered those unknown horse tracks. I don't know why I should, but I just have a feeling of bad things to happen."

Gathering her body, now bulging and heavy with the baby, into his arms, Harlan said, "Don't let your Indian way of life scare you. I won't let the evil spirits get you, not as long as I am alive and nearby to protect you. You have Timber at hand to warn you and your firearms in case things get serious. Martha, the bell mule, will let you know if anyone comes within seeing distance. If you like, go stay with White Bear and his clan. They would love to see all of you. But when you do, be sure to take some gifts of coffee, sugar, tobacco, and salt."

"Maybe you are right," Birdsong said. "This time when you are gone we will visit White Bear's clan. I will feel safer that way, with the baby and all. Autumn Flower and I will go visit, so when you come home, you will know where to find us. We will come back once a day to water and feed our horses and mules." She gave Harlan her usual beautiful smile.

Harlan gave Birdsong a loving pat on the bottom as Runs Fast let Autumn Flower go from his arms as well. Big Eagle and Winter Hawk just smiled from atop their horses.

It sure is good to be part of such a loving family, Winter Hawk thought proudly.

Entering the dark timber, Harlan, ever mindful of "the way," kept his eyes peeled and listened to the wildlife around him for any sign of danger. He wouldn't have said as much to Birdsong, but he too had felt a certain uneasiness, though it was nothing he could put his finger on.

The trapping was now at hand, and he put the bad thoughts out of his mind for the duration, blaming them on his worry about being a father for the first time.

Approaching their first snare, they discovered that it held a beautiful pine marten. For the next two days, the men found that their traps and snares had managed to catch numerous high- class furbearing animals. At night, they would sit around a small campfire designed not to draw any unwanted attention while they skinned and hooped the hides. By day three, the weather had turned threatening once again, with numerous banks of dark gray clouds stacking up in the northwest, from whence most of their storms came.

Realizing this could be the hard winter weather they had been expecting for months, Harlan told the boys, "Saddle up. We are heading for home in time to beat that weather, which can't be more than two or three days out."

Backtracking their trap-line, they sprang the remaining snares and deadfalls. In the process, they also picked up their valuable leg-hold traps for next season's trapping. As they headed out after finishing, Harlan was pleased. They were ahead of the storm, their pack animals were loaded with numerous high-grade furs, and none of the men had had any mishaps this time.

Rounding the meadow by their camp, Harlan was surprised not to see smoke coming from the cabins' fireplaces. After all, the wives had known they would be home this day. Guess the women are still at White Bear's camp, he thought.

Then he noticed that all the horses and mules were in the corral, looking a little out of sorts with impatient hoof stomping, eating the wood off the railings, and the like. That be strange, he thought.

Stepping off his horse, he walked over to the animals. The hobbles were still where he had left them three days earlier. That meant they hadn't been used. If that was the case, the horses hadn't been let out to feed or water since the men had left to go trapping three days earlier. That would explain their strange behavior in the corral, Harlan thought as worry began to build. That is not like those women to neglect our livestock because they are our lifeline, he thought with more than a little concern now welling up from deep inside.

The boys checked out the cabins and found all to be intact as they had left them. Then the men fell to hobbling the horses and mules in the corral to let them out to feed and water. They also hobbled their pack mules after unloading the furs and equipment from their recent trapping trip. Off those mules went to join their buddies, now happily feeding and watering in the meadow. Then the men remounted their tired horses and, without a word, rode toward White Bear's camp five miles to the east with more than a little apprehension.

Coming off the prairie rim overlooking White Bear's camp nestled in the creek bottom below, the men were shocked at what greeted their eyes.

Lying before them was White Bear's camp, or what was left of it. All the tepees had been burned, and clothing and equipment were scattered everywhere, as were the bodies of men, women, and children and the camp dogs.

Racing off the prairie rim and into the creek bottom, the four men stormed into camp, vaulted off their horses, and began searching among the bodies for their loved ones. Big Eagle found White Bear. His hands had been cut off, and he had been disemboweled and scalped. Next to him lay his wife and several other of the camp's women who had run to the chief's tent for protection.

Then Winter Hawk yelled. At his feet lay Timber, shot several times and filled with arrows. It was obvious that he had died defending his mistress. Next to him lay Birdsong. Her pistol was empty, and her knife hand was bloodied where she had obviously stabbed someone in the fight.

By her side lay her sister, Autumn Flower, whose pistol had been fired as well. Both women's bodies had been mutilated, and their babies had been cut from their bellies and tossed aside. Both babies were boys. They never found Autumn Flower's daughter. It seemed that every one of White Bear's immediate clan, about twenty-five in number, had been slaughtered by a surprise hostile Indian attack.

Harlan remembered Birdsong's concern over the evil spirits and the feeling he'd had of that he might be holding the love of his life for the last time before they'd left camp that morning. Runs Fast just stood with tears streaming down his face, saying nothing.

Winter Hawk was in shock and starting to tremble as he had as a boy after the attack on his village. Then Big Eagle yelled! He had discovered the body of the love of his life and turned away, vomiting. She too had been mutilated, but not before she had been ravaged many times.

Harlan was numb, raging, and stunned all at the same time. Never had he seen so much absolute destruction of a camp and the people living within. There wasn't one person who was not mutilated, scalped, or shot full of arrows.

Standing in the center of this butchery, Harlan found a towering rage building inside like he had never felt before. He wanted to kill those responsible for creating this scene, and he wanted the killing to take a long time and to be of the most violent kind. He found that he was incapable of tears, just the kind of vengeance, welling up inside like stinging bile, that is wreaked only on the most evil of things —and then only after asking God's forgiveness in advance.

With few words, the men begin burying their dead after wrapping them in buffalo robes. They placed the bodies of the women and their children in a nearby stand of oak trees, up off the ground and facing to the east, together as sisters for eternity.

Then the men heard the sound of horses coming across the shortgrass prairie. Grabbing their Hawkens, to a man they thought, If the horses belong to the men who did this, they will meet their maker here and now!

Over the ridge rode a band of Crow buffalo hunters, led by Limps-Ahead-of-His-Horses, who were coming to White Bear's village to see if anyone wanted to go hunting. They were not prepared for what they saw and almost turned on their trapper friends, thinking they were responsible for the carnage, until they realized what had happened. A runner was sent back to their village to warn the others of the deadly events in White Bear's village and to send relatives back to help in burying the dead.

Harlan, along with his boys, attempted to trace the signs of the attack before the sign was wiped out by the arrival of more Crow from nearby villages. Soon they discovered the route of attack and the place where the killers had holed up until daylight greeted them on that fateful day.

They had ridden over the rim and right into White Bear's camp before anyone could get organized and, being of superior numbers, slaughtered everyone. From examination of the ground, Harlan deduced that there had been about thirty Indians in the raiding party—and eight others riding shod horses!

The arrows in the bodies were those of the Gros Ventre, and many of the dead, including the women, had been shot at close range. As near as Harlan could tell, the trail was two days old at the most. Without a word,

Harlan remounted his horse and, with the boys trailing, rode over to Limps-Ahead-of-His-Horses.

"Do not send a war party after the killers. The boys and I will hunt them down if possible and kill every one of them. We will leave them in such a condition that even the wolves will not find enough to eat," Harlan uttered though clenched teeth. As an afterthought, he asked, "Would you send someone over to care for our stock? When I return, I will see that this person is richly rewarded."

A nod from Limps-Ahead-of-His Horses settled that deal.

Not another word was spoken, just a handshake of understanding, and the meeting was over. Then Harlan and the boys headed back to their cabins without another word. There they exchanged their jaded horses for fresh ones and saddled them for the hunt. They added extra powder and bullets to their bags of possibles, quickly filled the saddlebags with jerky, and tied several sacks of grain to each horse's saddle horn.

This trip would be a hard one, and the horses had to hold up on the long trail. The key to pushing the horses was the high-energy grain they now carried. Each horse was checked to make sure it had good shoes, and the men were ready for the trail. Each man carried two horse pistols and an extra Hawken. In addition, each wore a long-bladed gutting knife. Now that they were fully prepared for the trail, their eyes met, and that was enough.

Heading cross-country on an intercept course, Harlan and the boys soon cut across the track of the killers. They hadn't gone more than a mile on the cold track when they ran across the shallow graves of those killed in the battle at White Bear's camp. Digging up the eight graves, Harlan and the boys scalped all of the bodies. Harlan noticed one man with his belly ripped open by a knife. Birdsong had her revenge, he thought grimly.

They left the bodies exposed for the animals to have their turn, which in accordance with Indian tradition forbade those dead from ever roaming the Happy Hunting Grounds because their bodies would not be complete after the animals had finished.

Then they continued along that trail, and hard. After all, they had several days to make up.

That night, the pursuers cold-camped after heavily graining their horses. There was no open fire, and they quietly ate jerky that had been prepared in happier days. It was apparent that the killers had not expected pursuit because they were taking their time as they headed almost due north toward what Harlan figured might be the Judith Gap. The spacing of the tracks showed that their quarry had slowed their horses to a walk to save the livestock and themselves from exhaustion.

The men didn't get much sleep that night because of the family memories and what lay ahead. Four against twenty remaining men was tough odds, but every one of the pursuers welcomed the chance to close with those who had destroyed their little family.

By daylight, the men were hard on the trail once again as it casually continued north along many well-worn Indian and animal trails. Harlan's party doggedly continued the pursuit.

Kneeling by his horse, Harlan checked the tracks and horse droppings for freshness. Looking up to the boys, he said, "Maybe one day old. They sure aren't in any hurry. We best make sure we aren't walking into an ambush. We will start out wide and continue to cut back and forth across their trail. That way we can continue after them and not be led into an ambush."

The eyes of the men on the horses agreed.

Harlan swung back into the saddle and headed out at an angle, not directly on the trail in case someone was smart enough to watch their backs. Three hours later, the four men cut back to the trail and crossed it where the Indians and possibly their white partners had camped. There the tracks told another story. The killers had rested, and the ashes of their fires were still warm. But those riding the shod horses had split away and headed due west toward what is today White Sulphur Springs, Montana, and beaver-trapping country.

Big Eagle checked the Indians' tracks and, looking up at Harlan, said, "Four to six hours old."

Harlan sat on his horse for a second and then said, "Those eight are probably renegade trappers heading for the beaver grounds in the Big Belt Mountains. My guess is that is where they will hole up, especially with winter coming on. The Indians, on the other hand, will continue heading north to their stomping grounds in the hope that any Crows chasing them will be intimidated, since it is now the country of the Blackfoot, and will turn around and go back. My vote is to catch and punish the Gros Ventre and let others of their kind see what happens when they venture south. As for the trappers, if the snow doesn't get too deep, we can run them to ground in their winter camp later. Unless any of you have different thoughts, that is my vote."

———

COMING up on the south bank of the Musselshell River, Harlan and the boys smelled wood smoke! Quickly hiding their horses, Runs Fast and Winter Hawk sneaked up to the river's edge and peered into several campfires thirty yards away, surrounded by Gros Ventre cooking supper in a heavy growth of willows. There were eighteen men eating and two guarding their horse herd.

None looked like they were really on guard, the boys reported back to Harlan and Big Eagle. It was clear that pursuit was not on their minds this far north.

"We will wait until early morning, when they are sleeping the soundest, and then crawl into their midst and kill as many as we can before they kill us or run away," Harlan said slowly.

He spoke in such a way that the dark meaning of his words and the violence to follow would not be lost on the boys. This group of Indians had crossed the line, as far as

Harlan was concerned. They had ripped the hearts and souls out of his family, and now it was time to return the favor. Many would pay for killing Birdsong, Autumn Flower, and their children.

The two Gros Ventre guarding the horses died in their own blood gurgling from deeply slit throats before they even realized there was any danger. Falling asleep on guard duty had ensured them a long sleep! Runs Fast and Big Eagle held their heads and kept their mouths shut until they quit wiggling so they would not make any noise and arouse the rest of the camp.

Then the four trappers crawled in from one side of the sleeping Indians by the first campfire and with their knives commenced quietly cutting throats, holding each dying man still before moving on to the next in line. Soon the men were smeared with spurting arterial blood. Nine Indians, sleeping off a long ride and a big meal of venison, died around the campfire that morning.

Shifting their attention to the second campfire several yards away, where another nine Indians lay huddled together for warmth, the men rose to their knees as if on command and quietly shouldered their rifles.

"Hey!" yelled Harlan.

The Indians jumped up en masse from a sound sleep, only to be met by the blazing ends of four Hawkens and then eight horse pistols, quickly fired at very close range. None survived the onslaught, falling back and dying in the sleeping skins from which they rose.

Reloading their weapons in case there were more

Indians in the group or others within hearing distance, the men waited as their emotions ran wild for more killing. Upon seeing no one, the four men rose in unison and, as if following an unspoken command, scalped every man around the two campfires and the two by the horse herd. Then they cut off their man-hoods and shoved the organs into each man's pried-open mouth.

They chopped off the heads with their tomahawks and dumped them into the shallow edges of the Musselshell River for anyone to find. Then, off came the bodies' arms and legs, which were thrown into a pile with a stack of firewood over the top, which was then set afire. The torsos were stacked alongside trees as if they had crawled that far before dying, but not before their hearts were ripped out and placed on sharpened sticks for all to see.

With the carnage complete, the men set some of the Indian's venison on sticks around the campfires and ate a hearty breakfast. Still covered with drying blood on their hair, faces, and clothing, the four men made a hideous scene.

That is good, though, thought Harlan, because they were now trailing twenty Gros Ventres ponies as they started toward where he figured the trappers involved in the killing had holed up.

Now they could ride even faster because of the fresh mounts, and they did so, coming within twenty miles of where Harlan figured the trappers might have made their winter camp that first day. If any Gros Ventres or Blackfoot wanted to tangle with this group of grim mounted men, all they had to do was look at them—four determined-looking mountain men, all smeared with blood—and ask themselves if they really wanted a part of that terror.

But the killing of the rogue trappers was not to be. Mother Nature brought an end to the killing with two feet of heavy, fresh snow and foreshadowed a like storm on the way.

Winter is finally here, and in all its fury, thought Harlan as he sat on his horse looking in the direction he needed to go to get at those riding the shod horses. But from what snow lay on the ground now and what was possibly still coming, he decided against continuing the pursuit.

This was not the time to get caught in four feet of snow in the dead of winter in the high country, with just a few pounds of jerky among them and only several blankets apiece. They would have to come back in the spring, when the weather was better and the suspected white men were still trapping before the beaver went out of their prime.

He discussed the matter with the boys, and they also decided that it would be best to come back in the spring and settle up with those riding the eight shod horses, who had participated in the slaughter at White Bear's camp. Each man took one hard look in the direction their quarry had gone and resolved in his own way on a return that would be appropriate.

However, none other harbored the horrible dark thoughts Harlan had. When he finished, if he had his druthers, every man he was following would cry out to the devil to come take him to the fires of hell!

After a week of hard going south in snowstorm after snowstorm, Harlan and the boys finally arrived back at camp, exhausted, as were their saddle horses and Indian ponies. They had long since run out of grain, and the horses had been forced to fend for themselves in the ever-deepening snow. With nighttime temperatures dropping below zero, the men had damn near frozen to death every time the sun had gone down.

Thank heaven for the blankets we acquired from the dead Indians before leaving the Gros Ventres killing field, thought Harlan.

After unsaddling their horses, they hobbled them and let them out into the trees and field near the cabins to feed. The Indian ponies, not used to hobbles, were hobbled anyway with ones made from rope. There was a fair amount of bucking, snorting, and crow-hopping, but the ponies soon settled down and joined the other horses and mules. Now the trappers had a horse and mule string that numbered thirty-one horses and ten mules, which was of major value in the West, but it was a small thing in light of the loss of their loved ones.

For the first two weeks back at the cabins, the men had a hard time adjusting. It seemed as if everything they saw or touched reminded them of the two women who had been such a huge part of their lives.

It also made Runs Fast and Harlan think of their sons and wonder what they might have been like if they had been allowed to live and grow into young men. The dark thoughts of the two married men did not rival those of Big Eagle. His life had just started and had now been snuffed out, to his way of thinking, by those dead Indians to the north and the white men still living comfortably in their trappers' cabins in the Big Belt Mountains.

The fury they will feel to their bodies will be far from anything earthly. Big Eagle darkly thought many times a day and night with tear-filled eyes.

Come spring, Harlan took to looking daily at the new grass shoots poking their heads out of the semi- frozen ground. Without good feed for the horses, we will have a difficult time accomplishing our goals of hunting down and killing the trappers, he thought. This time we will not fail, and woe to those at the ends of our rifle barrels or blades of our knives.

His feelings, suppressed by the long winter months, began to rekindle and surfaced continually with a hatred not of this world.

Finally, the grass was of sufficient length for the trip north. Having made arrangements with their friends the Crow to once again take care of their cabins, stores, and livestock, the four men made ready to strike out for where they believed the trappers were living and trapping beaver in the Big Belt Mountains, or more probably along the waters of the Smith River, where beaver trapping would soon commence.

"Everyone loaded and ready to go?" Harlan asked grimly.

His three sons nodded as they sat astride their horses, each trailing a pack mule loaded with supplies. This time they had several months before the beaver went out of prime, and in that time they hoped to procure eight more horses, tack, and plews.

Carefully looking to see that each pack mule carried the boys' spare Hawkens, Harlan turned and walked his horse the five miles to White Bear's old campsite. As they passed slowly by the burial platforms of the women and their children, still high in the oak trees, each man made a pact with his God, a pact of promised revenge on those who had murdered their loved ones.

———

IN A CAMP along the Smith River, just north of what would become the town of White Sulphur Springs, Montana, were four trappers skinning, fleshing, and hooping out beaver plews. Quietly circling the men, Harlan stepped out from the surrounding brush and told them to air out their hands.

Surprised by the onslaught, one went for his rifle, only to have the unseen stock of Big Eagle's Hawken smash in the side of his face! That was all it took for the remaining three to do as they were told, seeing that they were surrounded and outgunned.

When Harlan looked at their faces, he nearly swallowed his tongue! These men were from the bunch who had tried to take Winter Hawk's Hawken at the earlier rendezvous. They had been with that venomous Patrick Bosco de Gamma! Harlan's eyes narrowed into killing slits as he realized the grade of men they were after was the most dangerous kind.

His killing feeling went double for their leader, who was still on the loose. Sitting down on a log after the men had been disarmed, Harlan took a big chew of tobacco and let it swirl around in his mouth for a few moments for the effect it had on his prisoners.

Then, with a big spit of juice, he looked each man in the eyes and said, "We tracked you men this far after you raided that Crow village down on Bear Creek Valley in December last." Pausing after those accusing words, Harlan watched for any reaction from the trappers.

The three who were still standing, without the bloody and sore-headed man who had been smashed by the rifle butt, took a hurried look at each other as if to say, "Who told this guy? How did he know what we did and where we were last fall?"

That quick, guilty look was all it took for Harlan to realize they were part of the group he and his sons had been looking for.

Then the man with the bleeding head growled his way into eternity: "What were it to you? Them was nothin' but stinkin' Crow Injuns, but they screwed good when we had 'em down and under us."

In a flash, before Harlan could say anything, Big Eagle

had drawn his knife and, with three quick swipes, cut off both of the man's ears and the end of his nose! As the man lay on the ground screaming in terror and agony, his three companions froze in abject panic.

Rolling the man over on his back, Big Eagle tore open the front of his pants and, grabbing the man's testicles, took them off with another quick swipe of his razor-sharp gutting knife. There was another screech, and then the man passed out from the pain. His bright red blood pooled between his legs until it ran no more...

That was all it took. The three remaining trappers told Harlan the whole story as fast as it could roll off their lips in the hope of saving their lives. It seemed that Bosco de Gamma had married a Gros Ventre, and her brother had been leading a war party south of their normal territory the previous fall.

Mindful of the fact that the Plains Indians scattered during the winter to better feed their horses, which placed them in smaller, easier-to- raid groups, Bosco de Gamma decided to strike while the Crow were ripe for the picking, and the unusually good weather had allowed Bosco de Gamma and his trappers to hook up with the Gros Ventre brother-in-law to raid the hated Crows for their furs and horses. In the ensuing battle, the white men were to have all the women they could handle and after that would kill them as one would a prairie dog.

Surprising the camp right at daylight, they had overrun White Bear's few defenders and then spent the day after the killing was done raping the surviving women and taking anything of value. However, they had spooked off the camp's horse herd and had therefore come away without the main reason for the raid.

The men, fearing they would run into more Crow, had not pursued the livestock. Afterward they had drifted north and finally separated, with the trappers going to their winter camp in the Big Belt Mountains, as Harlan had suspected, and the Gros Ventre returning home with their spoils.

"Well," Harlan said, speaking slowly for the deadly effect, "all your Gros Ventre Indian friends are looking for their body parts south of the Happy Hunting Grounds as I speak."

After a pause, Harlan asked "Where is Bosco de Gamma now?" as he ominously and calmly cleaned his fingernails with the sharp tip of his gutting knife.

"He is still at the winter camp with all our plews except what we have here, and most of our horses. He is just due west of the mineral springs. He will continue to trap the waters in the Big Belts and will meet us at the rendezvous at Ham's Fork come summer," said a man named Grudgley, who was shaking so badly he could hardly talk.

He must have figured out what's coming next, thought Harlan, observing the shaking.

As Harlan and the boys rode off toward the Big Belts, trailing their horse herd that had now expanded with the animals taken from the trappers, they could hear the three men still screaming.

With no fingers left on any of their hands so they could untie themselves and their hamstrings cut clear through on both legs, being tied alive to a tree in the wilderness with all the hungry varmints running around was not a good idea. And they knew it, if the tenor of their screaming was any indicator of the terror and pain they were now experiencing.

They had taken the men's riding horses and four pack horses. On those horses also rode their victims' fall catch of furs and their rifles. They had left the rest of the men's gear to whoever found the campsite after the animals cleaned up the four human carcasses.

For the next two months, Harlan and the boys searched for Bosco de Gamma and his renegade henchmen. They found his old camp, but the signs showed that it had been deserted in haste several weeks before the arrival of Harlan and the boys. It occurred to Harlan that Bosco de Gamma was somehow on to them and their bloody mission. But how could he know in such big country with few sources of information to divulge that secret?

Harlan and the boys did not realize that Bosco de Gamma had swung by his buddies' camp and discovered their remains shortly after the wolves and grizzly bears had finished.

Then one of his men had spotted Harlan and the boys in their neck of the woods and put two and two together. Realizing he was being hunted, especially when he saw his dead friends' pack animals in tow by the four men tracking them, Bosco de Gamma figured that if he and his men wanted to see the next sunrise, they'd best leave the country.

A spring snowstorm ended Harlan and the boys' cold-tracking of Bosco de Gamma and his remaining renegade buddies. That act of God allowed Bosco de Gamma and his killing companions to put a lot of ground between them and their relentless pursuers.

Harlan's party was held up by the deep snows as they tried to follow the tracks over the mountain passes. Realizing his quarry would have a big lead in escaping from them while they waited for the snows in the mountains and passes to diminish, Harlan grimaced.

Bosco de Gamma's haste to get across the country and to the south so his progress would not be held up by the snows told Harlan that the man had to know the hunters were hot on his track for something he and his men had done. With that realization, Harlan and his boys just sat on their horses in mounting frustration and violent, black-hearted anger.

"They are heading for the Madison River, sure, and then south. It will do us no good to pursue them any further, as Bosco de Gamma's lead is just too great. It will be best for us to return home and make ready for the rendezvous. If our paths ever cross again, we will take care of business at that time," Harlan grimly concluded.

2 6

A CROW SURPRISE

ROUNDING THE LAST TURN IN THE FOREST BELOW THEIR cabin, the men were surprised to see a young Crow teenager bringing their horses and mules back to the corral. Good old Limps-Ahead-of-His Horses, thought Harlan. His word was good when it came to taking good care of our livestock.

The boy, upon seeing the arrival of his trapper friends, spurred his horse ahead of the herd in his hurry to meet the returning men.

"Did you get the white men who helped in the killing of White Bear's people?" he eagerly blurted out, already aware of the Gros Ventre whom the four trappers had pursued and killed the winter before.

"We managed to kill four of the eight trappers who were involved," said Harlan as he tiredly dismounted.

"What happened to the rest?" asked the Indian lad, who was named He-Who-Shoots.

"They got away when it snowed, and we lost their trail," replied Winter Hawk as he also dismounted stiffly.

"Are you going back after them after resting up some and changing horses?" continued He-Who-Shoots.

"No," replied Harlan, not wanting to dwell on the subject. "We have work to do around here for now with our livestock, furs, and supplies before we go out once more to avenge White Bear, his people, and our wives and children."

Big Eagle and Runs Fast dismounted and began unsaddling the horses and mules.

"Have you been the one tending our livestock all these months?" asked Harlan.

"Yes," He-Who-Shoots answered proudly.

Looking out over the livestock and seeing that the animals were in good shape and all accounted for, Harlan was pleased.

"It looks like all our supplies are here and untouched except by a few mice," said Runs Fast coming out of the cabin they used as a storehouse.

"All our furs and hides are here as well," said Big Eagle as he came out of the fur storage cabin.

"All our tack appears to be all right as well," said Winter Hawk, who had been checking the storage tepee.

Turning, now more than pleased by what they had discovered upon their return, Harlan said, "He-Who-Shoots, you have done a good job taking care of our property. I appreciate that and have something to show my appreciation for your friendship and good work."

Walking to the four dead trappers' eight horses and taking their reins in both hands, Harlan took them over to the young boy.

"Here, these are yours!" said Harlan.

For a moment, the boy was frozen in his tracks, awestruck by the unheard-of reward for his work. One horse was a big present on the plains, much less eight! Plain and simple, he was looking at a fortune in Crow coin of the realm. Still not knowing what to say, the boy just stood with a stunned look on his face.

"Here," said Harlan, taking the boy's hands and putting the horses' reins into them. "They are all yours for a job very well done."

That broke the spell, and with a huge grin, He-Who-Shoots swung easily up onto the back of the closest horse and, taking the other reins into his left hand, let out a yell and headed for home at a trot with his unbelievable fortune. Harlan just grinned, as did the boys. It was their first set of smiles in many moons.

"Hell, he has enough horses now to buy the bride of his choice," thought Harlan.

Since they had already owned thirty-one horses and ten mules, more than enough, he felt it only proper to reward the young man for doing such a good job of protecting their homestead. Little did Harlan realize what handsome rewards that gesture would shortly reap.

For the next two months, Harlan and his sons tended

to their herd of livestock, horseshoeing, and such. Tack was repaired, as were the pack saddles, and then the furs and hides were prepared for the trip to the rendezvous. All the beaver furs were packed in tight packs, and the rest of the furs were bound in bundles. The buffalo hides were bound in stacks of ten, as were the deer and elk hides.

In between those preparations, the men made meat, but they noticed that their Crow neighbors never joined them. In fact, Harlan was aware that the tribe had never moved back onto its summer grounds, where White Bear used to put his tepee. It almost seemed as if the trappers were no longer welcome in the company of the Crow now that White Bear was dead.

That feeling was brought to a head when, now that the meat had sloughed away, the men went to collect the bones of their loved ones from the burial platforms and place them into Mother Earth, as was the Crow tradition.

As they finished covering the bones with soil, He-Who-Shoots rode up and stopped at a respectful distance. Sitting on his horse, he waited until the men were finished with their moments of sorrow. Then, riding forward, he said to Harlan, "You need to leave as soon as possible! The rest of the tribe thinks your presence here is bad medicine. It all started when White Bear's only son and seven others from the tribe went south two winters ago to take horses from our enemies the Snakes. He never returned, and neither did any of the others."

Harlan's thoughts quickly went back to the winter when his home-site had been raided by eight Crows who were trying to take their horses and mules. It now appeared that Harlan and the boys might have killed Chief White Bear's only son!

"Then," the young man continued, "the tribe had no such troubles as befell White Bear and his band until after you arrived. With their killings, many have had bad thoughts and feel the spirit world is angry with them for allowing the white man and his family to live among us in the land of the Crow. Now, many other bad things have happened, and the tribal elders think you are bad medicine. There is much talk among the young warriors that you need to be attacked and driven from the country of the Crow as soon as possible!"

Shocked but not surprised by the young man's words, Harlan just shook his head, wondering what else could possibly go wrong. Realizing the futility of trying to talk to the elders about such matters as bad medicine, he wondered if they really now wanted to stay in the land of the Crow anyway. It was a land of much sorrow for the remaining family, not to mention the everyday feeling of loss that surrounded the cabins.

"Thank you, He-Who-Shoots. What you said to us here today will remain with the soil and the rocks and will go no further. The boys and I will discuss this matter and let you know what our response will be," said Harlan.

He-Who-Shoots, his message delivered to his friends,

left hurriedly so as not to be discovered talking to the trappers and suffer the wrath of his band.

"Well, boys, what is it going to be?" asked Harlan.

Big Eagle slowly said, "We still have unfinished business to the south."

"Runs Fast and Winter Hawk, what say you?" asked Harlan.

"The business to the south needs to be taken care of," said Winter Hawk as Runs Fast nodded in the affirmative at the wisdom of his brother's words.

"Then so shall it be," said Harlan.

Saying their individual good-byes to the memory of their loved ones at the burial site, the boys, now more like white men than Crow Indians, turned their backs on that hallowed earth and, without words, rode slowly back to their cabins.

Two days later, the cabins, tepees, and horse corral were empty, and the trappers were no more in the land of the Crow.

THE RENDEZVOUS OF 1834

WITH EACH MAN LEADING A LONG PACK STRING LOADED with camp gear; trading goods, packs of beaver plews, buffalo, elk, and deer hides, Harlan and the boys headed south from their home in the land of the Crow. Retracing the route they had traveled the year earlier, they again traversed the east side of what is today Yellowstone National Park.

Heeding He-Who-Shoot's words and heading south toward Ham's Fork of the Green, site of the 1834 rendezvous in the Green River Valley, the men pushed their animals hard until they felt sure they were out of the quick striking range of any Crow Indians who might follow them. They were concerned about pursuit because the Crow might be angry that they had lost the opportunity to remove the now hated white men and share the spoils from their cabins.

Stopping at the 1833 rendezvous site, the men and animals rested for two days in the lush meadows. Killing a buffalo, the men feasted on the rich meat and got back some of their strength after the long, hard ride from Montana. Skirting the east side of the Salt River Range, they continued moving south, now at a more leisurely pace so as not to jade the animals or themselves yet still kept a sharp lookout for any hostile Indians.

When they reached Ham's Fork of the Green, they followed it southwest until they arrived at the site of the rendezvous. It had been a long and dangerous trip, and now the men were ready for some friendly company, good food, trading, and rum to help heal their war wounds.

Walking their livestock into the rendezvous area, Harlan and company soon realized they were leading the biggest pack string of all assembled. This will be the last time for such a large pack string, thought Harlan.

It was just too hard to manage and provided too tempting a target for those wanting to steal good horse-flesh. After trading off their furs and hides, he concluded, they would also sell fifteen of their horses and at least half of their mules. With the credit from those sales, he would purchase firearms, powder, lead, flints, nipple picks, and the like.

If he had learned anything during his nine years in the outback, it was that weapons were the main thing the Indians wanted, and they would trade high in furs and other items for them and for tack.

Locating a site in a small grove of cottonwoods, Harlan and company began to make a camp. Around them were tepees from at least four different tribes, not to mention at least one hundred trappers' lean-tos. Lacking wood to build a corral to hold their stock, they ended up tethering the animals next to their camp, where a close eye could be kept on them.

While the boys rested and guarded their packs of furs and horses, Harlan rode into the rendezvous area to gather any news relating to the event. He discovered that the Rocky Mountain Fur Company was located five to ten miles up Ham's Fork. Another five miles above that was another trading company led by a man named Wyeth. At the site where they were now camped, at the intersection of Ham's and Black's Forks, was the American Fur Company.

Because the traders were so scattered, Harlan figured he would have to do some riding to see how they graded furs and what they had in the way of trade goods. He also discovered, in talking with some of his trapper friends, that beaver pelts were hardly worth anything, but buffalo hides and furs from the river otter, coyote, wolf, and fox were bringing good prices. He also learned that next year's rendezvous site would be where the 1833 gathering had been, at Horse Creek in the Green River Valley.

Returning to camp, he relayed this information to the boys. The boys also had some information. Next to their lean-tos stood the camp of Jim Bridger and "Crooked Hand" Fitzpatrick, a man so nicknamed because of an accidental, self-inflicted gunshot wound years earlier that had deformed his hand.

Pleased with that news, Harlan tied off his horse, and he and the boys went over to Bridger's camp and before long were deep into eating, drinking, and catching up on the gossip from the previous year. Bridger and Fitzpatrick were saddened by the news of the loss of the men's wives and children.

For many long moments after that news was shared, they all just looked into the flames of the campfire as if in it were the answers as to why such a thing could happen. The two men were also surprised to hear whom Harlan and the boys blamed for their losses. Nothing, however, was mentioned about the killing that would follow if Bosco de Gamma and his companions were ever located, for fear of tipping their hand as word got out among the other trappers.

The next morning, Bridger and Harlan met over cups of scalding coffee and decided that Jim would venture upriver to Wyeth's to see what kind of offers and trades he was willing to make. Meanwhile, Harlan and Big Eagle would journey upstream to the Rocky Mountain Fur Company to see what it was offering. That would also give Harlan a chance to see his friend Gavin and gather any insider information regarding the status of the fur trade.

They also decided that since both camps were low on fresh meat, Runs Fast and Winter Hawk would head into the country to see if they could kill a buffalo or elk for their camps' communal supper that evening. Fitzpatrick, because he had imbibed too much rum the night before, would stay behind and mind his sore head while watching the two camps and their collective horseflesh.

Not long after that, Harlan and Big Eagle were on their way north to the site of the Rocky Mountain Fur Company. They rode along with Jim Bridger, who was going even farther north to visit Wyeth's camp. At the same time, Winter Hawk and Runs Fast, with an extra horse pulling a travois, were heading northeast, where they had seen a small herd of buffalo several days earlier.

Fitzpatrick just sat by the fire and did not move for fear his head would break into tiny pieces.

Separating with a wave of the hand for good luck at the site of the Rocky Mountain Fur Company, Bridger continued north. Meanwhile, Harlan and Big Eagle looked up Gavin and, over some strong, day-old coffee and cold, greasy buffalo-hump ribs, discussed the current fur trade. According to Gavin, buffalo hides were the big thing that year. Almost everything else was secondary in price but would still bring enough for them to spend another year in the backcountry doing what they loved if the hides were properly dressed—and if they had plenty of them, and of the right kind.

Gavin also filled Harlan in on why the buffalo hides were so valuable. It seemed a country across the Atlantic called England was buying every buffalo hide it could get its hands on.

Apparently, the industrial folks in that country

considered buffalo leather to be tougher and longer-lasting than items made from the hide of a beef. Therefore, to feed their new industries' leather-belt-driven machinery, they needed every buffalo hide they could get.

To Gavin's way of thinking, that was why buffalo hides were bringing at least four dollars each that year at the rendezvous. He also informed them that river otter, marten, and deer and elk hides were bringing top dollar as well. However, beaver was bringing only three dollars at top price, if that. And anything smaller than a blanket-sized critter brought hardly anything.

Slowly savoring the tasty fat from his hump rib, Harlan took too long figuring once again. He and the boys had done very well that year. They had over one hundred buffalo hides and at least another fifty elk and deer hides.

They had at least five hundred good beaver plews, not to mention many bundles of other prime furs. Yes, he thought, the boys and I will do very well this year even in light of some poor prices for beaver plews.

Looking further down the trail, he thought, *We also have at least twenty head of livestock we can sell. And in this part of the horse-starved woods, that ought to fetch a pretty penny in trade between horse-shy trappers and the always horse-hungry Indians.*

About then, the storm-threatening skies opened up, and Harlan, like all the others, found himself scrambling for cover. After an hour of heavy rains, the cold rains showed little sign of letting up.

Yep, thought Harlan, this will make for a wet ride home.

Four hours later, in a continuing cold downpour, Harlan and Big Eagle turned into the meadow just below their camp. To Harlan's surprise, about fifty fur trappers and Indians were gathered around Jim Bridger's and his campsites.

Spurring their horses, Harlan and Big Eagle rode into their camp at a gallop. Hearing the approaching horsemen and recognizing Harlan, the crowd of men quietly separated, letting them ride right up to their fire pit.

Lying there in a lean-to under two blankets were the bodies of two men. Jumping off his horse, Harlan recognized the Crow-beaded moccasins of Winter Hawk and Runs Fast sticking out from under the blankets! He froze in midstride as his heart almost stopped beating. Big Eagle, jumping off his horse at the sight, grabbed one corner of a blanket and threw it back. Lying underneath was the body of his brother, Winter Hawk.

Without a word, Big Eagle lifted the other blanket, only to find the body of Runs Fast lying on the ground staring sightlessly into the sky! Both Harlan and Big Eagle found it hard to breathe for the next several moments at this horrific discovery. Then Harlan exploded with grief and fury.

"Who the hell knows what happened?" he demanded in a dangerously cutting voice.

A slightly built trapper named Jim Hayes stepped forward and said, "Harlan, me and Pete here was a-comin' to the rendezvous and stumbled across their bodies by the carcass of a dead buffler.

From what we could tell, they had killed the buffler and were in the process of butcherin' it when ten shod ponies approached them. Then the ponies moved off into a nearby creek as if not wantin' to be followed by losin' their sign, and these two boys here'n laid dead. It almost appeared as if n the men on the shod horses killed the boys outright for no reason a 'tall! We brought the boys into the rendezvous to locate their camp and kin, which seemed the Christian thing to do."

He continued with a lowered voice, "Crooked Hand here recognized the boys right off and asked that we leave them here. He boarded his horse right off to back-track our tracks in order to find the culprits before the storm hit and asked us to stay here and watch the camp. We been here about two hours and will stay longer if'n need be for you."

Kneeling by the boys, Harlan noticed that each had two large holes in his chest. He turned them over and saw that each had been shot twice in the back at close range! The shots had been so close that their buckskin shirts had powder-bum holes where the bullets had entered.

"Where be their horses?" Harlan asked with eyes ablaze. "They be in your pack string, where we tied 'em," said Pete. "They was standin' by the boys when we found 'em, and we figured the varmints who shot the boys did not take 'em fearin' the horseflesh would be recognized in camp by their kin."

About that time, a wet, bedraggled figure on horseback was seen approaching Harlan's camp. Soon he could make out that the rider was Fitzpatrick.

Reining up by Harlan, Crooked Hand said, "Ain't no use in tryin' to backtrack the varmints. This here storm washed their tracks plumb away. However, I followed them as fer as I could, and when I lost their trail, they was headin' in this direction!

I did manage to pick up the boys' Hawkens. They was lyin' alongside where the boys fell and was unfired. It almost seems the rifles were left on purpose so as not to reveal who the shooters were because of the rarity of their make and scarcity of them among us."

As an afterthought, Fitzpatrick said, "From the looks of those bodies, they was shot at close range. It were almost as if they recognized the riders who did the shootin' at long range as fellow trappers and let them in close. Then it were too late to defend themselves once they was recognized.

According to Pete here, Winter Hawk had his rifle in his hands as if he might've recognized someone in the party at the last moment, but it was just too late to survive their intentions."

Harlan's racing heart had still not adjusted to the loss of his kids, but he had heard every word spoken regarding the killings. Big Eagle had grown quiet and sullen, and his eyes held a dreadful inhuman look. To his way of thinking, another killing was not far off—and a slow one if he had his druthers.

Seeing there was nothing they could really do, the crowd began to move off out of respect and to give Harlan and Big Eagle the space they needed. Fitzpatrick built their fire bigger and higher, realizing a long night was at hand. Plus, he was as wet as a drowned muskrat and needed some drying.

Jim Bridger returned later that night, expecting a big meal and a horn of rum, only to find a grieving camp. He listened to what Fitzpatrick had to say and knew better than to try to track the culprits in the morning. Crooked Hand was one of the better trackers he knew, and he quickly realized that if he had not been able to find the killers because of the heavy rains, no one else would be able to do so either.

It continued raining hard all night, and come the dawn there was an early capping of snow in the distant mountains. A large fire was built and coffee brewed that morning, but the camp lacked any laughter in light of the two dead men still lying a few feet away in the lean-to.

As hard as Harlan had thought during the hours of darkness and rain, he couldn't think of anyone who would want to shoot his sons. He had enemies, but for the life of him, he couldn't think of any who would want to back-shoot his kin. He knew one thing for sure:

whoever had done it was the calculating kind, especially in leaving the valuable horses and rifles on the scene.

They knew what they were doing, he thought, and if I or Big Eagle ever catches them, well, God had better turn His eyes away.

What had been a happy event and one of anticipation was one now of sorrow and heartache, made even more so the next morning when, away from the prying eyes of the camp, Harlan and Big Eagle wrapped the two men in burial robes and placed them high in a cottonwood side by side as the brothers they had become.

Standing below the boys, Harlan and Big Eagle bade them a happy journey through tear-filled eyes. Then they turned and rode away forever. They now had other business on their minds, and it wasn't the kind the good Lord favored.

Based on Bridger's recommendation, Harlan and Big Eagle decided they would trade their trappings with the independent trader, Nathaniel Wyeth. Pulling out of camp at daylight the next day, they headed their long pack string north to his trading site.

With heavy hearts for their friends, Jim and Crooked Hand watched the sorrow-filled men with their pack string head off to Wyeth's camp that cold, damp morning.

Life still has to go on out here, thought Bridger, but I sure as hell would hate to cross Harlan and Big Eagle now under these circumstances. And those who killed the boys, Lord have mercy on their souls because Harlan will find the killers, being the great mountain man he is, and mercy will not be on his mind!

Not a word was spoken as Harlan and Big Eagle headed toward Wyeth's trading site. Both men were deep in their thoughts, and those thoughts were black indeed.

Hours later, the two men and their livestock had moved into the trader's camp. Happy to see such a large pack string of plews and other furs, Wyeth was more than accommodating to the two men. Then he recognized Harlan and, having already heard the news about the deaths of his two boys, quickly filled two cups brimful of the flaming, uncut rum for the two wet, cold men.

"We come to trade," announced Harlan in a quiet, determined voice.

After taking a long pull on his cup of rum, Harlan brought his section of the pack string holding the beaver plews forward. Without a word, Wyeth and another fur buyer began grading the furs. Watching carefully, Harlan could see that they were more than fair in their grading.

"Can only give you three dollars each for this here pile and two dollars each for these smaller plews," said Wyeth, ever mindful of Harlan's reputation as one tough mountain man, especially in light of the recent loss of his two sons.

"That be fair," said Harlan in a flat tone indicating to one in the know the man speaking had recently lost part of his heart and soul.

Then Wyeth and his partner graded the other hides

and furs. They were placed by species and grade in several piles, and once again Wyeth identified what each pile was worth. Harlan had no problem with the grading or prices offered. Last, Wyeth graded the buffalo hides, which had been well dressed by the Crow women back in their Indian villages in Montana.

"Damn fine buffalo hides, Harlan. I can go four and a half dollars on every one of them," he said.

"That be a good price," Harlan mumbled, still not into this fur-trading thing right now but realizing life had to go on if he and Big Eagle were to survive another year in the West.

Then Harlan spotted something almost lost under a huge pile of furs sitting off to one side. Walking over to the pile, he jerked the fur that had caught his eye out from under several dozen others. It was a pure albino grizzly-bear hide with pink claws still attached!

Turning to Wyeth with blood in his eyes, Harlan bellowed, "Wyeth, where the hell did you get this here white grizzly bear hide?"

Surprised by Harlan's outbreak, Wyeth jumped like a bug on a hot rock. "We bought that hide yesterday. Ain't it a beaut!" he exclaimed, trying to hide his surprise and concern over Harlan's violent outburst.

By now Big Eagle had hold of the hide, and the look in his eyes told of a killing that was coming unless this trader was forthcoming in his information—and fast!

"Harlan, what the hell is with this Injun? He has a bad

look in his eyes, and you need to get control of him before he does something uncalled-for!" Wyeth whined.

"That isn't the half of it, Wyeth. If you aren't forthcoming about who you bought that hide from, you will have the two of us to deal with!" growled Harlan.

"Who did we get that hide from, Jeff?" asked Wyeth, turning to his other fur buyer, who was standing thunderstruck at the turn of events.

"We got that from Patrick Bosco de Gamma and his band yesterday," Jeff exclaimed with terror rising in his voice. "He told me not to say anything as to where it came from. Claimed he stole it off'n a dead trapper killed by varmints. That is why I hid it under those other furs, so as not to cause any unnecessary questions from other trappers," he concluded lamely.

Now everything is falling into place! thought Harlan. Bosco de Gamma stole the hide that I had given to Chief White Bear during last fall's raid and killing. Then by chance as he was coming to the rendezvous, he and his band stumbled across Winter Hawk and Runs Fast gutting out the buffalo.

Recognizing the two boys as part of the group that had chased his band over the mountain passes and down to the Madison, he took advantage of their situation and killed them both before they recognized him. That was why the killers didn't take their valuable horses or rifles. They figured I would be at the rendezvous as well and, recognizing the boys 'property, would go crazy and kill them like I did the rest of the party back up on the Smith River.

Looking over at Big Eagle, Harlan saw in his eyes the understanding of what had happened. Now someone was going to die for their back-shooting actions, and it was going to start with Bosco de Gamma!

However, they had a problem. They had a world of credit coming from their furs plus a large string of horses to sell before they could move on to the killing business at hand.

What to do with all these profits? thought Harlan.

Motioning Big Eagle off to one side, Harlan discussed a plan now swirling around in his head regarding the fur trade and the selling of the horses yet to come. This plan would allow them to procure the supplies they would need for a year of pursuit of Bosco de Gamma and his band of cutthroats, yet allow them a way, without trapping, to have access to enough supplies to survive the following year.

They also discussed what would happen if neither of them survived. Big Eagle agreed with the plan, and Harlan turned to Wyeth.

"Nathaniel, I will make you a deal, but first I need some information," said Harlan. "Do you plan on making it to the 1834 rendezvous at Horse Creek on the Green? And if so, will you allow Big Eagle and me to trade in part of our credit this year and the remainder at the next rendezvous?"

"Yes, I damn sure plan on making the next rendezvous on Horse Creek. I would be a fool not to with the price of furs the way they are. And if you want to trade part of your credit for this year and leave the rest hanging for next year, that would be just fine with me. Just understand that next year's prices for the goods you need may be higher than this year," Wyeth replied in a conciliatory tone.

"That be fine with us, and now the next part of the deal. We have a horse herd that needs to be sold. Most are horses, but we have a few mules to sell as well," said Harlan as plans for the next year spun crazily around in his head.

"You have horses and mules for sale?" blurted out Wyeth.

"Sure do," replied Harlan.

"I will buy everything you have to sell," Wyeth exclaimed excitedly.

"Then let's get to trading," said a now very determined Harlan, eager to get moving.

An hour later, the two trappers had more than enough supplies to pursue Bosco de Gamma and his band for at least another year. They also had a paper from Wyeth indicating that Harlan and Big Eagle had ten thousand dollars in credit due from his company during the 1835 rendezvous. The men had all put their marks and signatures on the paper, and Harlan tucked it away in his saddle bag. There was another signed piece of paper that deeded all of Big Eagle's and Harlan's credit to Jim Bridger in the event that they did not return.

Then Harlan strode over to Wyeth's fur buyer who had purchased the white bear skin. The poor fur buyer could see that Harlan still had blood in his eyes and was not to be fooled with.

"Jeff," said Harlan, "where did that bastard Bosco de Gamma say he was going?"

Jeff, realizing his life might be in doubt if he was cautious with his answer, said, "He told me he would kill me if I said anything to anyone as to where he was a-goin'!"

"Jeff, I will kill you in the next heartbeat if you don't tell me where he was going," Harlan said coldly as his hand went menacingly to the butt of his pistol.

"He said he were going to trap the Wasatch and then drop down and trade at Ogden's Trading Post near the Great Salt Lake after spring trapping ends. He figured you might be at the next rendezvous and had figured out something. I asked what that something was, and he just snarled and told me to leave it be!" Jeff blurted out.

Patting his shoulder to settle down the frightened little man and show that he believed him, Harlan turned toward Big Eagle. The smile on Big Eagle's face was not one of this world.

THE HUNT FOR THE MOST DANGEROUS GAME BEGINS

RETURNING TO THEIR CAMPSITE, HARLAN AND BIG EAGLE made ready to pack their remaining horses and mules for the trip soon to take place. Then, taking the ham from an elk they had killed en route to their camp, they staked great slabs of meat around the fire to cook for them and their campmates, Bridger and Fitzpatrick.

After dinner, Harlan motioned for Bridger to follow him away from the campfire. Harlan told Jim about his discovery of the white bear hide at Wyeth's. After explaining how he had figured out who the killers of his sons were, Harlan laid out his plans. He told Jim that he and Big Eagle planned to hunt down Bosco de Gamma and his killing bunch of friends in the Wasatch. Jim nodded in agreement and asked if Harlan needed any company, since varmints of such a kind always needed lots of killing.

Harlan said, "No, not this time. I thank you for the offer, but this time, Big Eagle and I will do what needs doing, and may God forgive us."

Jim nodded his understanding. Then Harlan dropped the other moccasin.

"Jim, you and me been good friends fer a number of years. What Big Eagle and I have at hand, it being four against two, may not do anything but add our carcasses to the soil down the road if we can't do the killing right off and first. If that happens, 1 have left ten thousand worth of credit from my furs and horse and mule trades in the hands of Wyeth and his fur company for release to be made to you at the 1835 rendezvous."

Jim took a step back at that surprising news. Ten thousand was a small fortune in that day and age, and both men knew it. He was so surprised by his friend's offer that he didn't know what to say.

Harlan continued, "You was always wanting to build a trading post when your old bones got the best of you, and now here is your chance. I figure we will be gone for at least a year tracking that varmint Bosco de Gamma and the rest of the killers. After that, if we don't show up, take the credit and do with it what you want."

With those words, Harlan produced the contract he had signed with Wyeth and handed it to Bridger. Jim just shook his head at his old friend's generosity as he looked at the document in utter disbelief.

"Harlan, you sure you want to do this?" he asked, still not sure he wanted to take his old friend's offer.

"Jim, you have always been right as rain in our dealings. If it takes the two of us longer than a year to get done what we have to do, we will return and you can stake us from the goods at your new trading post so we can last another year in the backcountry. How does that sound?"

Jim Bridger stuck out his hand; in those days a handshake was a contract not to be broken by any man, especially those in the mountain man fraternity.

The two men returned to camp as if nothing out of the ordinary had occurred. But before they did, Jim insisted on helping Harlan cut Bosco de Gamma's sign leading from the rendezvous toward the mountains of Utah. Harlan was known as an expert tracker, but it didn't hurt to have help from Bridger and Fitzpatrick because they were the best in the business, and the task at hand was a deadly one.

There were so many pack-string tracks coming and going into the Green River Valley from those trading at the rendezvous that it took the better part of a week for the men to cut the tracks of Bosco de Gamma's ten-horse party. Finally, with Fitzpatrick's expert tracking ability, they found Bosco de Gamma's tracks south of the rendezvous on Black's Fork, heading toward what is today known as the Unita Mountains.

There, over a final campfire and some fresh buffalo, the men split up. Jim and Fitzpatrick returned to the rendezvous, and Harlan and Big Eagle began their pursuit of Bosco de Gamma south to wherever it led and however it ended.

Cold-tracking Bosco de Gamma's ten-horse pack string led Harlan and Big Eagle south to the Duchesne River in what is today northeastern Utah. Every cold camp they came across had obviously been made without haste, so it appeared that once Bosco de Gamma had left the area of the rendezvous, he had not feared pursuit.

Nonetheless, he had taken care to mix the tracks of his men and pack string with every other one he could find in his travels south. Harlan and Big Eagle did not push their chase of the group for fear of jading their horses so badly that they would lose them and end up afoot in a hostile land.

Speed was not an issue since the crew they were following did not appear to know they were being pursued. To Harlan's and Big Eagle's way of thinking, it was just a matter of time before justice would be done. And when it was, Even God will turn away, Harlan thought coldly.

Camping along the Duchesne River one evening, Harlan built a small fire while Big Eagle hunted the adjacent willows with his bow and arrow for a fat deer for supper. Currying down the stock and checking the condition of the animals' shoes, Harlan was surprised at Big Eagle's quick return. Thrown over his shoulder was a small, fat doe, which explained Big Eagle's smile of success.

LAYING the deer down by their campfire, Big Eagle said, "There is Indian sign upstream all along that river. We had better really hard-stake our animals this evening; otherwise we will lose them to thieving Indians. In this neck of the woods, I imagine they are Paiute and hungry for good horseflesh and anything else they can steal."

Looking over Big Eagle's shoulder as if expecting to see the Indians charging over the ground in pursuit, Harlan said, "That we can do, and we will keep a small fire for cooking this evening so we don't advertise our position to unwanted eyes."

After dinner, the two men staked out their horses with Martha the bell mule in the middle of the livestock for the warnings she always offered when around Indians of any sort. Then, crawling under some nearby clumps of overhanging willows for the cover they offered, the two tired men rolled up in their sleeping furs and went to sleep alongside their Hawkens.

Eee-haaw went Martha in the darkness amid the nervous pawing of the rest of the horses' hoofs.

Both men were instantly awake but did not move for fear of giving away their positions before they could pinpoint the danger. It would do them no good to walk around presenting a target until they figured out what had riled up Martha, be it man or critter.

Soon a darkened figure slowly crept between Harlan and Big Eagle. Zip-thunk went an arrow from Big Eagle's bow into the darkness. Without a word, the figure pitched forward to the ground, wiggled some in his death dance, and then lay still.

Then another darkened figure, unaware of what had happened to his partner, appeared out of the willows right beside Harlan! Thwack went Harlan's tomahawk into the intruder, followed by an inhuman screech!

Then the darkness of the night closed in around the mountain men as if nothing had happened. Harlan and Big Eagle continued their vigil for the rest of the night. By dawn, it was obvious that there were no more Indians, and the two men rose from their concealment in the willows to look over their camp and animals.

"Paiutes," exclaimed Big Eagle as he rolled over the one he had shot in the head at point-blank range with his bow and arrow.

"The same for my man," said Harlan as he removed his tomahawk and wiped the blood and chunks of brains off the blade on the dead man's buckskins.

"Good old Martha," said Big Eagle as he took a clump of grass outside her reach and fed her out of satisfaction and respect.

"Time to move on, and fast," said Harlan. "There will be more where these two came from once the tribe realizes these are gone or killed."

"That being the case, we must try to hide our tracks and watch our back trail if we don't want to experience the same kind of treatment," Big Eagle commented.

Finishing the last of the venison from the previous evening, the two men hurriedly packed their animals and headed into the shallows of the river to hide their tracks after they had hidden the Indian's bodies in a small wash. Following the river for a good mile, they finally left the water in a dense, brushy area as they headed deeper into the mountains.

Four days later, the two men finally discovered Bosco de Gamma's permanent camp, complete with lean-tos and horse corrals, in a densely wooded draw out of sight of prying eyes.

From the tracks and warm fire-pit ashes, it was apparent that two men had gone farther into the mountains to find new trappings while the other two had set out on foot to follow a nearby stream full of beaver dams, ponds, and beaver. In the corral were the group's leftover seven horses. Three of the missing horses, by their trail, had struck out from camp scouting for other beaver-trapping waters to the south.

This is too easy, thought Harlan as he closely scanned the surrounding terrain for any sign of danger.

At that point, Big Eagle didn't care about caution or concern for danger because, to his way of thinking, a deserved killing of varmints was not far off.

Bring it on, he carelessly thought as his rage and lust to kill continued to grow. He had nothing but violence in his heart for those who had had a hand in the killing and raping of the love of his life, not to mention the rest of his family.

Now that he was this close to his quarry, nothing but a bullet or an arrow would stop him from killing those who had killed his loved ones. Soon someone is to die, he thought with narrowed set of eyes as the emotion rose in him to a dangerous, almost unthinking, fever pitch.

Staking their horses in a little meadow at a safe distance from the trappers' camp, Big Eagle and Harlan made ready. Stalking back over the hill and down into the creek bottom and beaver- dam areas, they moved carefully and quietly downstream. Below them about fifty yards away, they noticed some movement!

Two trappers could be seen setting their traps along several beaver dams and ponds. Big Eagle unlimbered his bow and handed his Hawken to Harlan. Then, sneaking around the two unsuspecting trappers, he disappeared into the undergrowth. Giving Big Eagle a few minutes to get into position, Harlan began sneaking downstream, using the beaver dams and clumps of willows for cover as he walked directly toward the two unsuspecting trappers.

The two men, having set out all their traps, turned and started walking back toward their campsite. Peering through the clump of willows hiding him, Harlan saw that one of them was none other than Dick Nance, a vicious individual and bully who loved beating the stuffing out of men smaller than himself.

The other was Jacques Puzier, a mean-ass Frenchman. Both men were longtime traveling companions of Bosco de Gamma and killers in their own right. In fact, they had been the ones at the rendezvous who had beaten Runs Fast while Bosco de Gamma had taken on Winter Hawk in the contest for the boy's Hawken.

No two men deserve dying more, thought Harlan with a look of clouded violence on his face.

Rising from his hiding place in the willow patch, Harlan faced the two men as they continued walking away from the trapping area. For a few seconds, the sight of Harlan standing before them did not register. Then it did!

Puzier began to raise his rifle, suspecting that he was looking at death. He never saw it coming as Big Eagle's arrow caught him right between the shoulder blades with a resounding whack! Lurching forward screaming and in the process dropping his rifle, he desperately reached behind his back in agony in an attempt to pull the arrow out. His effort was in vain as Big Eagle ran up to him and in one fell swoop spun him around and scalped him while he was still alive. His screaming was now ungodly, to say the least, and could be heard at least half a mile away.

Big Eagle let him go to roll around on the ground in pain and let out a yell of triumph as he waved the bloody rag of a scalp over his head. Nance, totally surprised by the suddenness and ferocity of the attack, slowly lowered his rifle to the ground in a sign of submission, but that didn't stop Big Eagle, who was on him in a flash.

Grabbing Nance's shoulder-length hair, he jerked his head back and, in several quick swipes of his gutting knife, scalped Nance as well. His screaming was unholy as he jumped around holding the madly bleeding top of his head in abject pain. It got worse as Big Eagle continued hacking at the man with his knife. First Big Eagle sliced off the fingers on Nance's right hand as he tried to disarm Big Eagle; then, with another swipe of his knife, Big Eagle hamstrung his right leg so he couldn't run. The sounds coming from the trapper were inhuman as the blood continued gushing from his scalped head and down over his buckskin shirt as he stood wobbling on his one good leg.

Harlan just stood there and let Big Eagle continue in an attempt to get the murderous fury out of his system. Puzier was gasping his last as the hemorrhaging in his lungs from the arrow caused him to drown in his own blood. Then, Big Eagle disemboweled Nance with another vicious swipe of his knife! With his intestines flowing over the ground and into the dirt, Nance fell onto the forest floor, writhing in pain as he also began to bleed out.

Lowering his rifle, Harlan watched the life run out of the two men. He felt a certain satisfaction that six of the eight who had wreaked havoc on White Bear and all the people in his camp and also on his sons, were now in the In-Between World. He felt even better that the stirring in him relating to the loss of the love of his life was also partially avenged. Only two of the original killers remained to be reckoned with, and he would not rest until Bosco de Gamma and his partner in crime were bleeding out on the ground as well.

Leaving the two men where they had fallen, Big Eagle and Harlan quietly began the long walk back to the camp of Bosco de Gamma. They hoped to ambush the remaining two killers and give them the same treatment rendered to their partners. In fact, Harlan had some special treatment for Bosco de Gamma when the time came. Treatment that would even make God turn away...

Zipppp went an arrow by Harlan's head, so close that he felt the sting of the wind from the shaft! Zippp-zippp-zippp went three more arrows by his body as Harlan quickly stepped behind a large tree for protection. An Indian exposed himself from behind another tree before him, and Harlan killed him with a quick shot from his Hawken.

"Hey-yeh-yeh-yeh," yelled two more Indians as they charged Harlan's position with tomahawks upraised now that they knew he had fired his one and only shot from his rifle.

Pow went Harlan's pistol as he shot the closest charging Indian in the face. Then he grabbed his own tomahawk from his sash and threw it at the next man rushing at him. That throw hit the man squarely in the mouth in a splash of blood and flying broken teeth.

He careened into the tree partially protecting Harlan in the shock of the impact. Turning in agony, he met Harlan's knife plunged deeply into his guts, splashing blood over the tree bark and Harlan's arm. A fourth Indian, seeing the quick demise of his companions, took off running through the trees in an attempt to escape.

Harlan, now in a killing haze, took off after him with his remaining unfired pistol in one hand and his knife in the other. Closing fast, Harlan fired one shot at the fleeing Indian, hitting him low in the leg and effectively slowing him down. Harlan was on him in a flash, cutting his throat with one swipe of his knife. When he did, the impact of the two bodies hitting each other spun both to the ground. Jumping up, Harlan saw that his adversary was dying as he gurgled his last through a set of wide-open and surprised eyes.

Then, remembering Big Eagle and wondering where he had gone during the fight, Harlan ran back to where the attack had started. Sitting on the ground with his back against a tree was Big Eagle. Driven deeply into his guts just below his breastbone was the shaft of an arrow!

"No!" screamed Harlan as he reached his son's side.

Their eyes met, and at that moment both realized that they would be separated for only a short time before they met once again on the Happy Hunting Grounds. Gathering up his son in his arms, Harlan cried like a baby as he felt the life go out of Big Eagle with just a last quiet gasp, a shudder, and no words. The surprise and agony in the dying man's eyes said it all.

It was an hour before Harlan let go of Big Eagle, finally letting him slip gently to the ground. Harlan's very heart and soul left with the loss of life from Big Eagle, the last of his frontier family.

29

THE FINAL TRIP

THE PAIUTES HAD THE LAST SAY, HARLAN THOUGHT bitterly as he surveyed the battleground around him. Even though the four of them died, they avenged their two brothers killed on the Duchesne River by killing Big Eagle. Not only that, they ruined any chances of surprise in catching and killing Bosco de Gamma with all the gunfire.

Shaking his head in disgust, he took two buffalo robes from the trappers' camp and buried Big Eagle high in a large oak tree on the hillside. As he stood there looking up, the tears flowed down his cheeks and onto his buck-skin shirt, leaving dark brown stains. God, how he hurt inside! He had lost everything dear to him, once again he stood alone in a land that was seemingly uncaring.

Those were the last tears he ever shed. With a hard-ened heart, he turned away from Big Eagle's burial site and walked back to his horses. I still have some unfinished business to attend to.

Returning to the trappers' campsite with his horses and mules in tow, he let the horses belonging to those whom he had pursued for so long loose from the corral so they could survive on their own. Then he turned to the trail leading away from the battle site to the one of the last two remaining killers. He was now on a hunt with a determination that was not of this world.

High up on a ridge, Bosco de Gamma, upon hearing the shooting, had started back to help Nance and Puzier. But the shooting was over so quickly that he stopped so he could watch his campsite from afar until events could untangle themselves and become clearer.

There on his trail far below was the lonely figure of one man, and from the looks of the intensity of his cold-tracking, it had to be none other than Harlan Waugh.

"What we gonna do, boss?" whined a nervous Pete Sites. "That bastard is gonna dog us until the end of time unless we kill him."

"That is just what we are going to do," said Bosco de Gamma with narrowed, hate-filled eyes.

"How we gonna do it, boss?" Sites asked with fear still in his eyes and in the sound of his voice. "He has killed all our pards, and now he is on our track. Is there anything that will stop him afore he stops us?"

"Since he is cold-tracking our trail, we will go up into those rocks yonder, and when he gets within range of our rifles, we will ambush and kill him. When that is done, I will tear out his heart and eat it like I ate the hearts from those damn Comanches back on the Arkansas who tried to kill me so long ago!" said Bosco de Gamma with a killing look in his eyes.

Strangely, it was the same look as that in Harlan's eyes at that very moment as he closely followed three sets of tracks.

The two trappers being pursued took their horses to the high ground and tied them off in the trees. Walking back down the mountain to a rocky point, the two men took up ambush positions and waited for the ever-patient, hard-tracking Harlan Waugh to walk into their trap.

Harlan, lost in his immense grief and not paying attention to the lay of the land around him as he should have, felt Martha pulling back hard on the reins. Looking back, he could see that she was looking up the mountain as she usually did when she spotted a grizzly.

Turning, Harlan looked hard in that direction but did not see any danger. Discounting Martha's warning, he continued following the fresh, clear set of tracks of two riders and a pack animal. He knew he had to continue his hard-on- their-heels pursuit, or they would get away once again. The last time Bosco de Gamma had escaped, it had cost him two of his sons. It would not happen again, he resolved bitterly.

However, Martha continued balking and pulling until Harlan got pissed and started to jerk her lead rope. Then it dawned on him: Martha didn't like Indians. Recalling that he had just been ambushed by Indians and suspecting more of the same, Harlan quickly got cautious as he moved along the trail of fresh horse tracks. All of a sudden, as if on a whim, he moved his horses and mules into the brush of a deep covering draw with a rocky overhang and out of sight of any prying eyes.

Boom went Harlan's Hawken, and a one-ounce slug of lead bounced off the rock just underneath Pete Site's prone body as he overlooked the trail below. The glancing impact of the heavy lead slug exploded his guts over the rocky face on which he lay. The impact of the big slug was so great that he rolled down the rock face and dropped eighty feet onto the talus slope below, then rolled down into a brushy draw. Pete was dead before he had hit the ground.

As he calmly reloaded the Hawken, Harlan got a deadly grin. His dad had taught him to shoot low on a rock on which a crop-eating varmint like a woodchuck was lying so that the slug hitting the rock would mushroom tremendously. Then it would ricochet upward into the body of the varmint, blowing the guts clear out of the critter!

From the way the killer lying in ambush sailed off the rocky ledge, Dad's theory has borne fruit once again, Harlan thought with a smile.

In the same instant, Bosco de Gamma looked wildly around for the white puff of smoke from the rifle that had just been fired. Seeing it high on the ridge above where he also lay in ambush and knowing he was in a poor defensive position, Bosco de Gamma scrambled to jump up for the run to his horses.

Boom went the reserve Hawken as the big slug whistled down, finding Bosco de Gamma's thighbone. The soft, speeding lead bullet shattered the thighbone into numerous pieces in a microsecond. Crashing back down on the rock face and screaming in pain, Bosco de Gamma tried to roll out of the way of what he knew was another shot to come.

However, he was unable to roll into cover because of the pain of the exposed bone, which was now sticking into a crevasse of the rock on which he lay. Boom went another shot from high above, and this time the bullet struck the rock at the base of Bosco de Gamma's left arm, shattering it instantly at the elbow.

Screaming in even more pain, he dropped his rifle, which clattered off his rocky perch into the canyon below. Still trying to move out of the line of fire, Bosco de Gamma heard another report from a rifle just as another heavy lead slug blew his other leg almost off at the knee. With that, he passed out in pain from shock and loss of blood.

When he came to, he saw Harlan quietly standing over him. Even in his pain, Bosco de Gamma used his one good hand to grope for a weapon. He discovered that he had been disarmed except for his sheath knife.

"Harlan, you bastard, finish me off," mumbled Bosco de Gamma in utter pain.

"Not before I let you know you killed my wife, daughter, granddaughter, and their unborn children in that raid on the Crow village with your Gros Ventre buddies last winter. You also back-shot my two sons at the last rendezvous while they were butchering a buffalo. And now you and Sites just tried to ambush and kill me. I want you to know, me and my boys killed everyone involved in that raid with the exception of you. Now," Harlan said coldly, "it is your turn."

Harlan took Bosco de Gamma's knife out of its sheath and dropped it onto his chest, where it could be reached with his remaining good hand. "When you are ready, you now have the tool to kill yourself," he said.

Turning, he walked off the rocks and headed back down to his horses and mules, which were tied below. As he rode off, he could hear Bosco de Gamma screaming for him to come back and kill him.

The wolves, grizzly bears, or cold of the night will do that in time, thought Harlan as he continued riding back down the trail. But whatever way you die, there is always your knife.

The screaming continued until Harlan rode out of sight and sound.

———

HARLAN WAUGH WAS NEVER HEARD from or seen again. He eventually joined the soil, as had so many mountain men before him—alone and somewhere in the mountains he loved.

Jim Bridger took Harlan's credit the next year once he figured the mountain man was lost to the ages and used it to build Fort Bridger. The crude trading post along the Oregon Trail was used for several years by the wagon trains of Argonauts heading west to make a better life on many trails blazed by the mountain men. With that and a few more short years, the glorious days of the mountain men faded into the soil from whence all of us came.

"Wagh!"

NOW LOOK FOR CROSSED
ARROWS, ALSO BY TERRY GROSZ...

In 1829, Jacob and Martin left Kentucky to become Mountain Men, trappers of the Rocky Mountains. The rugged mountains that lay beyond America's frontier remained mostly unexplored. In those days, when beaver were plentiful and the buffalo roamed freely, the killing was good. The two young men would also find that life would be hardscrabble in the high frontier. They would face grizzly bears and hostile Indians. And they would risk horse wrecks and mountain storms to trade their furs each year at "rendezvous." Crossed Arrows is the story of two adventurers who lived hard in the earliest days of the Wild West.

AVAILABLE NOW FROM TERRY GROSZ AND WOLF-PACK PUBLISHING

ALSO BY TERRY GROSZ

Defending Our Wildlife Heritage

Hell or High Water in the Indian Territory

Slaughter in the Sacramento Valley

Flowers and Tombstones of a Conservation Officer: Part I

Flowers and Tombstones of a Conservation Officer: Part II

The Adventurous Life of Tom "Iron Hands" Warren

The Adventures of Hatchet Jack

No Safe Refuge

The Saga of Harlan Waugh

Wildlife Dies Without Making a Sound

Wildlife On The Edge

Wildlife's Quiet War

Crossed Arrows: Mountain Men

Wildlife Wars

Josiah Pike

The Adventures of the Brothers Dent

Curse of the Spanish Gold

ABOUT THE AUTHOR

Terry Grosz earned his bachelor's degree in 1964 and his master's in wildlife management in 1966 from Humboldt State College in California. He was a California State Fish and Game Warden, based first in Eureka and then Colusa, from 1966 to 1970. He then joined the U.S. Fish & Wildlife Service, and served in California as a U.S. Game Management Agent and Special Agent until 1974. After that, he was promoted to Senior Resident Agent and placed in charge of North and South Dakota for two years, followed by three years as Senior Special Agent in Washington, D.C., with the Endangered Species Program, Division of Law Enforcement. While in Washington, he also served as Foreign Liaison Officer.

In 1979, he became the Assistant Special Agent in Charge in Minneapolis, Minnesota. Two years later in 1981, he was promoted to Special Agent in Charge and transferred to Denver, Colorado, where he remained until his retirement in 1998.

He has earned many awards and honors during his career, including, from the U.S. Fish & Wildlife Service, the Meritorious Service Award in 1996, and Top Ten

Award in 1987 as one of the top ten employees (in an agency of some 9,000). The Fish & Wildlife Foundation presented him with the Guy Bradley Award in 1989, and in 1993 he received the Conservation Achievement Award for Law Enforcement from the National Wildlife Federation.

Unity College in Maine awarded Grosz an honorary doctorate in environmental stewardship in 2001. His first book, Wildlife Wars, was published in 1999 and won the National Outdoor Book Award for Nature and Environment. He has had ten memoirs published since then— For Love of Wildness, Defending Our Wildlife Heritage, A Sword for Mother Nature, No Safe Refuge, The Thin Green Line, Genesis of a Duck Cop, Slaughter in the Sacramento Valley, Wildlife on the Edge, Wildlife's Quiet War, and Wildlife Dies Without Making a Sound (in two volumes) —and his Mountain Men Novels — Crossed Arrows, Curse of the Spanish Gold, The Saga of Harlan Waugh, The Adventures of the Brothers Dent, and The Adventures of Hatchet Jack.

Several of Grosz's stories were broadcast as a docudrama on the Animal Planet network in 2003.

Terry Grosz lives in Colorado.